JENNIFER ARMINTROUT

CHILD OF DARKNESS

A LIGHTWORLD/DARKWORLD NOVEL

MIRA

MIRA®

PLEASE RECYCLE · THIS PRODUCT IS RECYCLABLE

Recycling programs for this product may not exist in your area.

ISBN-13: 978-0-7783-2670-0

CHILD OF DARKNESS

Copyright © 2009 by Jennifer Armintrout.

All rights reserved. Except for use in any review, the reproduction or utilization of this work in whole or in part in any form by any electronic, mechanical or other means, now known or hereafter invented, including xerography, photocopying and recording, or in any information storage or retrieval system, is forbidden without the written permission of the publisher, MIRA Books, 225 Duncan Mill Road, Don Mills, Ontario, Canada M3B 3K9.

This is a work of fiction. Names, characters, places and incidents are either the product of the author's imagination or are used fictitiously, and any resemblance to actual persons, living or dead, business establishments, events or locales is entirely coincidental.

MIRA and the Star Colophon are trademarks used under license and registered in Australia, New Zealand, Philippines, United States Patent and Trademark Office and in other countries.

www.MIRABooks.com

Printed in U.S.A.

This book is dedicated to Tez Miller.
Not just because she won the Twitter contest
and this was the prize, but also because she is
one of the nicest romance bloggers I have met.

Prologue

On the night she was born, the Palace rejoiced.

But her mother did not.

Lying in her bed, the infant tucked closely to her side, Ayla despaired. *Protect her,* the Goddess had said. It had been so easy when the child had been a part of her. Now, she was a part of the world, a world that was more cruel and difficult than one of her race should have to face. Protecting her would not be as simple now.

The child was perfect, though more Human in appearance than even her mother. Faery babes were born pale, tinged with green, and spindly like the roots of a plant. This child was plump and pink, with a shock of flame-orange hair sprouting in tufts from her head. Two feathered, black wings were tucked against her small back, and they stirred as she slept, as though she dreamed of a day when she could use them.

The door to the Queene's chambers opened to admit the child's father. Malachi, once divine, now mortal. He approached carefully, as though afraid to see what lay beside Ayla in the bed.

"She is…whole?" He had voiced his fears to Ayla only once, late at night, when he'd recounted for her the sights of the pitiful children he'd had to escort to Aether, the domain of the Angels on Earth. He had been afraid that the child would be malformed, as a punishment for his fall.

It relieved Ayla that she was able to show him how foolish that fear had been. "She is whole." She hesitated. "But her wings…they are the same as yours. Everyone will know she is not Garret's child."

Emboldened by the news that his child was not deformed as a consequence of his actions, he came forward to see her. "I am glad they will know. I would not care if that traitor's name was never uttered in the Palace again."

Ayla stroked the downy skin between her daughter's wings. "No. No one must ever know. To keep her safe."

"It would be safer for her to be thought of as a bastard," he argued, and Ayla could not be surprised. She'd thought of it, herself.

"It would be. She would never be Queene, and so, she would never be a target for an Assassin's blade. As heir to my throne, she will be," Ayla mused aloud, as if thinking of it for the first time. "But if she were revealed to be a bastard, her inheritance of my throne might be compromised."

"Your throne," Malachi repeated. The words sounded like poison he needed to spit from his mouth.

Ayla did not bristle, as she used to. Over the months since her coronation, it had become clearer and clearer to her that while Malachi loved her and would stay at her side in the Lightworld, he hated the Faery Court. She'd feared, for a time, that it was her he hated, that he stayed in the Lightworld simply because he had nowhere else to go. But she had resolved to tolerate it, because she'd caused him to lose his immortality, and the kind Human who'd saved his life had died because of her.

It had only been when Cedric, her closest advisor, had politely suggested the real reason for Malachi's hatred of her position—that it kept her from him, in all but the physical sense—that it had become clear. And now, she felt foolish at the mere memory of those fears.

"I do not worry for myself. Or, perhaps I do. If the child is known to not be Garret's, those who wished to remove me from the Court could use it against me. If I were officially declared a traitor, think of what might happen to her." Speaking of death aloud, in this room where Queene Mabb had fallen under Garret's hand, sent a ripple of apprehension through her, as if her own death brushed over her on its way to the future. "No, it would be safer for her to be thought of as the heir to the throne, and endangered in that way, than to be cast on the mercy of the Court and be subject to their machinations."

She pulled the blanket over the child—her daughter, how strange to think those words!—so that her form was obscured. "Bring Cedric. I need his counsel."

Malachi's fists clenched at his sides. She knew his feelings for her advisor. Malachi wished to be the closest to her, in every way. And he was, in most ways, though he would not believe it no matter how many times she reassured him. But Cedric knew the Lightworld as no one else did, not even Flidais or the other members of the council, and Ayla called on him when a problem seemed too large or complicated to solve on her own. It was impossible to convince Malachi that she did not view his inexperience with Lightworld politics as a lack of ability.

He did not argue and, with a last, longing look at his child, turned and left. He returned with Cedric quickly; no doubt both men had waited in the ante-chamber beyond for the child's arrival.

When the door was shut, Ayla pulled back the covers to reveal the tiny babe at her side. She studied Cedric's expression carefully, but he gave nothing away.

"She is perfect, Your Majesty. You both should be

very proud that your union resulted in such a beautiful child." His tone was schooled through years of politics; he never missed a step by disclosing something too soon. "Have you a name for her?"

"Cerridwen," Ayla answered, though she had not thought of it until now. "After that face of the Goddess."

"It is a strong name," Cedric said with a Courtly bow. "The Royal Heir, Cerridwen."

"It is a mockery of the true God," Malachi put in, but without malice. He often made such pronouncements, without feeling, betraying that he had once been a creature without emotion or will, completely subservient to the One God of the Humans.

Ayla ignored him, choosing instead to press on with her advisor. "And what of her appearance. Do you not see anything odd, Cedric?"

As if freed of some invisible bond, Cedric spoke in earnest now. "She appears to be Human. That is explained away easily enough, as you are half Human yourself. Plus, most Fae have little experience with young of their own species to tell the difference readily, especially from a distance. But her wings, Your Majesty. There are already rumors that you will make Malachi your Royal Consort. If she is seen to have such a similar feature as him, especially one that is so unlike anything born to the Fae… No doubt you've thought of this already."

"She has," Malachi said, coming to sit on the bed beside Ayla, as if he could no longer stand the separation. "And we have decided that it is in the best interest of the child that no one discover her true parentage." He leveled his gaze at Ayla, and the sudden sorrow in his eyes jolted her. "Not even the child should know, lest she let the information loose by mistake."

"That is wise, Malachi," Cedric acknowledged with a nod of his head. "However, it is not practical to keep the girl locked away forever. The Court will question her absence at royal functions. Her existence might even be called into question. Even if hiding her was possible, she will have to be attended by servants, and servants do talk."

Ayla waved a hand to stop him. She was tired, and wished to be alone with her child on this first night of its life, without the nagging fear that so much was left to do. "I agree with you. We cannot hide her away. As for the servants, I will leave that to your discretion. You know which servants in the Palace can be trusted, not only to keep her secret, but to care for her as she deserves." She tapped one finger on her lips, as if considering, though her mind was already made up on the next matter. "I believe I shall enact a new law. All Faeries at Court shall bind and cover their wings. In homage to Mabb, of course, who always hid her own.

The anniversary of her death is only a few weeks away. Surely we can keep Cerridwen hidden until then?"

Cedric did not respond immediately, and he looked as though he worked over the problem of what to say to her in his mind. "I do not believe Your Majesty has thought of all the implications such a declaration will entail. There will be those who resist."

"And they shall be turned away from Court until they comply with my wishes. This is not unheard of. Mabb often used such tactics," Ayla answered quickly.

"With respect to Mabb—" and Cedric did not need to assure her of his genuineness in this respect "—do you truly wish to be seen as her equal in the eyes of your subjects?"

"My subjects clamor to be Human, though they don't admit it." She thought of the words of the Goddess, who'd delivered her from death, who'd revealed Ayla's purpose to her in the barren in-between of the healing Astral plane. Nearly struck down by Garret's ax, she had been spared to rescue the Fae from their obsession with Humanity, an obsession that the Goddess had blamed for destroying the Veil. An obsession that the exiled Fae races did not even see. Was such a proclamation, to dress in such a way as to appear more Human, a violation of the charge given to her by the Goddess?

No, it was for the greater good of her race. It was buying time for her tiny daughter. She continued,

"This will allow them to indulge their sick fantasy of mortality. I do not believe there will be so many protesters as you imagine."

Cedric did not argue, though whether he was in agreement or simply did not wish to pursue it further, Ayla could not tell. "I will make a pronouncement on the anniversary of Mabb's assassination. In that time, you may keep the child's wings disguised easily, and perhaps the Court will not link her birth as the cause for the new law."

"They will. And they will think she is deformed," Malachi said bitterly. "But if it is to protect the life of my child, I will bear it."

"You would bear it, no matter the cause," Ayla snapped, and she knew then that she was too tired, from the birth and from the meeting that had followed, to be reasonable any longer. "Thank you, Cedric. You may go and announce the birth of the Royal Heir, noting, of course, that she will be presented to all in a few weeks, when she's of an appropriate age."

"It would be my greatest honor, Your Majesty," he said, bowing low before exiting her chambers.

Malachi stayed at her side, looking longingly at his daughter. As though Ayla were not there to hear it, as though it were meant for no one but himself and the child, "It is for the best," he said quietly.

Her heart tore for him, but Ayla knew he was correct. Though it would pain him every day, disclos-

ing the truth about her parentage would only harm
Cerridwen.

The babe stirred, rustling her black feathered
wings. A small, angry sound issued from her lips, but
hushed as she drifted into sleep once more.

As they watched, awed by the mere presence of
their daughter, Ayla found she was not as tired as she
had thought. In fact, she felt she could study her
child endlessly.

One

It was easy to slip from the Palace unnoticed, when you knew exactly what to do. A mistake could get you returned to precisely where you did not wish to be— confinement, boredom, the duties of a Royal Heir— but she'd learned from her mistakes in the past. Now, it was nothing at all to duck her governess and gain her freedom.

It was especially easy on this night, when so many Faeries poured in through the Palace gates that the guards would not concern themselves with the ones going out.

And this was why Cerridwen did not object to yet another royal party. She'd complained on the surface, just enough so that her compliance would not arouse suspicion. And her governess had dressed her hair and helped her into her gown, all the while ignoring the expected grumbling and protesting that she had become so used to over the past twenty years.

Twenty years. Really. Who still had a nursemaid at twenty years old? Not even the Humans kept their children as children for that long!

Twenty years, this night, and a party to celebrate it. A party to celebrate one more year that the Royal Heir was not dead. What importance was an heir, really, in a race that did not die, or, at least, did not die naturally? There would be another party like it, and another, and another, always with the same Faeries, always in the same, boring pattern. A feast, then dancing, and conversation with the few faeries she was allowed to know, all of her mother's friends and advisors. How many evenings of her life had already been wasted in awkward chatter with Cedric, her mother's faithful lapdog, who never said or did anything interesting, lest he offend Her Majesty? Or Malachi, who glowered and stared in the most uncomfortable way, who, it was rumored, was not even a quarter Fae, but was kept because of some bizarre devotion to her mother?

"It is not a waste," Governess would say sagely while she pulled and pried at Cerridwen's tangles. "If it is the will of the Gods, you will never die. You cannot waste that which is infinite."

It did not make Cerridwen glad to know that her boredom would be infinite.

After she had been cleaned and dressed and made to look far more fine than usual for these occasions—which aroused some suspicion on her part that quickly faded when she remembered her plan to escape the party altogether—she had dutifully followed the guards that would escort her to the ball. Then she had promptly allowed herself to become separated from them by the chattering throng of arriving guests, and her escape was made.

It had not been hard to disguise her leather breeches under her gown, and when she reached an alcove, covered over by a tapestry of her mother, the Great Queene Ayla, slaying her father, the Betrayer King, she ducked behind the heavy fabric and shucked her dress, pulling on the shirt that she'd folded and hidden in her bodice. She kept her wings bound—where she was going, they did not know her as the Royal Heir to the throne of the Faeries, nor as a Faery at all. Among them, she was Human, and the ruse suited her.

The blowsy Human shirt—a ruffled, silk thing she traded with Gypsies for—would have covered her wings without their binding, but she had worn them bound since before she could remember. She felt almost naked without them secured to her back. Into her sleeve, she tucked a scrap of a mask. It would guarantee her entrance tonight, to a gathering much more desirable than the one she'd been expected to attend.

She left the dress and her shoes in the alcove. Better to go barefoot than break her neck in those flimsy slippers. She took a deep breath and slipped from her hiding place, but no one noticed her. As she wound her way through the crowd, deftly avoiding her abandoned and confused guards who stumbled, helpless, against the flow of bodies moving into the Palace, she pulled her hair over her shoulder and worked it into a loose braid, making sure to cover the wisps of antennae that sprouted from her forehead. By the time she reached the Palace gate, she could have been any Human slave being sent by their Faery master on an errand in the Lightworld.

Cerridwen spotted two such slaves following their owners into the Palace. In a time before her mother's reign, they all said, this would never have been tolerated. Queene Ayla herself did not care for the practice, either. It brought the Fae races too close to Humans, blurred the dividing line between them. No doubt the Faeries who brought Humans into the Palace tonight would either be turned away or have their names marked down somewhere to note that they were out of favor with the Queene.

Cerridwen's fists clenched at her sides as she marched away from the Palace. Her mother's hypocrisy never failed to ignite fury within her. She was half Human, and yet she criticized full-blooded Faeries for consorting with them? And she kept a Darkling at her side, yet railed against the Darkworld, as well?

The flames cooled as Cerridwen realized how far she had already traveled from the Palace, and how close she was to the freedom of the Strip. Already, she could hear the sounds of it echoing through the concrete walls of her prison world. She came to the edge of the Faery Court, nodded to the guards who stood dressed in her mother's livery, and broke into a joyous run toward the mouth of the tunnel.

The Strip was the neutral ground between the worlds of Dark and Light. A huge tunnel, reaching far over the heads of the creatures on the ground, with dwellings and places of commerce stacked on top of each other, the Strip was home to those who took no side in the ongoing war between Lightworld and Darkworld. Mostly Humans, the fascinating ancestors of Cerridwen's mother, and, she sometimes reminded herself with pride, of herself. Gypsies, who considered themselves apart from Humans, who claimed kinship to immortal creatures long ago. Bio-mechs, still Human, but fitted with metal parts.

Then, there were those that were not so fascinating, not so much as they were repulsive or frightening. Vampires, with their thirst for the death of any mortal creature. The Gypsies that even other Gypsies would not consort with, who lured creatures away from the safety of the Strip to harvest their parts. They pulled stinking carts, hawking their wares, eyes and teeth and horns, and nameless, slimy things that no one, at least, no one that Cerridwen could think of, would want. She could not fathom why any Human would chose to live in the Underground with the very creatures their race had banished below. After the destruction of the Veil between the world of the Astral and the world of mortals, the Earth had to be shared. The Humans had taken more than their share by driving the races of the Underground into their sewers and cellars. Why some of the Humans would follow the creatures into their skyless prison, Cerridwen could not explain.

She pushed her way across the wide tunnel, toward the stand that sold sweet Human bread, and the smell reminded her that she had not brought anything to trade with. She reached to her hair, where Governess had pinned a jeweled ornament. It was worth too much to trade for simple bread, but the sticky, spiced scent teased her empty belly. Tonight, she would be generous.

A soft, tutting sound came close to her ear, and a voice whispered, "You know better than that, Cerri."

She jumped and laughed as she turned. "Fenrick, you frightened me!"

As he always frightened her, a little. And thrilled her. He smiled, and his teeth stood out, brightly silver against the blue-black of his skin. "You should be frightened of me. You, Human, me Elf—we are, after all, mortal enemies."

"Mortal enemies," she agreed, good-naturedly, but she wished he would not make such jokes. They were enemies, more than he knew. Between Elf and Human, no love was lost. But the animosity between the Faery Court and the kingdom of Elves went back much farther than their confinement in the Underground.

He took the hair ornament from her hand and made a soft whistling sound as he examined it. "This looks like Faery craft. It fairly burns my skin to touch it."

"I found it in the mouth of a tunnel to the Lightworld." It was not a complete lie. She *had* found it in the Lightworld.

This impressed Fenrick; his pointed ears lifted as he smiled. "So much bravery for such a small thing! No doubt you'll be at the front line when the great battle comes."

The great battle. They often mocked it together, the lust for blood and war and victory that both the Lightworld and Darkworld professed at length. It was speaking out against such ideals that had gotten the Elves expelled from the Lightworld in the first years since the Great War with the Humans. And it was what had gotten Fenrick's father expelled from the Darkworld Elves only twenty-five years previous. Fenrick had grown, as Queene Ayla had, in the hardship of the Strip.

Strange, Cerridwen thought, that it made her

mother so angry and hardened at Humans, so different from Fenrick, who embraced the difficulties of his childhood and held no one unduly accountable.

Fenrick motioned to the stall owner and handed over his trade—a few water-stained packets of sugar from the Human world above, a booklet of paper scraps held together with coiled wire, and two or three small, coppery coins, also Human in origin—and waited for the thick-armed man to assess the value. He nodded, unsmiling, and broke off a large chunk of the sticky sweet bread for Fenrick.

Fenrick held up his hand. "For the Human. She was willing to part with something much more valuable for it."

At this, the shopkeeper's eyes widened in disbelief, and he made to pull the bread back, but Cerridwen snatched it and she and Fenrick ran laughing into the crowd at the center of the Strip.

When they stopped again, near one of the tunnels to the Darkworld, she meant to thank him for the bread. But Fenrick spoke first, and she used the opportunity to bite into the delicious Human confection.

"You look different tonight," Fenrick said, gesturing to her face. "You're wearing paint on your eyes. Trying to impress someone?"

She had forgotten to remove the cosmetics Governess had applied for the royal party. She swallowed carefully, the sticky bread sliding down her throat in a raw lump. Then, she put on a wicked grin, the one she had practiced in the mirror until it looked both teasing and good-humored. "Perhaps. Or several someones. The night is long."

He took a step forward, then another, until they were so close that his chest brushed hers. His gray tongue darted over his blue-black lips, his unsettlingly yellow gaze fixed on her mouth. He leaned down, and she did not know what to do, other than to flatten against the slope of the tunnel and move the bread to her side so that he did not crush it between them. His mouth covered hers—how often had she thought of this happening in the weeks since she'd met him?— and it was exactly like, yet strangely nothing at all like, what she had imagined it would be to be kissed. She heard a small noise from her throat before she could stop it; it was a shame, she wanted to appear experienced and unaffected.

When he moved back, it seemed to have been finished in a blink of an eye. For another blink, she waited, wondering what he would say, if this was when he would declare some feeling for her. Her heart stuck in her throat, or it might have been the bit of bread, but while she gaped at him wide-eyed, his serious, intense expression changed into one of laughter.

"Come on. The night isn't *that* long." He tugged on her hand and she followed him into the tunnel, bracing herself against the stench of decay that lingered in the Darkworld.

So, that was not what he meant by the kiss, though she did not know what he *had* meant. It did not matter. She could laugh and dance and be young, unencumbered by the strictures of Palace manners, the seriousness that pervaded every facet of her life in the Lightworld.

She let him take her hand and pull her deeper into the Darkworld, and she thought she could already hear the pulse of the music that awaited her.

"Your Majesty?"

Ayla looked up, away from the revelers who crowded the Great Hall. Cedric, seated at her side, turned his attention to the guard who had approached her, as did Malachi, who stood at the foot of the dais, in deep discussion with two other Faeries on her council.

Angry as she was with her daughter, she would not show it. Nor would she show any concern, though in the back of her mind it crept in to spoil her annoyance. "Yes? Have you found her?"

"No, Your Majesty. We did find a dress, which her servants have confirmed belonged to her, and shoes." He cleared his throat, obviously nervous to have to speak to his Queene thusly. "Is it possible that she has left the Palace? We do not wish to presume—"

Ayla cut him off with a glare. "If she is not in the Palace," she began, her voice low and serious, "then she has left the Palace. You do not need my permission to think so. Organize your men and find her!"

Cedric cleared his throat. He did not approve of her tone, or what she had said, that was certain. But she did not give him leave to speak. Nor would she meet Malachi's concerned gaze.

It was all too appropriate that her daughter would demonstrate her willful disobedience tonight, of all nights. It proved that she needed guidance, and if she would not listen to her mother, she would have to be influenced by someone far wiser, and more patient.

It had not been an easy decision to make. Ayla had first thought of assigning her a position on the royal council, but Cedric had warned against it. There would be too many opportunities for her to discover the truth about Ayla's past, too many chances for an untrustworthy member of council to flaunt their knowledge in an attempt to hurt the Queene.

A Guild, then, seemed far more appropriate. When Ayla had come to the Lightworld, the Assassins' Guild had taught her discipline, and respect for her race. But she could not choose the life of an Assassin for her daughter. It was too dangerous. The Healers' Guild accepted only those with an established gift for healing, and Cerridwen had not displayed such a talent. The other Guilds also fell under Ayla's harsh scrutiny, and were rejected.

Her only course of action, the only sensible course of action, was the one she had determined to take long before this royal feast had been planned.

"Perhaps," Cedric began quietly, "we should put it about that the Royal Heir is ill, and cannot attend this evening?"

Ayla drummed her fingertips on the table. Whenever Cerridwen went missing, there was some lie about her health to cover the disappearance. Doubtless, no one believed the stories any longer. "No. We've made her sound as sickly as a changeling as it is."

The servants cleared away the plates from the meal; already members of the Court stirred, restless for the dancing and merrymaking to begin. There would be no other opportunity.

"Cedric, tell the herald I wish to make an announcement."

An announcement her advisor would not, she suspected, be enthused about. But he was dutiful. He would obey her and put on a good face before the Court. She was sure of it.

As if sensing some unpleasantness to come, Cedric nodded warily and pushed back from the table. Though their wings were bound, the Faeries in the great hall perched upon low stools, so that the tips were not bent by the torturous contraptions that were Human chairs.

Within moments, the herald sounded the call that would bring the entire assembly's attention to their Queene. At the loud, metal clanging of the bell, Ayla rose and fixed her face with a serene smile.

As she opened her mouth to speak, panic hit her full in the chest. How could she do this? Only a handful of years separated her from the babe who'd snuggled at her side, the gangling, near-mortal child who had nestled clumsily in her mother's lap after a scrape. If she could have, she would have kept her daughter from growing at all.

Kept her from growing into the alien creature who had seemed to replace that sweet child overnight.

The anger at her daughter's ill-timed "disappearance" flared to new life and fixed her resolve.

"Friends," she began, her throat constricting as though to prevent her from speaking the words she was sure to regret. "My daughter, high-spirited as she is, seems to have slipped away from the festivities. That is unfortunate, as she is unaware that there is so much more to celebrate on this night. More than the reminder of her joyous birth, more than our gratitude for the continuance of the royal bloodline she descended from. Tonight, we celebrate her betrothal."

There was a rumble of approval. Every Faery

present would be delighted to hear this news first-hand, and relate it to those who were not fortunate enough to be there for the historic announcement themselves.

Ayla continued, "As I have said, my daughter has a reputation for high spirits, and that reputation is well earned. She is a creature more Fae than many of us, in many ways. Her mate should be, then, someone who remembers how to be the way we were. Someone who knows how to live with and appreciate the gentle nature that she exhibits, and who will respect her position as heir to a cherished bloodline." She took a breath, which others almost certainly judged a dramatic pause. Truly, she teetered on the precipice of a moment she could not reverse, words she could not revoke. "That Faery is my chief advisor and close personal friend, Cedric."

A mixture of murmurs, gasps and applause rose from the hall, but all of it sounded pleased, and the ball of anxiety in Ayla's chest unclenched.

And then she caught sight of Cedric, standing in the crowd, ignoring the congratulations of those who gathered around him, staring in shock and—*anger?* Was he angry—at his Queene?

Ayla looked away, too uncomfortable under Cedric's glare—for that was what it was, an angry, disbelieving glare—and found Malachi. His expression was much the same.

When she looked away, to Cedric again, her advisor pushed through the crowd, brushed aside all of those Faeries who wanted to congratulate and envy him, on his way to the doors.

Ayla waved to the leader of her musicians, and they began a lively dancing tune on their bells, harps, and whistles. The commotion around Cedric's departure wouldn't be forgotten, but for a moment, the dancing would take the place of the gossip.

Ayla looked for Malachi. But he, too, had disappeared from the gathering.

He stalked through the tunnels almost without seeing, so blinding was his anger. How could she have done this? Without consulting him, without warning him, at least?

He would not take this. For twenty years now, he'd stood by her side and played the faithful servant. When her regard had faded to expectation and every day she took him a bit more for granted, he had ignored it. When she had begun to question his advice, then blame him publicly for decisions whose consequences could have firmly been laid at her feet, he'd stayed silent. And after all he'd done. Without him, she would have been executed, or rotted away for the rest of her immortal life in King Garret's dungeons. This was how she repaid him.

No more. She would regret this callous disregard she'd dealt him.

He'd already passed through the Strip, into the tunnels of the Darkworld, more familiar and welcoming now to him than the place he called home. Perhaps it was because the menace here was on display, not hidden beneath layers of pretty trinkets and vapid treasures. Here, he could slay those who harmed him and not be fooled by his own sense of loyalty.

In the darkness ahead, a figure moved. Small, almost shrinking from the shadows, its voice called out in a ragged whisper. "Cedric?"

"It is," he called back, in the mortal tongue he had learned but not fully mastered. He often wondered if he sounded foolish or stupid to the Humans, the way the Queene's Consort sounded to his ears when he attempted to speak the Fae language. But his self-consciousness was forgotten when the figure broke into a run, and he braced himself for the slight weight of her body colliding with his, her arms twining in his hair.

Dika. An ugly, mortal-sounding word for such a creature. Soft, and somehow clean when all around her was sordid and filthy. Cedric buried his hands in the coiling fall of her dark hair, pressed his lips to hers, finding her mouth hot and eager under his, as it always was when they had been apart.

"I worried you would not come," she gasped against him, her hands clutching to fists in the fabric of his shirt. "That you no longer wanted me."

He would have laughed at her if he hadn't known that such an action would anger her. She, like many of the Humans he had met through her, did not enjoy being laughed at. But how could she have thought he would abandon her? The only thing that pushed him, mechanical, through his days and nights was the prospect of being with her.

"That is absurd. I would never wish to be parted from you." He inhaled the perfumed scent of her hair, wanting to hold the fragrance in his mind so that he would remember it in the smoke and spice of the Lightworld. He was never able to.

"I am glad to hear it," she whispered, still clinging to him. "Because we have confirmation from our Upworld contacts. We are leaving."

He stepped back, though all he wanted was to pull her closer. "When?"

"Soon." She reached up to touch his face, smoothed her hand over his antennae, which he knew glowed with his anxiety. "I want you to come with us."

They had discussed this before. He did not wish to do so again, and especially not now, when they had been apart for so long.

But later, as they lay together, awake but not

speaking, in the tangle of rough bedding in the secret room that was for them only, for their meetings, the unavoidable notion of her leaving the Underground could not be ignored. The thought nagged at him, like pain from a wound seen but not yet felt.

And yet, it was something of a relief, too. If she left the Underground, there would be no longing for her after the Queene's ridiculous proclamation was carried out. No wondering if she still felt for him, as he surely would, always, for her. And most importantly, no need to lie to seek her out. That was something he could never do, no matter how repulsive the thought of the marriage would be. Though his race might view the mortal concept of fidelity as antiquated and quaint, Cedric had lived long enough to know that lies, of any kind, destroyed one's self faster and more efficiently than a blade ever could. Though murdered, Mabb had brought on her own end through constant duplicity. Her brother, her murderer, Garret, had gone in much the same way. Cedric would not repeat their missteps.

"You could come with us, you know," Dika said quietly, her breath teasing the skin of his chest where her head lay. "I know you've said that you don't want to. But you could pass for Human, and my people will protect you. We protect our own."

"I will give it thought." He wanted to believe that were true. That he could go with her, escape what life had become all those hundreds of years ago when the Veil first tore in half. But he could guarantee her nothing.

He could guarantee himself nothing.

Two

The music thrummed through her veins like a secondary heartbeat, an all-consuming imperative to move among the seething mass of bodies around her. They were all different shades and varying species, not like the uniformly lithe and perfect forms of the Faery races.

Cerridwen had lost track of the time, and she did not care. She had lost track of Fenrick, too; that was more worrying. But the part of her that cared was enslaved by the part of her that wanted to remain where she was and dance. Fenrick would turn up. She did not want to stay at his side like a mewling kitten.

Unless someone else was at his side.

She stood on tiptoe to see above the heads that bobbed in time to the music around her. It was dark; she would not be able to spot him, another degree of darkness in all of the moving shadows.

The tunnel where they gathered was another of those crisscrossing tunnels that comprised the Underground, holes once made by the Humans above for their great trains to rush through. This one was not decorated with tiled patterns, or arranged like the Great Hall in the Palace. Here, they danced wherever they could find the space, and the music came from loud, Human machines, not tin-sounding whistles and bells. This music was alive.

Though she was loath to the leave the dancing behind, Cerridwen could not shake the thought that Fenrick might be one of those shadows, in one of those corners, with another. *And what will you do if he is?* she chided herself. *Demand that he turn his attentions to you?*

She shoved the voice of self-doubt away and pushed through the crowd. It was much harder to move in the room if one was not dancing, like pushing one's hand against a current of water. She reached an edge, the platform where the big trains would have stopped to let Humans on. She came upon it faster than she'd thought she would, and for a dizzying moment realized she could have easily stepped over. She felt her way to the ladder and followed something vaguely mortal—she hoped it was not a Vampire—down to the next level. Beyond the reach of the lights, a bit of a Human train remained, though the tracks had been scavenged by Gypsies and Bio-mechs long ago.

There was a door, and crudely constructed steps leading to it, and someone inside.

She knew, without actually knowing, that she would find Fenrick there. Once up the wobbly set of steps, though, she faltered. Did she knock, or simply barge in, trusting that her bravery and brazenness would impress him as it had in the past?

If he is with someone else in there, he might not appreciate the intrusion, the doubt crept in again. Before she had time to force it aside, the door popped open, nearly toppling her from the steps. She backed down as Fenrick emerged, his expression angry for the barest of seconds, then pleased and surprised.

"I'd thought I'd lost you," he said, the flash of his silver teeth the only indication of his smile in the darkness.

Cerridwen smiled back, to show she had not taken his disappearance too seriously. "I thought you were trying to lose me." Movement in the dirty windows of the train caught her eye. He had not been in there alone, nor in a romantic engagement. The movement was accompanied by a muffled shout of voices in unison. "What were you doing?"

Fenrick came down the steps, his body language easy, but he did not look behind him. "Just chatting with a few old friends."

A cry went up from the dance floor above their heads. Not the enthusiastic shout that sometimes came from a group having a good time. The screams of a crowd interrupted by something unexpected, unpleasant.

"Watch out," Fenrick said, strangely calm as he pulled her out of the way of a large, furred beast jumping down from the level above. He backed them into the safety of a narrow space between the train car and tunnel wall, even as those inside the train rushed out.

As they watched, more creatures jumped from the upper level, some landing on their feet and running off down the tunnel, others falling roughly, only to be crushed by the next creature who jumped down. The less-brave partiers swarmed another ladder, and slipped down it in a hurry to get away from whatever pursued.

"What is it?" Cerridwen whispered, aware, but only fleetingly, that their bodies were startlingly close together in this space, and that he had not let go of her.

"It could be anything," he whispered back, his breath stirring her hair. "Wraiths, maybe. Or Demons. But Demons are running from whatever it is…they would fight another Demon."

She shivered, from the fear and from the proximity of him.

And then, the pleasant shivers faded. Shouts, in the Fae language, angry male shouts, drifted to her ears, and soldiers, wearing her mother's seal, followed the crowd over the edge.

If not for the confusion of the scene, they might have spotted her, but they pursued the Darklings down the tunnel, away from her hiding place.

"Lightworlders!" Fenrick rasped vehemently in her ear. "What are those scum doing here?"

She knew what they were doing. She could not let them find her.

"Let's get out of here," she insisted, trying to move past him, down the tunnel blocked by the train. "Come on!"

She'd expected him to mock her. "Are you afraid?" she'd thought he'd say. But he did not. He gripped her arm and pulled her, inching their way past the train car, to the open tunnel where they could run. And he pulled his knife, a wicked, curved thing, from under his shirt.

They ran until they were out of breath, until her legs ached and her wings strained at their binding, as if arguing with her that flying would serve her better. She forced herself onward, until she could no longer stand it, and collapsed to her knees, her breath coming from her in loud, frightened sobs.

Fenrick knelt at her side, and tossing his knife away, put his arms around her. "It's all right. We're safe," he assured her between panting breaths. "It's all right."

He kissed her hair, held her head to his chest, kept

her close to him. All she had to do was catch her breath, and tilt her face up....

When she did, he kissed her, hard and furious, as if he could expel all her fear and exertion of their flight by channeling it into himself. And she melted under his mouth, his tongue. Melted into him.

She pushed her hands under his shirt, found the blue-black skin beneath warm under her fingers.

"You're shaking," he said against her mouth, and he reached for the ties of her shirt.

She caught his hands, her heart thumping hard. "Did you hear that?"

"I didn't hear anything." He leaned to kiss her again, trying to shrug aside her hands, but she resisted him and climbed to her feet warily.

Down the tunnel, where a shaft of light from another, intersecting route pierced the darkness, something moved. Cerridwen thought of Wraiths and the destruction they could wreak.

"What are you afraid of?" Fenrick asked, an edge of impatience in his voice.

It was not a Wraith. It bobbed as it moved, as though it were walking. The Wraiths glided above the ground.... At least, that was what she had heard.

"I am not afraid of anything," she stated boldly.

He rose to his feet and pulled his shirt over his head, tossed it aside. "Then come here, if you aren't afraid."

She looked away, for although she could not see

his, he would be able to read her expression in the dark. And she spied his blade on the ground.

She stooped to grab it and walked slowly down the tunnel, toward whatever the creature was that continued toward them.

"Cerri, what are you doing? Come back," Fenrick called.

The creature in the shadows halted.

"Cerridwen?"

Her heart lurched in her chest at the familiar voice.

"Cerridwen? The Royal Heir?" The creature stumbled closer, two spots of angry red light forming in the darkness, where his antennae would be. "Is that you?"

He stumbled close enough to see her, and she looked over her shoulder for Fenrick. He was invisible in the darkness, or maybe he'd left her there. She hoped that he'd left. She did not wish for her game to be given away so soon, just as things were becoming interesting between them.

Cedric gripped her by her arms and shook her, nearly knocking the knife from her hands. "What are you doing here?" he shouted, his hands crushing painfully. "Do you have any idea how dangerous this area is?"

Now, she knew that Fenrick had gone. He would not have let someone lay his hands on her this way. She pushed Cedric back. "How dare you!"

"I should do *worse*," he threatened, coming a step closer, looming over her.

She laughed, tried to make it sound as scathing and bitter as she had heard from Courtiers. "No, I mean how dare you follow me here, like my mother's obedient dog! How dare you show yourself such disrespect!"

"Your mother?" he asked, his expression suddenly confused.

Something mean and vicious blossomed in Cerridwen's chest. "Yes, my mother. She's sent soldiers here to find me. Her soldiers, into the Darkworld. And you…you didn't know?"

"If I had, be assured I would not have let it happen." He grabbed her arm again, and pulled her toward the crossing of the tunnels.

"You didn't know, and you didn't know to come look for me," she accused. It made more sense, now. Why he'd been so surprised to find her. Why he'd been in the tunnels with no guards. "You were here on your own business."

"Of a sort," he admitted sourly. They reached the intersection and he started off in the wrong direction.

She yanked him the right way, preferring to glare at him rather than argue, and tucked the knife into her belt. "And what business could you possibly have in the Darkworld, oh shining beacon of loyalty?"

"My own," he snapped. "This is not the right way."

"I was unaware that you were so knowledgeable about the Darkworld." She pulled free from his grasp. "I will be sure to tell my mother about your expertise."

"Your mother already knows." He followed her; she heard his boots splash through a puddle, and a curse. That made her smile.

"You could tell your mother about how I found you." He sounded no less angry, but it seemed as though he tried to mask his wrath. "Or I could tell her about how I found you."

"And you would be admitting to your own guilt," she reminded him, turning a corner. He was not expecting the bend, and she heard a loud exclamation as he collided with the wall.

"Which is why," he seethed through his teeth, "I suggest we reach an agreement. I will tell her I found you on the Strip, and you will not contradict me. The consequences of that accidental meeting will be far less than the ones attached to the truth."

"She will still wonder why you left the Lightworld," Cerridwen pointed out, feeling very satisfied to have the advantage.

But the advantage disappeared as he muttered, "Your mother will be aware of my reasons."

It was cryptic. Cerridwen did not like cryptic responses. But ahead loomed the path to the Strip.

"Do we have an agreement?" he asked her, no urgency in his voice, no pleading.

She crossed her arms, pretending to consider. But this manipulation failed, as well, for Cedric said nothing, made no further offers.

"We do," she said with a sigh. It would have been so sweet to catch her mother's favorite in a useful web, but he was right. The punishment her mother meted out to her would be far less severe if she'd been caught somewhere else.

They proceeded to the Lightworld and passed the borders without further speech, but when they approached the Palace, he stopped her.

"When we enter, go straight to your chambers. Wash all of that off your face, and change into something respectable before you are presented to your mother." He would not look at her.

She tilted her chin up, trying to look confident when now all she felt like was a child. "How do I know you will not simply run to her and break our agreement?"

"I will not. With more reason than you know." With that, he turned and stalked through the Palace gates.

"We have some reason to suspect that she has left the Lightworld."

The words froze Ayla, the way she imagined a prey

animal would cower before a beast. She'd long since retired from the party, but it continued, the noise thrumming like the workings of some great machine throughout the Palace. The dull pounding of drums, punctuated by the sharp staccato of voices raised in laughter, served to cover the startled thump of the blood in her veins. "Where is Malachi?"

"He has organized a few discreet guards into a search formation." The captain of her guard bowed. "We are keeping this secret, Your Majesty."

"As well you should," she said, amazed to find her voice working under its own power. "You may go, now, Captain. Keep me informed of your progress. And bring her to me the moment you find her."

The guard bowed as he left, but she did not acknowledge him. Instead, she waited, seated on the edge of her bed, staring at nothing. Waited for the guilt to come crashing over her, as it always did. The questions that she would torment herself with: How could she have let this happen? Hadn't she been a good enough mother to Cerridwen? Of course, she had not. She had been too wrapped up in Court politics and her own selfish pursuits! She could not blame Cerridwen, only herself.

But this time, the guilt did not come. She was angry, angrier than she had ever been with her daughter.

Perhaps it was because Cerridwen had left the

safety of the Lightworld. Perhaps it was fear that drove her anger. She certainly knew, better than most at Court, of what danger there was to fear beyond the boundaries of the Lightworld.

No, it was anger. An ugly, naked anger not polite enough to wear a mask of fear for her convenience.

She could not bear to stare at the walls of her room any longer. Beautiful though it might be, with its configuration of electric stars on the ceiling and the grass growing forever verdant beneath her feet, she did not take comfort in fine things the way Mabb had. Tying the ribbons of her bedrobe, she went to the passage in the wall, the one that Cedric had begged her to seal off, rather than risk dying as Mabb had. She had refused for a number of reasons that had sounded sane and logical on the surface. Truly, she had done it because the way to the King's chamber, now the chamber of the Queene's Consort, was too public, and she did not wish her servants to know her comings and goings. Mabb, though she had never had an official Consort, nor a King to rule at her side, must have felt the same.

Ayla slipped out of the secret door and walked cautiously, looking for guards. Revelers from the party would not be in this part of the Palace, but she did not wish to listen to another report of her missing daughter, or be reassured that she would be found.

She went through the passage to Malachi's chambers and fished the door key from her sleeve, where she wore it loosely tied at her wrist. The door opened and she stepped through just as the main door to the room slammed open and against the wall.

Malachi stood in the doorway, his expression changing from surprise to anger. Ayla moved to quickly close the door behind her, so that no passing servant would see.

They stood in the antechamber. Malachi had been Garret's prisoner there, until Ayla had come to save him. She remembered how she had trembled that night, in fear and uncertainty, and the feeling crept back to her now.

He stared at her, his face gray with fatigue. He looked different now than he had when he'd first come to live in the Palace. Since his fall from his former, Angelic nature, he'd aged as a Human, rapidly. In what had seemed a blink of an eye, his features had become sharper, etched with hard lines. A streak of silver stood out from the ink-black of his hair, and though he was as large and physically powerful as he had been twenty years before, he did not exert himself with the vigor that he had in his youth. Every day he seemed older, the way mortals, distressingly, became. Ayla did not wish to dwell on it, and she looked away from his hard expression.

"How could you do this?" he asked in a raw whisper.

Ayla snapped her head up, glared back at him. "Cerridwen has run off on her own! If you wish to blame anyone, blame her governess, blame her guards!"

"I am not talking about her running off!" He slammed the door closed behind him, and it shook as though it would fall from its hinges. "Do you have any idea what you have done? To her? To Cedric? They have both run off now, and if I were him I would never return!"

This stunned her. Over the past twenty years, they had disagreed. And how they had disagreed, and over such petty things. But while he'd raged at her—his emotions ran high, another mortal trait—what he said now was somehow more hurtful.

Most hurt was her pride, and she sought to defend this crumbling wall without reason. "I did what I had to do! Cerridwen is out of control. She runs from me, she runs from this Palace. At this very instant she is out of the Lightworld altogether. She needs someone who will be better suited to keeping her here, and safe."

"And she won't run from Cedric? He is centuries old! She is a child!" He swallowed, and looked as though it pained him. "And what is to say that Cedric would not run from her? And from you?"

"Cedric will do as I command. *I am Queene!*" It sounded so meaningless, like a child threatening during a tantrum.

Malachi laughed. "Yes, he will bow and scrape, as all of your Courtiers do—because he must. How does that feel, Ayla, to know that those closest to you only do as you ask because they are accustomed to being ruled? To know that they do not do these things out of any love or respect for you?"

"My Court respects me! If they did not, I would no longer be Queene!"

"You would not be Queene if Cedric had not willed it so!"

A knock sounded at Malachi's door, and they both fell silent, not wishing to continue the fight, but not wanting to admit defeat, either.

"Malachi, I have news." It was Cedric.

Ayla's anger had not abated, and she glared at Malachi, defiant, as if daring him to open the door, warning that if he did, she would not relent in her argument with him.

"Come in," Malachi said, all the fight gone from his voice. He looked tired, as if every mortal cell of his body were weary. And in that moment, Ayla lost her anger with him, and it was replaced by that fear which had become all too familiar. Fear that he would succumb to his mortality soon, and that she would waste the time they had in petty arguments. They had already wasted so much time.

Cedric entered, and, spying Ayla, carefully masked his expression. "She has been found."

Relief weakened Ayla's knees, and Malachi uttered a quiet, "Thank God."

"Where was she?" Ayla would not allow even the ghost of the earlier tension to remain. She would not discuss the betrothal now.

"She was on the Strip. Disguised as a Human, watching a game of Human gambling." He cleared his throat. "I found her there, and brought her here."

"Thank you." The fear in Ayla's breast loosened its hold a bit. She had not ventured into danger, not as much as she could have. "Malachi, do you have a way to contact your search party? To call them back? I do not wish them to go far."

She did not wish them to go into the Darkworld, where their presence could begin a war.

Wearily, Malachi rose. "I know where they plan to search. I will go to them."

"No," she said, realizing too late how commanding she'd sounded, and how little Malachi would appreciate her tone. She forced herself to soften, willed away the anger and anxiety of the night. "You are tired. Send someone, but do not go yourself."

He should have argued with her; it alarmed her that he did not. He waved a hand to Cedric. "Can you find someone?"

"I will see to it myself." He turned toward the door, and paused. "Your Majesty, I did not tell the heir of what transpired at the feast tonight. I sent her to her chambers… I thought perhaps you would wish to speak to her, before she heard it from another source."

"I will speak to her. About your betrothal, and about her disappearance." Ayla loathed the need to apologize that clawed its way up her throat. She forced it down. "I hope you realize that I am only thinking of what will be best for my daughter. And for you."

His wings, confined by his robes, rustled under their fabric prison. She saw the movement, a furious shrug, and again the apology that some regretful part of her knew should be delivered tried to escape.

She was Queene. She would not let him force his guilt onto her.

Cedric did not face her. The weight of his words was measured carefully. "I realize that you believe you know what is best, and that you are acting under that belief."

When he left, he did not slam the door, but it was, without a doubt, closed.

"I do not do this to hurt either of them," Ayla said helplessly, turning to Malachi. He'd already removed his robe, revealing his now-scarred skin and the metal-patched black wings that had not been seen by the Court in over twenty years.

He looked up at her, not bothering to conceal his anger or hurt. "Get out, Ayla. I am tired."

She could have reminded him that she was

Queene…. But she had never been his Queene. She
could have ignored him and stayed…. But she had
done so before, and had accomplished nothing. No
subtle shift of power between them, no grudging recon-
ciliation. He would forgive her when he chose and no
sooner.

Three

It was simple enough to find the search party Malachi had ordered—what had he hoped to accomplish by sending them into the Darkworld?—and convince them to give up their search. He insisted on staying behind, in case there were stragglers, even after the soldiers insisted there would not be.

And there would not be. That was not Cedric's purpose in staying.

When he'd put enough distance between himself and the guards, he changed direction, and pulled from his shirtsleeve the rolled paper diagram that would lead him to the Gypsy camp.

The tunnels were not named on the drawing. Many of them went unnamed in the Darkworld, so it would not have helped. And only a few symbols, known only to those who were intended to find the place, indicated that it was a map at all. Dika had gone over it with him many times, though he'd protested ever needing to use it. He did not like to be in close proximity to mortals—at least, not large groups of them—and did not know how they would react to his presence. She'd been correct in her assumption that someday, his need to find her would be stronger than his desire to stay away.

He followed the map, doubting every turn, fearful of what might lurk in the shadows. It had been a long time since he'd had to use his battle training, and despite what most outside of the Guild believed, he'd rarely gone on missions as an Assassin, content to orchestrate the assignments and send others to do the fighting. He knew of the horrors that could lurk in these tunnels, knew in theory how to protect himself, but he'd not had the practice for a long time.

It was a relief when the tunnels became less dark, less damp. He knew it was a trick of his mind to equate light with safety, for untold horrors already stalked through both dark and light. But there seemed to be a life energy pulsing along the walls that Cedric could see in bright handprints and hurried smears where shoulders and limbs had brushed the cement in passing. These mortal imprints did not flare with terrified or angry energy, but happy excitement—the feeling of being home.

It was a feeling that Cedric could easily recognize

but not truly understand. Faeries did not have homes. A dwelling to return to every night was a prison. The true joy of their existence had always been in the roaming, the never knowing where you would wake that morning or sleep that night. Trooping, that was what they had been made for. It made their lives in the Underground a particularly cruel hell.

Here, the feeling of home was pleasant, not stifling, and he continued on, alert for the rising of sound, which always accompanied the living spaces of mortals. The tunnel bent, and there were no more electric lightbulbs, but grates that let in the starlight. The scent of wood smoke, a smell he hadn't experienced in decades, drifted up the tunnel, and, sooner than he expected, the buzz of mixed music and conversation. He rounded another bend and staggered on his feet at the sight of his destination.

It was as if the Underground had disappeared. The ground was Earth. Hard packed, dotted with bits of crumbled cement at intervals, but real Earth. The walls were not the carefully constructed tunnels the Humans had burrowed through the ground for pipes and trains and sewage, but rough rock walls that arched high, surrounding a hole with irregular edges and no grates, no barriers between the Upworld and the Underground. Through it, the view of the starry sky was blocked only by the black shapes of trees, reaching into the night above the heads of the mortals below.

And how many mortals! Cedric was certain the Humans here numbered far more than all the creatures on the Strip. Their dwellings were clustered in untidy, winding rows, pieces of property claimed here and there by stakes in the ground. Some of the dwellings were simple cloth tents. Others were built side by side and joined together by common walls of cinder-block and other materials. There were roofs made from blue sheets of mortal plastic or metal hammered flat, and some homes had no roofs at all. Mortal children ran without heed past mortal women stirring pots over communal fires or hanging sodden garments over lines stretched between tents. There seemed to be fire and joy and life everywhere, and for a moment, it truly overwhelmed him.

There was something else, too.... A sense of expectation, of a burden lifted. He remembered Dika's words, and it froze the joy within him to ice.

He remembered why he had come. It occurred to him for the first time that, although he had found his way here, finding Dika would be a much different task. He would have to enter the settlement, not just survey it from afar.

Dika had never told him what to expect of her home, nor what to expect of the people there. It was possible that she had not properly thought through the consequences of his being there, that she had no idea how other mortals would react to an immortal creature in their midst. But such carelessness was not like Dika, and so he concluded that it would be safe to enter the camp.

There were no guards; at least, no formal display of armed might, but a few males wandered at the outskirts of the camp, and one, upon spotting Cedric, approached.

"Do you speak our language?" he called, pulling something off of his back. A gun, one of those strange Human weapons that incorporated the magic of fire and force. Cedric stepped back instinctively. He did not care for such objects.

"I have this," he called out in lieu of answering the question. He held out the map, and when the mortal came close enough, he let the man take it.

The man frowned at the paper. "Who gave you this?"

"Dika." It was the only name he had. Did mortals, Gypsies, have other names? Secret ones that only they used with each other? "She told me her name was Dika."

The mortal laughed. "Dika is a very common name. I suppose next you will tell me that she has dark hair and eyes?"

Cedric had nothing to say to this. The man continued to regard him with wary amusement. He did not return the map.

"I can walk you back to the Strip, friend," he said,

tucking the folded paper into the pocket of his shirt. "But you cannot become lost in our land again."

"I must speak with her." Though Cedric tried to keep his voice even, he heard the desperation in his words. "She has told me that you are leaving soon. That this will all be gone. I cannot chance not seeing her... I have made a terrible mistake."

The mortal's eyes narrowed. "How do you know of our leaving?"

"Because Dika told me. She told me. I can't give you proof, but please, I must find her." Cedric could say no more, only look to the man with what must have been pleading on his face, and wait for his decision.

Finally, the man sighed the heavy sigh of something giving way. "You are an outsider. You will have to take your case to the Dya."

"Dya," he repeated the word, rolled the unfamiliar shape of it around his mouth. "Dika did not mention this."

"If you wish to see Dika, you will have to obey our rules, friend," the mortal said, his smile not so kind.

There was little else Cedric could do but agree and follow the man through the maze of the mortal city. They passed the rough dwellings, came to cleaner, neater homes—as clean and neat as anything in the Underground could be—made from the same mortal materials, but with a certain air of pride about them.

The children running the winding paths here were not as dirty, and the garments hanging to dry were much finer.

The people stared at Cedric as they passed. Mortals were roughly shaped, as if each was cut from a spare scrap of cloth, rather than crafted from the finest bolt. Of course, his appearance would stand out to them. Could they tell he was not mortal? He was built larger than most Faeries, but he stood only as tall as an average Human woman. The Gypsies were small people, though, wiry and compact, and Dika had not known him to be Fae, when they'd first met. He'd thought then that it was something of an insult, to look mortal. He still did, when other Fae muttered it about him. But now, now it might serve him to appear Human.

The mortal man led him to the center of the city. Only here did the plan of the settlement make sense. All of the winding streets led to the center hub, where a huge, communal fire blazed. Groups of singing, dancing, feasting Humans clustered around the wide pit of flames, mortal bodies writhing like salamander shadows in the firelight. Cedric's guide skirted these groups, smiling or calling out to wave at someone, but he never veered from his path.

It was only after they had rounded the fire pit and started down a wide avenue that Cedric noticed people following them. On the other streets they'd taken, he'd assumed the traffic behind them had been the normal progression of bodies moving to their intended destinations. But this street was empty of dwellings, lit only by the flickering light from the communal fire, and the trailing mortals were evident. Cedric looked over his shoulder once, saw the eagerness and anticipation in their eyes, and did not care to see them anymore.

At the end of the path loomed the ancient, gnarled roots of a tree, the top of which would stretch into the Upworld sky, but the trunk and branches were not visible here, beneath the ground. The looping tentacles lay like the sleeping form of a Leviathan, those underwater creatures that mortal men no longer feared, though they should. It caused a shiver to crawl between Cedric's wings; Faeries, too, feared the horrors of the deep.

A Gypsy wagon, like the ones Cedric had spied tramping through the forests of the mortal realm centuries ago, sat beneath the cascading roots, dwarfed by the coils that unfurled around it like embracing arms. This was where the mortal led him, and the people behind them stopped, either from respect or fear.

A small fire crackled beneath a smoke-blackened cauldron, and a female knelt beside it, the flames gilding her glossy black curls. Cedric stopped, though the Human continued on without him. "Dika?"

She turned, seeming to see the other Gypsy man first, then himself, and then the crowd at the edge of the camp. Her smooth face creased with confusion. "Cedric? You've come here?"

The answer was obvious, as he stood before her, but he did not say so. "You are the leader here?"

She came forward slowly, shaking her head. "No. No. I stay here with her…to help her."

The mortal who had led him there drew himself up to his full height. "This stranger has come to this camp uninvited, and he must face your grandmother's judgment."

"He was not uninvited. I gave him a map to find us. *I* invited him here." She squared her shoulders and glared at him, unblinking. It seemed neither of them would ever look away from the other, then the door of the wagon opened, and their attention shifted.

A lamp of many-colored glass hung beside the wagon door, and it swung wildly, sending a rainbow of shadows across the figure that emerged. At first glance, the figure seemed not even Human; a hunch-backed thing, like a rune stone jutting up from the ground, with a head covered by a leather cap with dangling flaps that obscured her face. She shuffled, and with each step the shells and trinkets wound on cords around her neck and arms clanked and jingled. The Humans waited with speechless patience as the woman made her way forward with a maddeningly slow gait.

When she was close enough to be heard, she pushed the flaps of the cap away from her face, revealing a countenance so marred by age that it resembled to Cedric some kind of rotted fruit shrinking in on itself. Two shrewd black eyes peered out from beneath eyebrows grown thick and white with age, and her seemingly toothless mouth worked from side to side as she regarded the mortals. "Dika, go and stir the stew pot."

Dika left. In her obedience, she did not say a word for Cedric's defense, as though she was not concerned about leaving him to this crone's devices.

Then the old woman looked past the mortal who had led him there and declared with delight, "Why, Milosh! You've brought me a Faery!"

This was obviously a surprise to Milosh, as well as to the audience clustered behind them. But to the Dya, this development seemed as natural as if she'd found a coin in the street. "I think," she pronounced with gravity, "I shall call him Tom."

This, finally, moved Cedric to speak. "I am Cedric, lady. Of the Court of Queene Ayla of the Lightworld."

"Yes, yes, and before that the Court of Queene Mabb, far beyond the Veil." She turned to Milosh. "Go. And take them with you. I don't suppose this one Faery is going to invade our camp. And if he is, well, I shall have to take him hostage."

Milosh, his chest swelling with anger, would not

be dismissed. "Your granddaughter gave him our location. She led him here and told him of our migration plan."

"She's told him more than that, I'll wager." The Dya raised her voice so that it would be heard by not only Milosh and Cedric, but Dika as well. "I'm sure she's told him a great many interesting things."

Dika's head and shoulders sagged as she stirred the cauldron.

"Come, Tom." The Dya no longer spoke to Milosh, as though he'd obeyed her and already left. "We shall talk about this transgression you've committed."

She shuffled toward the side of the wagon away from the fire, where a small iron table and chairs sat rusting in the shadows. "You aren't really allergic to iron, are you?" she asked with a wink, already knowing the answer.

"It is true, we can touch it. We are not fond of it," Cedric said through gritted teeth as he sat down on the unforgiving metal. "Why do you keep calling me Tom?"

"I saw a Faery once, when I was a girl." The Dya's expression took on a faraway look. "I strayed from my family's camp, lured by the sound of Faery music. And I saw the sweetest Faery you've ever seen. She had golden hair, and wings made of light. And a fiddle! She had a Human fiddle, and she plucked it with her fingers. She didn't know what to do with it.

But the music was so beautiful. I will never forget that sound."

Cedric did not know how to respond. The age of this mortal made him uncomfortable...though she was far younger than his years, he did not doubt that. But her flesh had aged. It was an experience that Cedric had nothing to compare to. Perhaps that gave her wisdom he could not claim.

After a long silence, he said, "Dika did nothing wrong."

The Dya chuckled, a bubbling, wet sound. "You know our ways so well, do you, that you can school the Dya of this camp on what is right and wrong?"

He said nothing.

"Why would a Faery come into the Darkworld, Tom?" There was no humor in her face, nor the far-off look of a Human with a wandering mind. "Why would he come and seduce our secrets out of a girl stupid enough to give them freely?"

"It was not my intention." He thought back to that first day, when he'd strayed over the border to follow Dika. He'd seen her on the Strip many times, but they had never spoken. She'd taunted him with teasing glances, and once even dared to toss him a beaded scarf that she'd used in her hair. The hours he'd spent stroking that scarf, pressing it to his face and inhaling the scent of her. Long, torturous nights that drove him from his bed and to the Strip in the vain hope of seeing her.

And she'd been there, coy and teasing as ever as she'd led him on a dancing chase toward the boundary of the Darkworld. A boundary that, it was apparent, she didn't believe he would cross. But he did cross it, without a second thought, and caught her in the tunnel and took her there, without even knowing her name, against the rough concrete wall.

A shudder he could not suppress went through him at the memory. "I was bewitched. I did not seduce her."

"And you did not press her for our secrets?" It was an accusation, not a question. "You did not make Faery promises to dazzle her?"

"She loves me," he said, coldly, haughtily. It was all he knew to be true in this place.

"She is elfstruck."

"She *loves* me! And it was *she* that sought *me* out!"

The old woman nodded, as if somehow satisfied. "You do not love her?"

He thought of it, carefully considered what she asked. "I do not believe we can love as mortals love. Your love is bound by time. That makes it more constant. Perhaps desperate. But in the way I am able, I love her."

"Your love is also bound by time." The old woman looked toward the flickering firelight. From where they sat, they could not see Dika tending the cauldron, but the Dya's gaze was pulled that way, just the same.

"Shorter time than you know. If she were to grow old, withered like a grape left on the vine, would you love her then?"

He could not say. "I would cherish her as something dear to me. It is all I can promise."

"And that is a promise that you must make to her, and make clear." The Dya's voice was sad, but that sadness fled as she turned back to him. "I wonder, though, what your purpose is, coming here. Though we live in the Darkworld, my people have no quarrel with you."

"I am not here to quarrel. In truth, I do not believe my Queene has so harsh a view of the Darkworld as her predecessor. I am here for Dika." He looked down at his hands. "I am here because I no longer wish to be a part of the Lightworld."

"Wishes are what *your* people deal in, Tom. Not mine." The Dya fixed him with a cold stare. "You cannot choose to be apart from your kind. You could not survive."

"I can no longer survive among my kind, either. Perhaps you would let me choose the course of my own future." He nodded toward the fire. "Perhaps you would let Dika choose hers."

He had the old woman at a disadvantage now, and they both knew it. "My Queene will be able to take no action against you. You are leaving, and will be gone long before she can find this place."

"You will be hunted on the surface," the Dya remarked, not wishing to relinquish her hand so soon.

"You are hunted there, as well. Your people tell fortunes and create elixirs. The Enforcers could not let such a thing go." He leaned back in the chair, though the iron made him uneasy and his paper-thin wings bent under him, and crossed one leg over the other in a Human gesture. "You will be in a unique position, though. You will have a Faery to hand over to them. A Faery who was close to the Queene, who knew her plans. They may not bother with us on the surface, but they do not like us. You could make a valuable trade and protect your people, if it should come to that."

The Dya chortled. "And how do you know I would not simply sell you to the Enforcers the moment we stepped on Upworld soil? I thought Faeries knew better than anyone what tricks could be played in a deal."

"I am aware of what tricks you could play on me," he stated simply. "And I am aware that your people fear my kind. You will not play me false, lest you suffer unintended consequences."

She smiled at him, displaying a mouth that was toothless but for two golden stubs that peeked over her bottom lip. "You would find your footing among us, in time, I suspect."

For a long moment, she contemplated him, then

called for Dika. The girl could not have been far, certainly not as far as the stew pot, for she appeared, as
if a shade summoned from the Ether, at their side.

The Dya pointed a gnarled finger to Cedric, and
did not look at the girl. "Dika, Tom wishes to stay with
us."

"Oh?" She tried to sound disinterested, either for
the Dya's benefit, or for his.

"What say you in the matter?" The Dya turned and
fixed a critical eye on her granddaughter. Her mind
was made up, that Cedric could tell. But Dika did not
realize it.

Cedric saw the turmoil behind her eyes and almost
smiled. But he did not wish to offend her, or the Dya.
He could wait a moment to express his happiness.

"I think that if…Tom…wishes to stay with us, it
is not our way to refuse him." She said it as though it
were an answer she'd been taught.

The Dya nodded. "That is what I thought, too." She
turned to Cedric. "Well, Tom, it seems we can
welcome you into our clan. For now."

"For now," he agreed. He had no doubts that,
should there come a time that handing him over to the
Enforcers became convenient, they would do so. But
that time was not now, and he would deal with the Enforcers if they came for him.

"I am tired, Dika," the Dya said, rising to her feet.
"Bring me my dinner inside."

The old woman held out her arm, and Dika helped her rise, casting a look to Cedric that implored him not to leave. He waited until they were gone, then rose, brushing the feeling of the iron from his body.

When Dika emerged, she looked for him, held out a hand with her index finger raised, and hurried to the cauldron, where she dipped a dented metal cup into the pot. She rushed this back into the wagon, and did not emerge for a long while.

As he waited for her, he settled into the curve of one of the ancient tree's wide roots, and closed his eyes. If he ignored the cavern ceiling high above, he could almost imagine how it would feel to be outside once again, to feel the wind, to speak to the trees. He would have to live as a Human, but it was a small price to pay for the freedom so long denied him.

And what of the price she will pay? the tree asked cheerfully, in the quiet way trees had of invading Faery thoughts. *To give up her one life bound to a lover who cannot love her in return? Doesn't seem fair, that.*

Then the tree, apparently pleased to see something passing through the forest above them, began to speak of rabbits. Dika emerged from the wagon, looked about, confused, until she saw him, and ran toward him, her face alight.

Cedric forced the tree's unsolicited opinion from his mind and met her halfway.

"I can't believe it!" She threw her arms around his shoulders, kissed his face. "I can't believe you really are here."

"I am here." He smoothed her black curls from her face. Unfathomable as it might have been to him previously, he wanted nothing more than to never return to the Lightworld, to stay here, with these strange people, to insinuate himself into their company. "There is something I have not told you about my life in the Lightworld."

Where to begin? Would he tell her how many years he'd existed? That he'd seen women as old as her grandmother born and dead ten, fifty, a hundred times over? Should he tell her of watching the Earth slowly shift apart, of walking the Human world and watching them "discover" the magic in plants to cure sickness, the sun to tell time?

No. All of that could come in good time. Now, she needed to hear this, without any embellishment or Faery tales to dazzle her. "In the Lightworld, I am not an ordinary…man." What a strange word when applied to himself. "I am an advisor to the Queene of the Faery Court. Her closest advisor. And recently she has charged me with a very important task." He wondered if the stories of jealous Human women were true, and if this would seem to her as ridiculous as it did to him, or enrage her. "She wishes that I should mate myself to her daughter."

"Oh." She did not meet his eyes.

"I will not. She is a mere child." He stumbled over this, as he wasn't certain Dika was much older than Cerridwen. He wasn't sure how Human age worked, really. "She is old enough to find a mate, but she has been coddled and spoiled. I do not wish to spend an eternity with her."

Dika looked up, a glint in her eyes that was caught between amusement and anger. "And me? Would you wish to spend an eternity with me?"

He opened his mouth to answer, and realized it was a trick. He could no more spend an eternity with her than she could spend one with him. "If it were possible, yes."

"Then you content yourself to living with me until I am as old and withered as the Dya?" She came closer now, and gripped the front of his robes to pull their bodies together. "Will you still love me then?"

"I will love you for as long as I am able." He knew now what had taken so long in the caravan, what the Dya's muffled voice had been saying. "You know that I am merely an inconstant Faery, with no heart for Human love."

"I know this," she said, rising on her toes to touch their mouths together. Her breath moved over his lips. "I wanted to know that you knew it."

Four

~~~~~~

Cerridwen did not go to her mother that night. She didn't have the stomach to, after the scare in the tunnels, and after she'd left without telling Fenrick goodbye.

Fenrick. His face tumbled over and over in her memory. She brought her fingers to her lips to better remember the touch of his mouth. In the safe darkness of her room, her refusal of his advances made no sense. Why had she not let him do what she had secretly wished he would do—what she had been wishing he would do for the long weeks since they'd met?

She was a coward, she decided. And she did not like cowards.

You are furthermore being cowardly by not going to your mother and facing whatever punishment she has in store for you, a nasty voice taunted in her head, and she blocked it out.

She would face her mother. After the Great Queene made her morning audience, before the Royal Heir's day became another endless series of dutiful appearances at her mother's side.

It was so she could learn the way to be Queene, or so everyone told her. When would she ever need such knowledge? The Queene that had ruled before her mother, Mabb, had only fallen when slain by her brother.

Cerridwen did not like to think of her gone father murdering his own sister, so she put that from her mind.

But Fae were an immortal race, and, despite her mother's half-mortal blood, she had never grown older once she'd come of age. No one would kill Queene Ayla, worshipped as she was. And if someone did, well, there were others who were more qualified for—and interested in—ruling the Faeries. Cerridwen would happily quit the Faery Court altogether.

These thoughts, and thoughts of her impending punishment, and thoughts of Fenrick—she tucked his knife under her pillow and rested a hand on it—kept sleep from her. By the time it arrived, it seemed only to pay her a short visit before Governess was shaking her awake, muttering angrily about her mother wishing to see her.

Cerridwen sat silent through Governess's torturous grooming, though she scrubbed her skin raw and pulled at tangles mercilessly. She was thinking of a plan.

Cedric had made a bargain with her. Had he kept to it? What if he had not? Should she barge into her mother's chambers and tell her exactly where she had been, stand defiant and argue that it was her right as a grown Faery to go where she pleased and do what she wanted? Or would it be more prudent to stay silent, play the wide-eyed innocent if her mother already knew of her stray into the Darkworld? She'd overplayed wide-eyed…perhaps outrage would suit her. Wait and see if her mother knew about the Darkworld, about Fenrick.

She smiled at her freshly brushed and scrubbed reflection in the mirror. No matter what took place this morning, she would not let her mother get the upper hand. She would pretend to be the dutiful daughter for a few days, perhaps a week. And then she would resume her life as normal, and as she pleased.

The morning audience was over, but the guards led her to the throne room and not to her mother's chambers. Courtiers clustered outside of the doors, whispering behind their hands at the sight of her. This was not unusual, and she ignored it, lifting her chin as though she could not even deign to look at them.

"Congratulations, Your Highness," someone called out, and this bizarre exclamation was met with a smattering of applause and few huzzahs. For the most part, though, the Courtiers kept up their malicious whispering.

"Congratulations?" she muttered under her breath, wondering what she'd done to be congratulated on, what foolish new story her mother had concocted to excuse her absence.

The guards standing at the doors pushed them open, while the guards at Cerridwen's back kept the Courtiers from streaming in. A private audience between the Queene and the Royal Heir in such a formal setting? This would certainly set the whisperers gossiping at a frantic pace.

Her mother sat on the throne, an uncomfortable-looking rock thing covered on the sides by clumps of quartz. She dressed in less formal robes than she would don before her evening audience with the Court. The morning audience was when everyday business was proposed to the Queene. In the evening she would hear more important petitions.

The rest of the room was empty, not even a guard remained. But her mother's faithful mortal servant stood at her side and showed no signs of leaving. There had long been rumors that he was the Queene's Consort, and the thought of it, once she had come to understand the term, made Cerridwen ill.

"Is he going to stay?" she asked, and cursed herself inwardly. She'd already gotten her back up, as she had sworn to herself she would not do.

Her mother nodded, seemingly unperturbed by her daughter's strident tone. "Come closer, Cerridwen. You do not stand awaiting your execution."

It certainly felt like it. Normally, her mother was in a full rage before the doors closed, screaming down the walls over whatever transgression Cerridwen had committed. This solicitous nature made the skin on her neck creep.

"You missed an important announcement last night," her mother said, still in that maddeningly kind tone.

Was this the time, then, to burst out in her own defense? To break her bargain with Cedric? She opened her mouth to protest.

Her mother shook her head. "I do not wish to hear your excuses. I was angry with you, but now that anger has passed. I trust you will not leave the Light-world again."

And that trust was woefully misplaced. "Of course not, Mother."

"Cedric brought you back to the Palace?" Though phrased as a question, it was a statement of fact, so Cerridwen did not answer. "Did he tell you anything of what occurred at the feast?"

Cerridwen shook her head slowly.

Taking a moment to rephrase her question, her mother asked again, "Did he tell you why he had come looking for you?"

"I was unaware that he looked for me." The traitor had spun the story in his favor! How like a Faery male. "I thought his own business had brought him…to where we were."

Beside the throne, Malachi spoke up. "Likely, it did."

Her mother ignored him. Of course, the one time he seemed to be on Cerridwen's side, the Great Queene Ayla would consider his opinion beneath her. "He looked for you because of the announcement I made. Last night was a celebration of your coming of age. I had hoped you would have been proud to show the entire Court the fine Faery you have grown into.

"Instead, you showed the Court the reason I had to make a very difficult decision. I know you cherish your freedom, Cerridwen. I know you feel you are stifled by life at Court, but if life at Court had *truly* clipped your wings, you would not have been able to fly from the Palace at a whim." She stood and came down from the throne, down from the dais. Malachi stayed behind, watching the exchange from beneath his dark, furrowed brows.

"I fear I have not taught you the discipline you need to grow into your full potential as the Royal Heir. And I've come to accept that I am not the one to teach you. The influence of someone more experienced with Court manners and life, but someone who has also managed to balance the demands of Court with the demands of a happy life, is what you need." Her mother reached out, touched Cerridwen's face briefly. "That is why I have chosen Cedric to be your mate."

Individually, all of those words made sense to Cerridwen. She knew what it meant to choose something, knew what it meant to choose a mate. She understood that, occasionally, Faeries decided to bind their lives to each other for reproduction and mutual gain.

What she did not understand was the concept of someone making this choice for another person. The idea that her mother had chosen a mate for her. And that the mate she had chosen was…Cedric.

The room seemed far warmer than it had a moment before, and her feet did not rest easy beneath her. She pressed a hand to her stomach and took a step back, hoping her balance would return. She closed her eyes, but it only made the feeling worse, so she opened them again.

"It seems that, despite your confidence, the Royal Heir does not see it from your perspective," Malachi said and laughed bitterly.

"*Shut up!*" Cerridwen shouted, hearing the tears in her voice. That he had uttered his opinion, that he'd been privy to this humiliation at all, was more than she could bear.

"I did not make this decision to punish you!" Her mother held out her arms, as if to comfort her.

Cerridwen backed away. "No!" Her breath burned in her lungs, and no words, no matter how hurtful she might be able to make them, would put out the fire. "No! You do this to…to push me off on someone else! To get rid of me!"

"Cerridwen, please." Queene Ayla did not look so queenly now. Just pathetic and sad in her daughter's eyes. "You cannot understand—"

"No, I cannot understand!" Cerridwen's fists pounded her thighs of their own volition. "I cannot understand how you think I could love him. That I could…lie with him. It's disgusting!"

Her mother's expression grew hard at this. "To become Queene, I had to do a great many difficult things."

"I do not wish to become Queene!" Her shrill scream rang off the stone walls of the throne room. "And yes, you did a great many difficult things! How difficult was it to kill my father? If he were still alive—"

"Your father is not still alive, and thank the Gods I saw to that!" Her mother's words, dark with rage, rang out even over the loud crack of her palm colliding with Cerridwen's cheek.

She expected the blow to her pride to be greater than the physical pain, but the intensity of the sting shocked her. Tears sprang to her eyes, and though she wanted desperately to stop them falling, they poured onto her cheeks.

"I hate you," she spat, and turned to flee the room.

Her hand still throbbing from the slap, Ayla stared at the closing doors her daughter had fled through.

"You did not have to strike her so hard," Malachi said quietly from his place on the dais.

Ashamed, Ayla could not face him. "I should not have struck her."

The sound of his descending footsteps echoed through the empty hall, but they did not drown out the searing memory of her daughter's invective. "No, you were well within your right to strike her. I've wanted to, myself, on occasion."

"I am a poor mother." Self-pity was not becoming of a Queene, and Malachi certainly did not allow her to wallow in it in his presence, but she did not care at the moment.

He took a breath, his mouth close to her ear, and placed his hands on her shoulders. "You are stubborn. And prideful. So is she. But you cannot truly judge yourself a poor mother, as you had none, and I cannot judge you one, either."

"Twenty years have slipped through my fingers

like water. Try as I might, I cannot hold on." She closed her eyes. "I am a fool to think that Cedric will be able to hold her, either."

"You are fool to ask it of either of them," Malachi agreed with a gentle squeeze. "I will put an extra guard at her door. No doubt she will run away again."

"And this time, for good." Shaking her head, Ayla turned. "Perhaps she is right. Perhaps, if her father were able to have a hand in raising her…"

Malachi frowned down at her, and the frown deepened the faint lines on his brow. "If Garret had lived, he would have killed you and her both."

She had not meant Garret. It surprised her how easily Malachi confused their daughter's parentage himself. But now was not the time to correct him. "Cedric did not return last night. He was not at my morning audience. Do you think—"

"I think he is still angry with you. And I think you would do well to avoid each other for a while. But he is too loyal to ignore your orders for long. He will return."

Malachi spoke of loyalty as though it were something foul. It seemed strange to her that he, of all the creatures in the Lightworld, would have this opinion. He'd been wholly, unquestioningly subservient to his One God—he still was, she knew, having overheard his whispered prayers—and content to stay that way, it seemed, mourning his separation from that life of duty. If he looked down on such a quality in Cedric, she could only surmise that it was because Cedric's devotion was to his Queene, a being Malachi knew as imperfect and prone to mistakes.

In truth, Ayla would not have preferred the same slavish dedication from Malachi. It was one of the things she treasured most about his company; he did not find her infallible. The adoration and confidence the Courtiers all showed her seemed to disappear at the worst of times, and Malachi would not disagree with her then. But when the Court loved her, he became critical, lest she forget how tenuous her grasp over her kingdom was.

As they were alone, she let him take her into his arms. Closing her eyes, she remembered a time not so long ago, when she had run through the perils of the Darkworld for him. There were moments she wished she could escape to that time again, to not know of the dangers that had laid ahead of them or of the hardships they would endure. To not have the worries of running a kingdom, raising a daughter, being under constant scrutiny…feeling suffocated by duty.

There were times that that escape seemed possible, when they lay together in the dark, limbs twining, skin sliding over skin. Though so much had changed over time, that never had changed, and she was glad for its familiarity.

His mouth moved against her ear as he spoke and

he did not speak to her as her advisor or her friend. He spoke to her now as her lover, her life mate, and without judgment in his tone. "If I do not understand your choice in this, I do not doubt you mean only good. Do not grieve the loss of my faith in you, for it is still strong."

The doors of the throne room scraped open without a warning from the other side. Ayla and Malachi stepped apart quickly, their reaction honed by years of practice.

Though the doors were barely parted, a slender figure slipped into the throne room. Flidais, a member of Ayla's council, recently charged with the important task of Lightworld defenses, ran down the polished aisle, toward her Queene. She bowed with uncharacteristic agitation before hurriedly asking, "With your Majesty's permission, might I be granted an audience?"

Ayla had never seen the Faery in such a state. Her yellow hair floated around her head as though it had been invigorated by the run to the throne room and did not wish to settle down. Her antennae buzzed against her forehead and shone startling green.

"Of course, of course," Ayla said quickly, motioning that she should follow her to the dais. "Shall we call in the Court?"

"No, Majesty, I beg you, not right now." Flidais's tone was grave, pleading. "I hope you will understand my caution."

Ayla could only nod in response. She sat on the throne and beckoned Malachi to stand beside her. "Tell me, what has vexed you so?"

As if suddenly aware of her appearance and manner, Flidais quickly smoothed her hair and visibly tried to calm herself. When she spoke, it was in her usual, measured tones, though it seemed a strain. "There is news. From the Upworld."

Ayla tensed. For over a hundred years, the Upworld had not interfered with the world below. It would only be a matter of time, she had assumed, before they grew tired of ignoring the pests below them. "What news?"

"There is news," Flidais took a gulping breath, "that Faeries remain on the surface."

Ayla took a moment to be cautious, thoughtful. For many years now it had been common knowledge that some Fae lived on the surface, masquerading as Human. If this was Flidais's news, then it was nothing to cause a stir over. However, Flidais was intelligent enough to know this, and so Ayla asked, "In what capacity do they remain?"

"Free. Living as Fae in small groups." Thank God she did not say as prisoners. That would have been Ayla's worst fear, that they would have impetus to go to battle with the Upworld.

"Are they…do they have political motivations?" When the question escaped, she knew how it could be interpreted. That she feared someone would come for her throne, someone with a more valid claim. And that was not what she feared. "They do not wish to overthrow the Human world?"

Flidais shook her head, calming some. "I do not believe so. That is, they have not announced any such intention at this time. They have, however, sent an Ambassador and entourage, in the hopes of making contact with you."

"An Ambassador?" She wished Cedric were not missing. She needed him, desperately. "Without sending word ahead?"

Flidais considered. "When the Dragons came to us during Mabb's reign, they sent several of their Human servants uninvited, in the hopes of expediting a meeting."

"But Dragons…they do not expect to be turned down for an audience," Malachi said quietly. "I believe this puts Her Majesty in a difficult position. If she does not wish to have contact with this Upworld settlement, she cannot politely refuse contact. They are already here, and already awaiting her reception."

"I do not believe they mean any malice," Flidais protested. She had never liked Malachi's presence at the side of the Queene and considered a Consort's place to be in the bedchamber only.

"I will need time to think on this," she pronounced. It would keep the peace between Malachi and the Faery. "Flidais, tell the Ambassador that she—or he—

is welcome in the Lightworld, and see that the entire party is provided with appropriate accommodations. But on the subject of a meeting, you must be vague. I have not—and will not—make up my mind on this matter until I have given proper thought to what their sudden appearance might mean, and to what it might mean for all of us to come into contact with the Upworld. Also, I wish this to remain as secret as possible. I want no plotting behind my back on this, which I fear will happen if the Courtiers are informed before I make my decision."

Flidais bowed and left to do her Queene's bidding. She would do it well, of that Ayla was certain. Of all her council members, Flidais knew best how to handle a delicate situation, and she would do whatever needed to be done in order to see that her Queene's wishes were carried out.

As soon as the doors were closed behind her, Ayla rose from the throne and stalked toward the doors that led to her chambers. Malachi followed, as she knew he would. "I need Cedric," she said, not bothering to couch her command gently. "Bring him to me. I'm sure you know where he's gone."

"I do not," Malachi responded smoothly. The liar. The two of them were thick as thieves most days. "But I will find him."

"Good." She stopped, halfway through the little hallway to her chambers, and turned to face him.

There was no sense in parting angrily with him, when it was not him she was angry at. "Thank you. I…appreciate that you are willing to do these things for me. And for the Faery Court."

"I do these things because I love you. I do not care about the Faery Court." A smile ticked the corners of his mouth, where the ghosts of smiles past lingered. "Shall I come to you tonight?"

The words elicited a spark that flared to full flame in her, and she nodded. She would be grateful for the respite of his arms, his body, his presence after a day that had already, in its infancy, proved trying.

He stepped forward and drew her into his arms, his lips finding the skin between her ear and the high collar of her robe. Her Guild mark was there, indelible black against her skin, covered unintentionally by her hair and her robes, but the part of it he could reach he touched, traced with his tongue, and she shivered.

Just as abruptly as he coaxed the flame to life within her, he doused it by stepping away. "I will find Cedric for you," he said with another smile, and then turned and left in the direction they had come.

Five

No matter what Ayla accused him of, Malachi did not know where Cedric hid. It was a testimony to how very easily her suspicions gripped her, that she imagined her two closest friends and allies somehow plotting to hide themselves away from her.

Cedric had every right to leave the way he had. But leaving once was one thing. Leaving again, and staying away, was another altogether.

The best place to start looking, Malachi supposed, was with the guards he had been sent to call off the search the night before. He made his way to the barracks, a distant part of the Palace that was too close to the dungeons for his tastes. He found, as he had expected, that the guards who'd been sent off to search for the missing heir had been granted a day of rest. They were making use of it, too, as evidenced by the Faeries lounging on their crudely constructed bunks.

"Do not rise," he said, holding up a hand when they first noticed his presence. As Consort to the Queene, he was due a certain amount of respect from the Court, but display of that respect seemed cheap to him, and made him uneasy. He would rather they respect him not because of their Queene's preference, but because of the times he had fought at their side in the past twenty years. It was a vain hope, he'd concluded, but that did not stop him from wanting it.

"Last night, Master Cedric found you in the Darkworld and ordered you to call off the search, yes?" He watched as they nodded uniformly in response. "And did he return to the Palace with you?"

"No, Sire," one of the soldiers spoke up. "He stayed behind, to look for any of us that got separated."

That did sound like something Cedric would do. "Had any of you become separated?"

"No, sire."

That, also, sounded like Cedric. "And did you tell him this?"

"Yes, sire."

"Thank you." Malachi nodded to the guards and turned to go, when a voice stopped him.

"Sire, I may know where he is."

There was a noise of clearing throats and the rustle

of movement. Out of these, Malachi distinctly heard someone whisper fiercely, "You keep your mouth shut!"

Malachi turned. A young Faery—or perhaps he just appeared young, as Malachi could never tell the difference—stood apart from the others. The rest all watched him with daggers for eyes.

"You know where Cedric is?" Malachi asked, flicking his gaze over the guards who sat in sullen silence behind him.

"Do not tell him," one of the guards advised the young-looking one. "He is not one of us. What Cedric does is between himself and the Queene."

"What do you know?" Malachi asked the young guard again, ignoring the others. "I need to find Cedric. I seek him on the Queene's orders."

The Faery squared his shoulders. "On our patrols near the border, we have observed Master Cedric in close contact with a Human. A Gypsy. He has been spotted meeting with her on the Strip. I believe…we all believe…that he goes to the Darkworld to be with her."

That, of all things, did not sound like Cedric. But Cedric had always been private. And he'd been so angry at Ayla's announcement the night before….

No, Cedric had enough reason to be angry at that, without a Human mistress. Cedric, the most noble and incorruptible of all the Fae in the Lightworld, toppled from his virtuous pedestal by a mortal? And a Darkling?

"That seems…very unlikely," he told the guard, though he still let the thought tumble around in his mind. "But I thank you for your trust."

He left then. Let them think what they would of him. He'd become so used to the disdain the Fae showed toward all mortal creatures that it only surprised him when one of them treated him with respect. Not Ayla or Cedric, of course, but they alone knew what he had been in his former life. If the rest of the Court knew, well, they might not respect him, but they would fear him.

He shook off the self-pity that would usually follow such thoughts. Right now, his only concern was finding Cedric. The guard's story—and the zeal of the other guards to suppress it—troubled him. This was not the first time Cedric had left the Lightworld with no explanation. He always turned up later, but never offered where he'd been. Ayla had not pressed…perhaps she knew any answer would be a lie?

It would not be like Ayla to voice concerns about Cedric, who was, at times, closer to her than Malachi himself. She rarely questioned him and had never, to Malachi's knowledge, voiced any displeasure with him, even in private. The Queene bowed to Cedric as much as Cedric bowed to his Queene.

But now, the faithful servant had gone missing. The guard's story did not make so little sense, in this reasoning.

The years had flown—over half of Malachi's own mortal life—but it had not been so long that he could not remember the ways through the Darkworld, to the Gypsy encampment. He made his way through the Strip, to the entrance of the Darkworld, to the place where the Gypsy markings began. Symbols meant to ward off evil—to ward off the Death Angels whose ranks he'd belonged to—all the things that crawled and slithered in the Darkworld that were so hazardous to mortal life. The symbols were useless. Malachi did not like them, did not need the reminder that there were things capable of destroying him here in the Dark-world.

He had not been across the Darkworld border since before Ayla had officially become Queene, when he'd returned at Cedric's pleading. Now, he hoped Cedric would return at his pleading.

After hours of walking, he found that the camp was the same as he remembered—dirty, crowded, smelling of fire and too many unwashed bodies. It was also guarded still, though on his last visit those guards had not seen him slip in, their eyes blind to the messengers their God sent to bring them home.

They were not blind to him now. And they were not blind to what he was.

A group of children chased each other near the mouth of the tunnel, and a Human woman ran to them, crossing herself, looping her great fat arms around them and clutching them to her as she backed away, never taking her eyes from Malachi.

A warning call in a language Malachi could not understand rang out from one guard to another, and they came toward him warily, as if recognizing him as mortal, but unable to reconcile that with what their stories and legends told them about the Death Angels' purposes.

"I am looking for one who is not of your kind," he called out in the mortal language before they could get too close, before they could seize him, do him harm. They still might; their fear glittered in their dark eyes like the glimmer off of spilled blood.

"You are one who is not of our kind," a thin man called to him. "And you are not welcome here."

"I will leave, and gladly, once I find who I came for." He considered for a moment that Cedric might not have told them his identity, that he was masquerading as Human. Among these people, as keen and superstitious as they were, it seemed unlikely that they would not know what Cedric truly was. "He is a Faery."

A murmur went through the Gypsies who stood before him. Something that sounded suspiciously like "Tom."

Had another Faery come to live among Humans? To
have tracked the wrong Lightworlder into the Darkworld would be the perfect end to an absolutely fruit-
less day.

The thin man nodded, once. "We cannot take you
to him. We can bring him here, to you."

"That will be enough for me." Malachi bowed his
head briefly, to show them deference. "I will go into
the tunnel, and wait there, so I will not further upset
your people."

"And after that, you will not come this way again."
It was not a question, but Malachi answered with a
nod, all the same.

He waited, as he had promised, in the tunnel. What
would have possessed Cedric to come here, to cast his
lot with these strange creatures? All mortal beings
were strange, and Malachi did not excuse himself
from that description, but Gypsies were among the
most bizarre. And for a Fae to knowingly pursue one,
when mortal lives were so terribly short and fragile...

It was something Malachi found himself thinking
of far more often lately. The fragility of mortal life,
the interminable length of immortality. He was not
unaware of how his mortal body had aged. What had
been full and strong in youth was now lean and tough.
Lines marred his face. Those lines had not been there
before, nor had the strands of silver that had grown
into his hair. He had more years to live, true enough.

But he could not imagine what it would be like to watch Ayla age, wither and die, as she would watch him fade away. Their circumstance, he had thought, was exceptional. Why would another immortal seek out such an unhappy situation?

Footsteps in the tunnel brought Malachi's mind sharply back to where he was. His mortal life would be much shorter if he let his attention wander in the Darkworld.

The figure that approached was unmistakably Fae, from the way it moved as though somehow not a part of the space it inhabited. And it was Cedric. He was distinctive among the other Faeries that Malachi had seen, in that he was not as wiry, as short and slender, as the others. At first glance, someone who did not know better might mistake him for mortal. But Malachi would never tell him so.

"What are you doing here?"

It was not the greeting Malachi had expected. He'd thought that, upon being found out, Cedric would beg forgiveness. He seemed, instead, to demand apology. It took Malachi a moment to adjust his response. "You are needed, back at the Palace."

"I am always needed at the Palace," Cedric said, but did not move, or offer any other explanation.

"I understand you are angry." And Malachi did understand. What he did not understand was why the Faery did not rush from this place, as he would have done before. "But this has nothing to do with the betrothal."

"It does not matter what it is. I will not return." Cedric stepped into the light. He wore Human clothes, and they looked strange on him. His mothlike wings were unbound, powdered blue dust falling from them where they touched the fabric.

The Humans permitted him to walk among them this way? It almost made Malachi laugh, but that would have been disastrous now. "Your Queene needs you."

Cedric's hands balled to fists at his sides. "My Queene must learn that she cannot abuse her servants so. That she cannot reorder their lives at her whim."

"She *can* reorder your life," Malachi stated calmly. "She is your Queene. How often have you given her that power over you, Cedric? And it surprises you that she uses it?"

He did not answer.

"You have the right to be angry with her," Malachi continued. "But you cannot endanger your entire race, the entire Lightworld, simply because you are angry. I know you too well, friend.

"A settlement of Faeries from the Upworld has sent an Ambassador. An uninvited, unannounced guest seeking an audience. Ayla does not understand the ways of Faeries as well as you do. She has been Queene a short time, and the ways of your Courts are hundreds of years old. Every step she has taken so far has been guided by your patient hand. She will badly mangle this on her own, and you know it."

Cedric appeared to consider this, though Malachi knew he'd already settled this in his mind. "I had planned to return, you know. I would not have left with things unfinished."

It was a lie, but Malachi would pretend to believe it if it ensured Cedric's return. "It makes me glad to hear it."

"I will not stay, though." Whether Cedric said this so that Malachi understood, or so he, himself, understood, Malachi could not tell. "I will return here, and I trust you will not come to find me for her, or tell her where I have gone."

Malachi did not like to keep things secret from Ayla. But if she knew where Cedric had gone, she would seek him out for eternity. "I will not lie to her. If she guesses where you have gone, I will not lead her false. But I will not help her divine your location, either."

The heavy breath Cedric let out was a sign of his concession. "I will return, to lend my help in this. But I urge you to promote Flidais above me in the Queene's esteem. She is far wiser than I."

"Clearly," Malachi said with a nod toward the Human encampment. "She is not rushing off to live with mortals."

* * *

The Ambassador from the Upworld was received at the evening audience. Cerridwen did her duty by her mother, standing at her side in the stifling, crowded throne room. She held her head high, so that she would not have to see her mother's eyes, which flicked furtively to her now and again. Judging her, no doubt, looking for ways in which her daughter was failing yet again.

She also ignored the open stares of the Courtiers who'd witnessed the aftermath of her earlier humiliation. They, too, judged her, as if they had the authority. If she could burn them with her hatred, she would, but cold indifference was the only weapon she had against them.

Their harsh stares and gleeful whispers were diverted, thankfully, when the herald announced the entrance of the Upworld Ambassador and his entourage. The throne-room doors scraped open and a hush fell. From the corner of her eye, Cerridwen noted her mother's posture. Stiff. Formal. Intimidated.

The Faeries that approached the dais seemed far different than the Fae Underground. They were smaller, cleaner. Their clothes were made, it seemed, from natural materials found in the world above, rather than crafted from fabric the Humans above cast into the garbage. Their wings were unbound, their hair fell in tangled ropes, as if they had never cared to brush it out.

The one who led the group was quite handsome, Cerridwen decided, taking in his matted black hair and glowing skin. But he was not as handsome as Fenrick.

"Your Majesty," he intoned with a deep bow, which seemed to somehow hold a hint of mockery. "We are honored to be received in your Court, having been sent by Her Most Glorious Majesty, Queene Danae—"

Queene Ayla snorted to interrupt him. "Queene? Thank the Gods, I thought only we lowly Lightworlders had succumbed to such mortal nonsense."

She was, Cerridwen realized, jealous at the thought of another Queene. That thrilled an evil place in her, deep down, to know that her mother could be shaken.

The Ambassador bowed again. "It is true, what you say, Your Majesty. We have found that, for our survival, leadership was necessary."

"What is your name, Ambassador? Or shall I call you by your title?" The Queene leaned forward on the throne and made a show of examining him.

"You may call me Bauchan, for I am of their number." The Ambassador, this Bauchan, was far wiser, in Cerridwen's estimation, than her mother. This should have pleased her, but it frightened her, as well. Though she loathed her life in the Lightworld, in the Palace, she had never given thought to what might happen if it should one day come to an end. Is that what this visit portended? Would these Upworlders come here and take the Faery Court away? Would they go to live in the Upworld, away from everything that was, if loathsome, at least familiar? Away from Fenrick?

She would run off before that happened.

The throne-room doors opened again, this time without announcement. Cedric entered, hastily tying the sleeves of his robe.

At the sight of him, Cerridwen's stomach dropped. He looked so angry and serious. Her thoughts had strayed several times over the course of the day, directly where she had not wanted them to go. She'd imagined, against her will, what it would be like to mate with him, and the imagining had been awkward and terrible. The reality would not, she assumed, be much better.

"I apologize for my lateness, Your Majesty," he said, without bowing, and mounted the steps to the dais. He looked, very briefly, at Cerridwen, then looked away as if disgusted.

As if he had a right to be disgusted! He was not being mated to a creature older than her mother, older, probably, than her father.

Her mother nodded to her faithful servant. "You are forgiven. You have missed introductions. This is Bauchan, an emissary from the Court of *Queene Danae.*"

"Queene?" Cedric laughed, as though the Ambassador did not stand right before him, as though he were not normally well-mannered and thoughtful. "And how long did Queene Danae wait to proclaim her sovereignty after Mabb and her Court were forced Underground? A week? Two?"

The Ambassador's antennae showed as two livid streaks of red against his hair. "Queene Danae has not sent us here to quarrel—"

"You are certainly here to quarrel, if you come here thinking to gain tribute from us." Cedric's voice echoed around the shocked room. "Our Queene will not kneel."

"Mother," Cerridwen whispered, as close to the Queene's ear as she dared. "Stop him."

She held up a hand, but said nothing.

Silence fell over the throne room—even the whisperers held their breath—as Bauchan and Cedric glared at each other. The former had a look on his face as though he'd tasted something nasty. The latter looked almost triumphant.

Finally, Bauchan spoke. "It is with great regret that we must come to our unpleasant reason for our visit here."

"I think coming to your reason would be very wise," Cedric said calmly. He bowed to Ayla. "Your Majesty, I apologize for my rudeness."

Ayla nodded. "Do not let such an outburst happen again."

The goal, Cerridwen realized, had been to destroy all pretense of politeness. That was why Cedric had been so late to the meeting and was so rude when he arrived. To let the Ambassador know that the Queene and her Court would show them no favor.

"The reason for our visit," Bauchan stated, loudly, as if attempting to once again control the situation in the throne room, "is that we have received some very troubling news. On the surface, we Fae have kept the Elves in our good graces. We were unaware of the tensions that existed Underground, and the steps that the Elves here might take against our Fae brethren.

"In the Upworld, both Faery and Elf alike wish to avoid any conflict below. In the words of our wise Queene Danae, how can we expect to reclaim the Earth the Humans have spoiled if we cannot cease the fighting between our races?"

"Truly, your great Queene is wise, in as much as she can fathom," Queene Ayla said, sounding almost bored. "She has no concept of the hardships faced Underground, yet she speaks with great authority on that which she does not know."

"She knows that to be unified against an enemy is to be stronger," Bauchan corrected. "But we do not seek to unify the warring Elves and Faeries of the Underground. We seek to prevent a tragedy to come."

He turned to one of the Faeries who stood behind him. Though the Faery's wings were unfettered, it wore a hood over its face. One could not tell if it was male or female. Bauchan gripped the hood and pulled it away, revealing a sight that made the Courtiers recoil in horror as Cerridwen did.

The creature barely resembled a Faery. Its head was bare, ridged white skin stretching in uneven furrows over the crown of its skull. Where the eyes had once been, now only a rumpled seam of ruined flesh remained. It was as if a giant claw had swiped all of the pitiable creature's face from his head.

"What could have done this?" Her mother's voice was hard as stone. She had not recoiled from the sight. She did not look horrified. She looked angry.

"Waterhorses." Bauchan pressed the hood into the maimed Faery's hands, one of which was nothing more than a stump.

Cerridwen had never heard of Waterhorses, but she could gauge the seriousness of the situation from the reaction of older members of the Court. A terrified scream sounded over cries of disbelief and despair.

The Ambassador did not react to the stir he'd caused. "We believe that the Elves of the Underground have raised the Waterhorses, and plan to use them to attack the races in your Lightworld."

"Your Majesty," Cedric said quickly, kneeling beside the throne. "I suggest we convene the council and meet in private, to avoid further panic."

"Yes. That would be best." The Queene nodded in agreement. "Have the herald dismiss the Courtiers. Malachi! Gather my council and have our meeting place prepared. Ambassador Bauchan, I will ask you to discuss this with no one save myself and my council."

Elves of the Underground had done this? The image of the Faery's horrible scars swam in Cerridwen's mind. Certainly that was not true. She'd seen Elves. Fenrick was an Elf. He'd never have done something so horrible, would have never allied himself with monsters capable of such evil. Decisions were made on behalf of the Fae race every day, and not each Faery agreed with those decisions...surely, every Elf would not be held accountable for this horror?

The herald sounded the Queene's dismissal of the Court, and the Courtiers, for once, were anxious to leave. Her mother turned to her, a mask of false reassurance over her face. "Go back to your rooms. This meeting will be long, and it will not amuse you."

"I do not need to be amused, Mother," Cerridwen protested, but before she could argue further, her mother's mortal pet grasped her arm and steered her toward the doors.

"Your presence is not required at this meeting," Malachi hissed through clenched teeth. "Go now, as your mother says."

Things had moved so quickly, from annoyance at being made to stand beside her mother, to embarrassment at having to face Cedric, to fear at the thought of Fenrick and what would happen to him when her mother took some rash action against the whole of the Darkworld. Whatever plans her mother would make against the Elves of the Darkworld would be made tonight, in that room, and she had to be there. She would not be able to change her mother's mind once the Ambassador poisoned her against the Elves, but she could arm herself with knowledge and warn Fenrick, save him. "I will do no such thing! I will stay!"

Malachi gripped her arm, as if meaning to pull her through the crowd. "You will do as you are told!"

The Courtiers, once eager to run to the safety of their homes to forget the horrors they had seen, now stopped, gleeful at the scene before them.

"Malachi!" It was Cedric, not the Queene, who took the situation into hand. He came down from the dais quickly, casting predatory glances to the Courtiers gathered around, causing them to shrink back. But only a little.

"That is enough," he said, loud enough to be intimidating without shouting. "Go, do as Ayla bade you."

Reluctantly, as if he had a right to challenge Cedric here, but was loathe to take it, Malachi stood down. He gave Cerridwen a last, angry look, and stalked away.

Now Cedric would take her from the throne room. He probably sought to assert his rights as her betrothed, to show the Court that he would keep his mate under his control. The thought made her gag.

"Your mother does not wish you to come to this meeting," he began, predictably. Then, quieter, he said, "I will come to you later and tell you what transpired, if that is your wish."

The kindness of his gesture, the fact that he treated her, suddenly, as though she were not a petulant child to be ordered to bed, struck her dumb. She could only nod, mute, and watch as he walked away to join the others.

For a moment, she wondered if she should follow them, try again to argue with her mother. But she stopped herself. If she failed, perhaps Cedric wouldn't keep his promise to her, and then she would have no way to warn Fenrick.

She went back to her room, shook off Governess and her attempts at conversation. She climbed into her bed, still dressed, and pulled the curtains closed around her. She inched her hand beneath the pillow, felt for Fenrick's knife there, closed her fingers around it, and waited.

Six

"The Waterhorses." Cedric dropped the open book onto the table in front of Ayla.

It was a Human book, written in Human hand, about the various monsters of the Astral. One of the books that helped cause the rift in the Veil, by sparking more Human interest in the world they were not meant to know.

"Where did you get this?" she asked, barely glancing at the text.

"It has been in our treasury for some time." He tapped the page. "It is frighteningly accurate."

Ayla could not read the words, but the illustration chilled her blood. The creature stood on two hoofed legs. Its torso was that of a well-muscled mortal warrior, rising up to a thick neck topped with an equine head. The lips were pulled back;

rows of sharp teeth seemed to glitter on the stillness of the page.

"Notice the webbed fingers, with claws," Cedric said, something akin to awe in his voice. "And the teeth. They are the only creatures known to inflict damage such that even our healers cannot correct it."

Ambassador Bauchan, who had, until now, sat in silence, his entourage assembled behind him, held up his hand. "We have brought proof enough of the damage they can cause. Let us not relive it."

Ayla was glad for his interruption. The sight of the maimed Faery's injuries had been enough proof, on that score Bauchan was correct.

"Queene Ayla is a young Faery," Cedric said patiently. "She has not encountered these creatures, and I felt it important that she know exactly what we are dealing with."

Though it made sense to Ayla, it would not do for Cedric to point out her ignorance to the Upworlders. She cleared her throat and fixed him with a warning gaze. "I appreciate your concern, Cedric. But I have ample understanding of the severity of this threat."

Cedric nodded, and she continued, "Ambassador Bauchan...surely Queene Danae sent you here with a greater purpose than to merely warn us of the danger."

Maddeningly, Bauchan feigned a look of astonishment. "My Queene would never presume to send orders to another who equaled her rank, Your Majesty."

Ayla sighed. The day had begun so simply. No, not so simply. But better. And it seemed a lifetime had passed, and she felt every moment drive into her weary bones. "That is a shame. Perhaps she is not so wise and great as you claim. If she were, she would have sent you here with an offer of aid, or at least a suggestion as to how we could avoid this catastrophe."

"Her Majesty does not wish to be involved in an Underground war. She proposes only that you and your Court come to the surface, and take shelter there."

This was something she dreaded most of all. The reaction of the Court had been instant and panicked. This new Queene offered protection from what they feared most, something that Ayla could not give them.

At her side, Cedric restlessly tapped his fingers against the table. He wanted to respond to Bauchan, but he waited for the Queene's approval. He would wait a long time. Ayla was not inclined to let another outburst stand, even if the one in the throne room had been to her benefit. She did not wish for Bauchan to see her as weak, or believe she was a puppet for her advisor.

"It is a generous offer. But I will need all of my Court here to defend our race during an attack." She stated it as though it were something she did not expect him capable of considering.

He shifted uncomfortably on the stool he perched on. "You misunderstand. My Queene wishes for your entire race, from you, Your Majesty, to the lowliest Faery in the Lightworld, to join her on the surface. To unite, as it were, under one banner."

"Unite? Against who should we unite? It was my understanding, as you have made it very clear thus far, that your faction holds no quarrel with Elves. She does not wish to war with the Elves aboveground or below…so what goal can she seek to achieve through our unity?" Ayla did not look away from Bauchan, did not flinch as he stared back at her.

Finally, he spoke. "On the surface, our resources are limited. We are hunted by Enforcers and other bands of antimagic Humans. We do not live in such circumstances where raising and training an army would go unnoticed. We cannot provide the aid you require. That is why Queene Danae wishes you to bring your subjects to the surface."

"And would we not also be hunted? Wouldn't a higher concentration of our kind bring more attention to your presence there?" She tried for a kind smile, and feared it came across as hard and ruthless as she felt. "And what of the rest of the Lightworld? Should we abandon them against these creatures? The Dragons, the Trolls, who have always been our allies…what have they done to deserve such treachery?"

"On the surface, we could unite against the Humans. Reclaim what they took from us during the

Last Great War." Only now did Bauchan's face show genuine animation. This was the real reason he had come. This was his Queene's true proposal. Not one of aid, but one of fealty.

"And your great Queene Danae can ride into battle at the head of our unified race, and slay the demon Humans and save us all." Ayla shook her head. "Do not think that I am stupid. And do not think that I turn down such a modest proposal out of mere pride. Why should I not wish to hand my subjects over to your Queene, to wash my hands of leading them?"

"It is not Her Majesty's wish to—"

"Silence!" She stood, knocking aside the stool she'd sat upon. "You come here with tales of monsters, incite hysteria in my Court and ask me to bow to the wisdom of your Queene. You claim she sends her emissaries in good faith, to warn us of a danger far greater than we can manage on our own, and then you tell me that the only aid she will supply is at the cost of our lives in the Underground?

"Your Queene has no understanding of the world down here. I do. I have never lived in the Upworld. I have never seen the sun and sky but through grates that separated me from it. I have never lived in the Astral, and I have not had to adapt myself to Human domination. But I do know those who have, and their pain is far too great to mock by engaging in your selfish Queene's silly games. Go back and tell your

Queene that we will not fear monsters of the Human imagination, and that it will take more than an injured Faery to incite us to run from our homes!"

Bauchan stood slowly, spread his hands helplessly before him. "If Your Majesty does not wish to believe the danger you face, that is your own choice. But I could not leave here without offering to your subjects that which you have turned down on their behalf."

He would offer to take Faeries to the Upworld, to join his Queene in her campaign against the Humans. They would go. She had no illusions to the contrary. Life in the Lightworld was unpleasant for even the richest Fae, and if offered the chance to live as they once had, in the time just after the Veil had torn, before they were forced Underground, they would embrace it.

Perhaps she should have been more prepared for this day. She had known, ever since Mabb had shared the words of the prophecy, that her race would return to the world above. Ayla knew, also, that she would not lead them there herself. But she had not known how quickly this time would come.

That was not the only shock. That a Faery colony existed on the Upworld surface and had survived since the rest of their race had been banished to the Underground, seemed fantastical. That they had not known of it seemed impossible. Queene Danae, if Bauchan was to be believed, had sustained this colony and resisted Human oppression for centuries. Their ignorance was shameful, and that shame fueled her angry pride.

The rage that had been building in Ayla reached its breaking point. Her limbs trembled and her vision blurred red. "Guards!"

The doors to the council's meeting room opened, and soldiers appeared. "Take our guests back to their accommodations. See that they do not speak to anyone on the way, and, once they are returned to their lodgings, that they do not leave."

"This is an *outrage!*" Bauchan shouted, pounding his fist on the table. It was the last he managed before the guards dragged him from the room. His entourage followed willingly, likely out of a desire to avoid being so roughly handled.

When they had gone, Flidais spoke up from her seat at the table. "Your Majesty, a word?"

"Yes." Ayla righted her stool and sat. Her anger had left with Bauchan, and now she was more tired than she had been before.

"It is possible that the Waterhorses were not a simple ruse to frighten us. No other creature could have caused those wounds to a Faery. We are not damaged by the ravages of time, and mortal weapons might kill us, but I have never seen a surviving Fae with scars. We heal completely, or we die. And I know of no Fae who would consent to be altered through magic to become such a disturbing vision." She spoke so sensibly, it was as though the inner workings of her mind could be heard clicking away throughout the otherwise silent room.

After a long moment of consideration, Cedric spoke. "You are right, Flidais. A Faery could have healed from wounds worse than those if caused by sword or spear. But even if those injuries were caused by a Waterhorse, that is not proof that the Elves have made any pact with them. If the Elves on the surface do not have a quarrel with Faeries, why would they have used the Waterhorses against them?"

"Perhaps we should ask the creature itself," Ayla wondered aloud. "If it can still speak. Only it can tell us how it became so mutilated."

"If he does not simply repeat what Bauchan has coached him to say," Malachi added quickly.

Cedric stood, his hand going to the knife at his belt unconsciously. "We should go into the Darkworld and abduct some Elves. Interrogate them, torture them, see if there is any truth to these rumors."

"But how will we know which Elves are responsible?" Flidais asked, tapping the ends of her antennae absently with a forefinger. "Surely, not every Elf in the Darkworld is privy to this plot, any more than a Faery beggar outside the Palace gates is privy to what we say here."

"Abduction could cause retaliation," Ayla mused.

"Retaliation could also indicate whether or not there is a real threat from these Waterhorses."

"Precisely," Cedric agreed.

Flidais sighed, the way she often sighed when she knew she was about to make an unpopular point. "This is true. But if they have raised the Waterhorses, they are in as much danger as we are from them. If this attack happened on the surface, where the Elves have no quarrel with Fae, then they are unable to control them. Or, the Ambassador is not being honest in his tale. Should we not follow the course of action that would not lead to war, and see first if Bauchan is telling the truth?"

"Perhaps we should wait, just long enough to pull members of Court and the Guilds into militia service," Cedric agreed. "In that time, we can investigate Bauchan, and we can defend our borders in case of attack. And we should let the Trolls and Dragons know that we've been threatened."

"The Dragons, yes," Ayla agreed, "but not the Trolls. They are likely to start a war for the sake of violence. Besides, they supported Garret while he was in exile. They may turn against me as easily, again. We need not involve them until all other options are exhausted."

"I will go to the Dragons and seek an audience," Flidais volunteered. "Give Cedric the time he needs to fortify our borders, Your Majesty. But do not let this

Bauchan go. If he has brought lies from the Upworld Queene, then our quarrel is not with the Elves, but with our fellow Fae. He could be made an example of."

It was not a possibility that Ayla took lightly. It haunted her even after her council had departed. Malachi followed her, without speaking, to her chambers. He knew her mood well enough to know that there was nothing he could say, and so he remained silent.

What did this Upworld Queene wish, besides to rule over the Lightworld, as well? Perhaps Ayla had lied when she'd told Bauchan she did not turn down Danae's offer of aid out of pride. The gall, to send an Ambassador to her Court in the hopes of luring away her subjects—after all she had done to earn her throne!

What did you do, besides kill your mate? And nearly get killed yourself, doing it? the familiar voice of doubt chided her. But she had earned her throne. Now, twenty years after she had killed Garret, she could finally say that. She could not have remained Queene, even for this short time, if the Court had not had faith in her and her abilities. She would have been assassinated, if they thought her weak or incapable of ruling.

This false Queene, who wished to lure her subjects away from her, would have to do far more than simply scare her with monster tales.

But if they were not tales, and if the Faeries of the Lightworld were truly in danger, what then? The Dragons were their allies, true, but would they be moved to actually defend the Fae? The Trolls would no doubt relish the chance to go to war with anybody, but they often made more problems than they solved.

No answers would come to her. They would come, as they always did, in their own time, and Ayla's impatience burned her. Even though a plan was in place, and even though that plan was the most sensible course of action they could take, it had not unfolded in her view yet; she could not see what lay on the other side of it. That was the true torture of her position. She could make all the decisions and declarations that she might like, but she could not control the outcome. In a few weeks, would she be the slave of an Upworld Queene? A trophy of her victory over the Faeries of the Underground? Or would her own Court lay in ruin, a monument to her pride and unwillingness to bend? Or would some unguessed third outcome be her people's fate?

She would not be able to sleep this night, probably not the next, either. But she went through the motions of climbing into bed and closing her eyes, and, though she knew he was aware that she did not sleep, Malachi stayed at her side all through the night.

* * *

Though he was tired, and though it was the last thing he wished to do, Cedric had made a promise to the Royal Heir, and it had to be kept.

He knocked on the door to her chambers, and the governess—the child was too old for a governess, really—opened the door and eyed him with suspicion.

"I am here at the request of the Royal Heir," he stated without conviction, half hoping he would be turned away. Instead, the dour-faced servant opened the door wider and motioned him into Cerridwen's antechamber.

He'd never been in these rooms, even when Mabb had been Queene and his visits to the royal quarters had been frequent. The antechamber was smaller than the one afforded to the Queene and her Consort, and it was overrun by all the trappings of a young female Faery. Baubles and hair ornaments lay discarded on the tables and stools. A drum, limned in a fine jacket of dust, sat abandoned and unpracticed against the curved wall. The ugly gray of the concrete that enclosed the room had been stained in an attempt to make it white, a color far more appealing to a child.

Cedric stood in the middle of this unfamiliar chaos, helpless, while the governess went beyond the little wooden partition that separated the antechamber from where the Royal Heir slept. There was a shushing of raised whispers, the content of which he could not

make out, and movement. The governess returned and
said, though it was as though each word pulled a tooth
from her mouth, "You may go into the royal bedchamber."

He nodded to her. She did not follow. Did she think
that her charge's betrothed had come to mate this very
evening, without the benefit of ceremony in Sanctuary? The thought was as humorous as it was sickening. He would sooner bed the old Dya than the spoiled
princess of the Lightworld.

Inside her bedchamber, the Royal Heir stood beside her bed. Her dress was rumpled, as was the
coverlet, which had not been turned down. Her face
was drawn and gray. If she had slept, she had not
intended to, and whatever sleep had visited her had
been fitful at best.

Cedric almost pitied her. What must it be like, he
wondered, to be the heir to something held captive by
an immortal? Cerridwen's entire existence was that of
a child waiting and watching, preparing to take over
a throne that might never become vacant. To be caught
that way, always a child, always waiting, would have
to be a particular sort of torture.

She nodded to him, and he bowed his head, though
there was no one in sight to demand such protocol.
"What has the council decided?"

The reason for his visit, which he had not realized
he'd forgotten, came back to him with a peculiar tinge

of suspicion. What did she care what went on behind the closed doors of the council? It did not affect her. But perhaps that was why she wished to know it—to finally be involved in something, to finally have something affect her. "The Ambassador has been imprisoned. He came with the goal of luring your mother's Court to the surface, to induce their fealty to another Queene."

Cerridwen's grim demeanor changed. Her shoulders sagged and her breath came out as a sound of relief. She pressed one hand to the rumpled fabric of the bodice of her dress and struggled to speak over the rapid exhalations she'd held in while waiting for him to speak. "Then the Elves…it is not true that they will use force against us?"

It had not occurred to Cedric that the Royal Heir might have been frightened by what she had seen in the throne room. Hadn't she been present when the horrible, malformed Faery had been revealed? And certainly, in her haste to convene the council and empty the throne room of Courtiers, Ayla had not bothered to reassure her child of her safety.

He wondered for a moment if he should calm her fears now, and tell her it was not for her to worry over. But then he would be as bad as everyone else who patronized the Royal Heir and expected her to think only on childish things. "We do not know. Your mother wishes for us to form a strong militia from members of Court and the Guilds, and then we will begin capturing and interrogating Darkworld Elves to see if there is any truth to the rumors Ambassador Bauchan planned to use against the Faery Court."

Her relief fled, all at once. He knew he should not have told her that a danger still remained.

"Interrogate them?" Her voice wobbled on the word. "You mean torture them?"

"It is a necessary evil, unfortunately," he told her apologetically. "But you need not fear retribution from the entire Darkworld. They are unfocused, and unorganized. Any strike that is made against us will be from the Elves alone, and they are dealt with easily enough."

"I am sure they are," she said angrily, though he could not fathom what he could have said to anger her. "Thank you, Cedric. I appreciate that you kept your promise to me."

"I would be a very poor Fae indeed, if I did not keep my promises." He tried to smile, hoping to see some of the tension in her expression ease, but it did not.

"Truly?" She seemed more angry now than she had been. "It seems to me that treachery and lies are the hallmarks of our race."

The bitterness in her tone shocked him, until he thought of the reason for it. "I am aware that you do not agree with your mother's decree that we should be mated." The words were so difficult to say. He wanted to tell her that he also disagreed, that he planned to run from the Lightworld and never return, that she had no reason to fear that her mother's wishes would be carried out. But he could not risk her revealing all of that to Ayla, out of anger or spite. So, he settled for, "But you must believe that things will work to our mutual happiness."

"You could not possibly know that," she insisted, a sadness so deep that it shocked him coming over her face. "You may leave now."

"Your Highness," he tried again, but she stopped him.

"You may leave now."

He had no other choice, though for some reason, he was now reluctant to obey.

There was not much time. She thought of writing a letter, sat down with the pen in her hand.

Whom could she address it to? Her mother could not read. And she did not wish for her mother's Darkling to be the first to find this confession.

She began her letter to Cedric, but didn't really know what could be said. She tried a few lines—

I have gone to the Darkworld. I am in love with an Elf. I will warn them of the treachery you are about to commit against them, and then I will disappear into the Darkworld forever.

—but they rang too simple, like a story she might have told as a child, one in which too much was revealed all at once to be believed. She tried again.

In the time since I have come of age, I have learned a great many disturbing things about the way this Court is run. I have learned that while we fancy ourselves to be greater than those who live in the Darkworld, we act with less honor than the lowliest Demon. We feed from others as though we were Vampires. And we hate and fear those who are most like us, the Elves.

For too long, the Elves of the Darkworld have been separated from the Fae races, and now our Queene seeks to destroy them. I have left this place to warn them of the coming assault against them, and to join in their cause.

Did she, though? Could she really declare herself a traitor to her own race? It seemed such an absurd and lofty goal now that she had printed it out.

Another thought occurred to her: If she told where she had gone and for what purpose, would that not increase her mother's desire to attack the Elves, and bring her back?

She crumpled up both letters and began anew. This one, she would address to Governess, to thank her for her kindness in raising her, to praise her and let her know that she had fled of her own doing, and that Governess was not to be blamed, or blame herself, for her going. But those lines never touched the page before her tears did, and she silently commanded herself to stop.

As if summoned by her tears, Governess came in, frowning. "Do you wish for your breakfast now? It's almost morning."

Cerridwen surreptitiously wiped her eyes and nodded. While Governess was gone, she could slip out. It would not allow her much time, so once she heard the door to the antechamber close, she abandoned the idea of a letter altogether. She tore off her gown and raced to her wardrobe, rummaging through it until she found the clothes she'd used to disguise herself as a mortal servant. She also found the cloak of a Dragon emissary, which she had stolen from the Darkling's chambers long ago. She wrapped this into a bundle and shoved it into her shirt. She tucked Fenrick's knife into her belt and looked over her room. Was there anything else she would need? No, she decided. If she was to start a new life, she would not need the trappings of her old one. Just a few pieces of jewelry to barter for the things she would need. Fenrick would help her, she was certain, if she needed help.

A sudden, shocking feeling of elation crested over

her. It was truly happening, now. She was truly beginning her life.

In the time it had taken her to dress and collect what she needed, Governess was surely returning with her breakfast. The crumpled letters remained on the desk, and Cerridwen shoved them hastily beneath her bed.

If they were found, it would not be in time to stop her.

Seven

Ayla did not sleep, but Malachi could not go so long without it. He lay at her side, knowing that she would be content merely with his presence, and when he woke, he saw she had finally succumbed.

Not for the first time he marveled at how unchanged her appearance was. Her hair was not as tangled as the first time he had seen her, and she was not as dirty. He remembered the sight of her, fighting against him in the tunnel…seconds before he had become mortal…the way she had emerged from below the surface of the water in a great burst, her hair flaming red in the strange glow of the light she had summoned. In his mind he saw the curve of her arched back, the strained column of her throat leading to an open mouth pulling in a great breath of air…droplets of water flung by her haphazard braid circling her in a glistening arc.

That was what he had seen, but he had not been able to appreciate it then, nor in the days after, when he had believed his only desire was revenge, to take her life as punishment for the immortality she had taken from him.

He laid his head beside hers on her pillow and traced the line of her shoulder, wincing at the sight of his scarred, mortal flesh against the smoothness of her skin. Mortal. He would not have been loved by her any other way. If she had not caused his fall, he would be a Death Angel still, collecting departed souls and keeping them safe to await the return of the absent God. He would have existed beyond the end of the universe, but he would not have been able to love her. In his mortality, he could only love her for a short time. And that time, he knew, was drawing to an end.

He flattened his palm against her pale arm, studied the differences. Was there no part of him that did not betray his age?

How could she love him, still desire him, as she watched him wither?

She stirred, but did not open her eyes. "Why must you stare at me? I only just fell asleep. You know I can feel your stare."

Though her words held a sleepy anger, she reached for his hand and pulled his arm over her, as though pulling on a blanket. He rolled to his side and lifted one wing, felt the heavy tug of the metal in them. The canopy of ebon feathers arched above them and she opened her eyes just a fraction, smiling before letting them drift closed again.

"I wish I could spend today pretending that yesterday did not happen," she said with a sigh.

He pressed a kiss to her shoulder. There was no need to remind her that such willed amnesia was not possible. She was painfully aware of her responsibilities.

"I think Cedric and I should separate that wretched Faery from the rest of Bauchan's group. Win its trust," she mused.

"*His* trust," he reminded her gently. As a race, Faeries valued perfection. Something so twisted as the scarred Faery they'd seen in the throne room was regarded as an object, at best, an abomination, at worst. "Do you think he would tell you if Bauchan is lying?"

"He can tell us whether or not the Waterhorses have really been raised." Another sigh. "I do not know what we face, Malachi."

"You have had a quiet twenty years," he pointed out with a chuckle. "You were not entitled to a worry-free reign."

"You have a much different idea of quiet than I have," she argued. "You have fought in many battles yourself in the past years. The Vampire invasion, the uprising of the Humans on the Strip. Perhaps I flatter myself, but the Faery Court did have a large hand in taming those conflicts, did they not?"

"Minor squabbles in the larger scheme of an immortal Queene's reign."

She smiled and stretched, some of the gloom fleeing from her. "You speak the truth. I do not care for truth."

"You do not care for a great many things, yet they still exist." He sat up, swung his legs over the side of the bed. "You must get up now, and do your duty as Queene."

She made a frustrated noise behind him and kicked her legs free from the covers, throwing an exaggerated tantrum. Finally, she said, "Yes, I suppose you are right. Do not expect to spend the day lazing about, either. You have a militia to begin organizing."

Something in the pit of his stomach dropped. He had thought, for as long as he could stay awake the night before, about what would happen when the Faeries went to battle against these Waterhorses, and Elves.

Ayla was correct; her reign had not been completely without incident. There had been other battles, small in scale, handled by her guards, but battles nonetheless. And he had been proud to participate in those and had earned the scars he'd gotten.

But after the last one, nearly three years before, Ayla had no longer allowed him such freedom. "You are getting old," she had scolded him. "You cannot fight as well as when you were younger."

That had wounded him far worse than any blade could have. Not because she had pointed out that his body was slowing, his skill fading. But because she had spoken as a warrior, herself, and not as a female desperate to keep her mate safely at home. He had not pressed the issue.

Until now. He could not fathom staying behind when a threat so great loomed. He could not conscience it.

"I had a thought," he said, keeping his tone conversational, "that perhaps I could lead the militia into battle."

Ayla slid her legs over the edge of the bed to sit beside him, and said nothing for a long while. That was fine. He could wait.

"I do not suppose you have forgotten what I told you after the clash with the Vampires?" she asked, pushing her feet into the little jeweled slippers beside the bed.

His conscience forced him to honesty. "No, I have not."

"Then why do you ask?" She was not angry; he had expected anger, and this startled him.

There were so many reasons she would not be able to argue with. The militia would not include the Palace guards, who would fight under their usual command. Thus, his fighting force would be plucked from the Court and those outside the Palace walls. They would be...*inexperienced* was the incorrect word to describe the state they were in. Many of them had fought in the war that led to their banishment Underground, and long before that, the war in which they had claimed the Upworld and forced the Humans below ground. They had fought epic battles on the Astral—battles to mark the seasons, the changing of the winter to the summer. They were not inexperienced. But it had been so long, and Malachi could not believe that the pale, painted fops of the Court, with their fine silks and jewels salvaged from the mortal world, would be able to defend their Queene, even if they could be pried from their frivolous mortal pursuits.

There were other reasons, like vanity and his desire to forget, for just a few hours, that the Faeries who fought beside him despised him for what he was. But he had to give Ayla the reason she would understand, the one she was most likely to bend to.

The waiting, knowing the battle had commenced, yet waiting for any scrap of news, would kill him. He would go crazy before the first casualty was brought back.

"I wish to fight, because if I do not, I will feel useless and helpless during the battle." He knew this would speak to her, more than any of his other concerns. Since becoming Queene, she no longer fought, unless it was a war of words. And she hated to watch her soldiers march off without her, knowing that she could fight as ably as they.

He studied her profile, watched as she mulled over her answer. When she thought about something hard enough, he could almost see those thoughts forming and tumbling over each other, crashing like waves within her.

"You will not be useless. You could help here, guarding the Palace." But even she could not believe her words would appease him.

He played the game, anyway. "You will have your private guard. They will protect you, and me, though I would not wish them to. You do not need me here."

"I do not." She smiled, sadly. "I do, but not for protection. You are mortal, Malachi, and fragile. You've seen what these enemies can do to us. I would not have them do worse to you."

"Time will do worse to me on its own," he said gently. "I would rather be useful while I am here."

She leaned her head on his shoulder and her body heaved with a silent sigh. "I understand that, all too well. Help train them. Go into battle with them, if you wish. But swear you will return to me."

"You know that is something I cannot swear." But he could not imagine being dead, could not imagine the black wings of his former bretheren rustling in the darkness to take him to Aether. Could not imagine being separated from Ayla.

The thought of his inevitable demise, perhaps not in this battle, or the next, but lurking, waiting for him somewhere in a future he could not prevent, turned the moment maudlin. "How long..." he asked, clearing his throat around an unexpected knot of sadness. "How long will you remember me, after I am gone?"

She sat up, her face drawn with shock, as though she'd heard something so unbelievable that she had been rendered speechless. And she did struggle with her words. "How long? Malachi, I will never love another."

It was a pretty sentiment, but never did not hold as much promise in an immortal life as in a mortal life. "You will. You have an eternity. I will not blame you for it. But I worry that you will forget me, and I will have no way, where I will be, to remind you."

She climbed to her knees beside him, placed her hands on his face to force his gaze to hers. "I will never love another. I have loved no one the way that I love you. And when you die, that part of my life will be closed off, never to open again."

As if she needed to seal her promise through physical action, she kissed him, hard and deep. The familiarity was almost painful, because it reminded him that someday, he would be taken from it forever.

It was almost enough to change his mind, to make

him recant his silly desire to rush headlong into battle out of pride and boredom. Almost, but not enough. He felt some current the immortal creatures could not, something that perhaps only mortality could sense, with its innate knowledge that death was unavoidable, and that current pulsed with warnings of their doom.

If he would die soon, he would die fighting.

The Darkworld had always, in Cedric's sight, seemed filthy and foreboding, even when he was on his way to meet with Dika. Now, with the new suspicions he harbored against the residents of the Darkworld, it seemed far more sinister.

He followed his little map, sprinting through the darkness. At first, as he neared the Gypsy encampment, he wondered if he had made a wrong turn. No lights were lit, and the noises of Human activity were not the same joyful sounds of a people at peace. There were tense shouts—the sounds of labor.

He made his way through the final tunnel and expected some resistance from the guards who had not wished to admit him the first time. But no one stopped him.

They were too busy, he could see, throwing their belongings onto wheeled contraptions, pulling them deeper in the camp. He hurried past whole families piled onto carts, their belongings clutched to them as a strong man or woman pulled the whole along behind them as though they were beasts of burden. Women carrying crying babies on their hips, packs tied to their backs. And they came forth from each spoke of the giant wheel that made its hub at the central fire pit, which was cold.

He made his way through the crowd gathered there, headed to the path that would lead to the Dya's wagon. But a voice called out to him over the panicked noises of the crowd, and he stopped.

"Cedric!" Dika struggled past a stubborn clump of Gypsies moving in the opposite direction.

He went to her, though it was difficult to focus on her face when the crowd was so distracting. "What is happening?" he demanded as he pulled her to his side.

She clung to him, as though afraid herself. "I thought you would not return in time! I worried, I wanted to go get you, but Dya said they would kill me at the border!"

"In time?" He surveyed the chaos around him, looked to the hole high above the central hearth, where the mortals now clustered.

"We are leaving, Cedric!" Her voice was a mixture of joy and terror. "We are finally leaving!"

"Leaving." He could do little more than repeat what she had told him. "You are leaving the Underground?"

She nodded solemnly, the expression in her eyes uncertain. "You are still coming with us? You haven't changed your mind?"

"No." The answer was mechanical, so he tried again, with more emphasis. "*No!* No, I only thought that there would be some time. For planning. This seems…disorganized, at best."

A man with a caged chicken pushed by them, grumbling that they were in his way. Dika took Cedric's hand and led toward the wide, deserted avenue that he had sought in the first place. The Dya's wagon was parked there, blocking the path, and they ignored the cries of people who clustered near it.

"We were not thinking we would leave this soon." She examined the disordered throng and wiped beads of perspiration from her brow. "Not that we would have done things any differently. It may look chaotic to you, but we are a race meant to be nomads. This is routine, and everyone knows what they are doing."

"But what has moved you to leave now?"

Dika looked away, as if an answer other than what she wished to give would come rushing out of the mass of Humanity seething around the communal hearth. When that did not happen, she wetted her lips nervously and glanced toward the wagon, as though the old woman, presumably inside, would overhear.

"There have been rumors of something horrible, here in the Darkworld." The gravity she gave the words suggested it was something even more horrible than the horrors that already lurked in her home realm. "Gaido found a Demon on his way back from the

Strip…it had been…gutted. Eaten. And this was a Demon. A Demon! They are the worst you can imagine, huge, impossible to kill!"

"Not impossible," he corrected, but she did not hear him.

"My grandmother fears the creature that could have done such a thing, and worries that it might have already taken some of our men. A group left to go scavenging two days ago. They have not yet returned. She fears—"

The sound of the wagon door banging open cut off her words and pulled her attention away. She stared wide-eyed at the darkened portal.

The Dya emerged from her wagon, her motions setting the little lamp beside the door swaying. In the slow, deliberate time it took her to descend the steps from the wagon door, Cedric was sure the gathered crowd would rush to her, box her in. But they stayed back, kept the respectful distance they always seemed to allow her.

She looked at him, pasted on an expression of surprise that her eyes betrayed. "Tom," she said with a smile in her voice, "I didn't expect to see you again so soon."

He waited, his anger a hot coal inside of him, smoldering while she made her clumsy, old way toward him. When she reached the place where he and Dika sat, the smolder gave way to flame.

"Is that why you command your people to leave now? Because I had not returned, and you hoped I would not?"

The Dya made a motion, and Dika rose from her seat, helped her grandmother to sit there, instead. The old woman made a noise, "tcha, tcha, tcha," that held all of the disappointment in the world of both the Underground and the Upworld.

After a long while of catching her breath and adjusting her posture, she said, "And why, Tom, do you believe you are such an influence on our lives? Because you are a Faery? Because you shine as we cannot?" She made the sound again. "I had greater hopes than that for you, Tom. You really are like all the others of your kind."

It was a surprisingly effective insult, and Cedric felt at once ashamed of himself for his accusation and ashamed that he would let a mortal mock his race. "I only thought—" he began, but he stopped when he realized that what he thought did not matter. He'd already told her what he'd thought, and the reason for thinking it would not make him seem less self-important.

"I was going to tell him why, Grandmother," Dika said quietly, as though confessing. "I thought he had a right—"

"He already knows why we are leaving," the Dya rasped, suddenly seeming more powerful and dangerous than an aged mortal should appear.

It was magic, Cedric realized. That was what she held over her people, and that was why she was given a feared and revered position of leadership. Dark, powerful, ancient magic flowed into the Dya from some distant and unknowable source. The kind of magic that even the Fae had not learned to predict. They could harness it, get a glimpse of the future worlds, but only at the whim of the magic; they could not control it.

The Dya could control it. The power writhed and twisted in her invisible grasp, raged and screamed against its bonds, but ultimately bent to the will of its captor.

"You know of the Waterhorses." It was not a question.

At the mention of the creatures, Dika shivered where she stood. A mortal might have reached out an arm to pull her close and comfort her, but now was not the time to pretend he was mortal. Not when facing something so intimidating as the Dya's new appearance.

The old woman nodded, the dangling flaps of her leather cap dancing with the motion. "I have seen them in my dreams, coming ashore. They saw available prey in the daylight, but ignored it. They sought their masters, your enemy, ignoring all else until they were weak and emaciated. That was the spell that commanded them. Now, they have found those they sought, but they are in no position to do battle. They hunt, here in the Underground, every night, so that they can become strong again."

"They are here? Now?" It was enough to know that they were not an empty threat from a power-hungry Queene. But to know they were close, so close as to frighten away other denizens of the Darkworld, was far more troubling. "We had warnings, but—"

"But you could not trust the word of an Upworld Queene." The Dya nodded. "Oh, yes, I see more than what affects our little camp. I see your past, present, and your future. I see the lies you tell yourself to come here, and the ones that make you stay at your Queene's Court. I see the girl who waits for you, but does not want you."

"There is a Faery I am promised to," he admitted clumsily. "But I have no intention of honoring that imposed betrothal."

"It is true," the Dya told her granddaughter reassuringly. "He has no intention to. But clever Tom has yet to learn, with all of his hundreds of years behind him, that his will and the will of fate sometimes disagree. In that argument, fate will always win."

"So, you will leave me, and marry one of your own?" Dika's voice held the threat of tears. She did not understand, Cedric realized for the first time, how different the ways of their races were. He looked to the Dya, silently imploring her to cease her predictions.

"He does not believe he will honor this promise, but he will. You will be long returned to the Earth, so rest your fears." If the Dya felt any sadness at the thought of her granddaughter's death, she did not show it. "He will be faithful to you for as long as you live."

Heaving herself to her feet, she shuffled a few steps toward her wagon. "Something you should know, Tom," she began, leaning on Dika's arm, "your Queene will not be long for this world against these creatures. I have seen into your soul, so much as a creature of your kind can have one. You are loyal to her, you see her as helpless without you. If you go now, we will not wait for you. But if you venture Upworld on your own, and you travel tirelessly west, you will find us. We will welcome you back, if you choose."

Dika reached for her grandmother's elbow and helped steady her to the wagon. When she returned, tears shone in her eyes. "Don't leave. Go up with us."

Something tugged in him, something Humans would have attributed to their emotional heart, no doubt. He knew better. It was his loyalty to Ayla, pulling him away from his desire to be among Dika's people. He wanted to take that loyalty, to shake it apart and stomp the pieces.

But he could not. "Go up ahead of me. I will follow close behind."

"You will never find us!" Dika's voice took on a pitch Cedric had never heard before. Something desperate and angry boiled inside her, struggling to break free in her words.

Cedric did not like that hysterical edge, and sought to calm it. "I will go west, as the Dya said. I do not need to sleep, if I wish not to, so I will be able to travel night and day until I return to you."

"There is nothing in your world for you now," she insisted. "Unless you hurry back to be with your betrothed. Is that it?"

"No!" The very idea was absurd, and he wished he had the time and ability to show her why. "You heard your grandmother. I will be faithful to you until death."

"Faithfulness can be achieved even if you are not with me." Tears spilled over her cheeks now.

Those tears should have inspired his pity, but all he felt were the black embers of his anger at the encounter with the Dya. "They will destroy my Queene. Possibly my kind. Would you have me abandon them without warning?"

"And after this warning, you will stay with me until the next one? When she will pull you away from me again?" Dika shook her head. "You do not truly wish to be one of us. You do not truly wish to be with me."

He gripped her shoulders and shook her. He did not care if the others saw. "Stop this! I will return to you! But I will not be moved to do so out of guilt and obligation!"

She pulled back, hurt plain on her features. "Go then! You have made your choice!"

"I will return," he called to her as he watched her go back to the wagon. She walked quickly, her head down, arms wrapped around her waist. He wanted to go to her, then, but that pull kept him back.

He would be faithful to her until death. Her death. The Dya had assured it, and he did not doubt the truth of the magic that flowed into her.

Still, as he left the Gypsy camp, as he felt the pull toward Dika lessen and his sense of duty to his Queene build, almost crushing him, he doubted the old woman's words.

Eight

In hindsight, Cerridwen decided, the plan to leave the Palace, the Lightworld, would have worked far better if she'd known where to find Fenrick.

The Strip was far more crowded than usual, and hot. She lifted a lank strand of hair from her forehead and tried to peer through the impenetrable wall of traffic before her. Something had stirred the Underground. She only prayed it was not due to some move of her mother's.

Usually, when she escaped to the Strip, it was with no agenda. Most times, she found Fenrick, or he found her. On a few occasions, she had not seen him but ran into other acquaintances she had made and gone off with them for a time. Of course, she always hoped she would find Fenrick…but if she did not, her life did not crumble around her.

Tonight, it felt like it would. A thousand horrible thoughts curled through her mind like insidious vines breaking through pavement; her mother had already sent troops, they'd already captured Elves. Though she knew that Cedric would not have lied to her—and she did not know how she knew this, but she simply knew—she still feared that her mother might change her mind and order an all-out assault on the Dark-world in reckless pursuit of Elves, no matter how innocent they might be. If such a thing happened, if she could not find Fenrick first—

She choked back a sob that caught her by surprise. The panic that rose in her was due in part to the little sleep she'd managed, the weariness in her feet and the horrid temperature. But the root cause was her fear that she would not find Fenrick, and she could not force the other contributors to silence. Heedless of the crush about her, she pushed her way through the bodies, her heart pounding in her chest as though it would explode. Each new form that came into view, if it looked even a small bit like Fenrick, threw her into terrible hope, hope soon dashed at the sight of a pale brow or mortal face.

Someone stepped on her cloak, and she pulled against it without knowing. The clasp broke at her neck and the garment fell. She barely had time to pick it up before a Goblin marched across the place where she had stooped. The creature had no intention of stopping and hissed at her as it bumped past. She ignored it and spun to catch sight of a dark-skinned form. It was only a mortal. To her side, something white flashed, and she turned again, stumbled into a Vampire woman with silver hair. The creature shoved her, and she fell, became trapped by a forest of feet that did not care what they trampled.

Rolling to her knees, she crawled blindly toward where the crowd thinned, where only a few creatures stood around a wooden cart. Someone's boot caught her in the ribs, and a voice high above her head cursed her in a language she did not understand.

Her breath came hard as she made the clearing and pushed herself up, struggling to get even one foot beneath her.

"Cerri?" The voice caught her attention, turned her head when her body was not ready to respond, and she fell to her hands and knees again, the impact sending shocks up her arms.

Fenrick was at her side in an instant, his face twisted in concern and some amusement. "Cerri, what are you doing down there?"

When he helped her to her feet, she threw her arms around him and held on to him tightly. "Something has happened! I had to warn you—"

But he did not return her embrace. Instead, he pulled free from her, looked a bit embarrassed and even annoyed as he held her arms at her sides. "Warn me of what?" He was not unconcerned, but he seemed…preoccupied.

A flash of black caught her eye, and she looked beyond the cart, where a merchant had set up tables outside of his stall. There was a girl there, a Vampire or a mortal doing a good job of pretending to be a Vampire, and she watched Cerridwen and Fenrick with bored hostility.

"Who is that?" Cerridwen asked, her bones turning suddenly to ice. Then, she shook her head. There was something important that she must tell him, and she did not want to dwell on trivialities now. "No. I came to tell you something, and it cannot wait."

"Then tell me." He seemed more irritated now. The girl tossed her black hair lazily, turned away as though she were annoyed, but unworried, at Cerridwen's intrusion.

There was so much to confess to him first, before she could tell him of the events that drove her here. She supposed she could spill all to him standing right there on the Strip, but it seemed that to rush such an announcement—"I am the daughter of the Faery Queene and I have learned that you are in great danger"—would make it seem a joke, at best, or a lie, at worst.

"I cannot tell you here." When he made a noise of impatience and moved as if he would go, she grabbed his arm to stop him. "Please! Please, this has as much to do with your father, your family, every Elf you know, as it has to do with you. I cannot tell you here, on the Strip. But if we go away somewhere, I can explain."

He looked as though he were considering, his expression moving from angered to uneasy and back as his gaze moved from Cerridwen to the girl at the table. "Stay here," he said suddenly, and was gone before she could protest. He went to the Vampiress at the table and bent down to speak to her. That he did not touch her, did not appear to show any affection to her, soothed Cerridwen's bruised heart a bit. The girl pouted, twined her arm around his and tried to pull him down to a stool beside her, but he resisted, and with a cry of outrage, she stood and left. Fenrick threw some coins onto the table and lifted the tin cup that had been sitting beside the girl, downing the contents in a long swallow.

When he returned to Cerridwen's side, he seemed larger. Or perhaps that was just because she felt so very small.

Without speaking, he took her by the wrist and maneuvered through the crowd smoothly, until they came to a Darkworld entrance. They were barely inside when he stopped and let her go, demanding, "So, what is it you wish to tell me?"

Before she could speak, though, he said, "You look like the worst bits of the Darkworld, you know. I don't think I've ever seen you in such disarray. And you seemed so…worried. It's frightening me a little, Cerri."

"Cerridwen," she said stiffly. "My name is Cerridwen."

He shrugged. "I always assumed it was short for something."

"It is. Short for Cerridwen. Do you know much about the Faery Court?" She bit her lip and waited for him to answer, bracing herself for the rejection that was soon to come.

Another elegant shrug. "I know that they are Lightworld traitors. That they exiled my kind a century ago, and fought against us in the war when we sided with the Humans."

"And of their Queene?" As she spoke, she unbuttoned her shirt, her fingers trembling. "Do you know about her?"

"I do not know what game you are playing," Fenrick said with a slow smile. "But you play it better than the mortal I was just with."

She did not give him the benefit of a blush. "This is not a game." She let the garment slip from her shoulders and reached for the binding that held her wings in place. She pulled it free, finding the work awkward; Governess usually did it for her. "The Faery Queene, Queene Ayla, has a daughter. The Royal Heir. Got on her by her former mate, King Garret, who ruled only a few days before he was killed by his Queene. He was fully Fae, but the Queene is not. She is half Human. Her daughter…she can pass for Human, if she truly tries."

The binding fell free, and she stretched her wings, the feathery black things always bound to her back as part of her mother's obsessive need to make members of the Court appear more Human. They stretched wide and heavy, nearly upsetting her balance, and then she closed them around her nakedness.

"Cerri," Fenrick said, his usually arrogant, knowing expression obscured by a mask of shock. "Are you saying that you…you are a Faery?"

"A Faery, and the daughter of Queene Ayla." She took a deep breath and reached for her shirt. "I did not tell you before, because it was easier to pretend that I am a normal…that I am not destined to live out my life in my mother's Palace. I did not mean to lie to you, I swear. I would never seek to deceive you out of cruelty. I just wanted to have an adventure, to have friends outside of the Palace walls. You must understand, I did not lie to hurt you."

"I am not hurt," he said, his gaze falling to a place near her feet. "Is this the news you had for me? I thought you said it concerned—"

"No, there is more. And it does concern your race, and mine as well." She had thought it would be more difficult to confess her charade to him than to tell him of the coming danger, but now, she found that was not true. "A visitor from the Upworld came and warned us that Elves in the Darkworld would take action against us. I do not believe it, of course…they accuse your people of being in league with monsters. But my mother and her council believe it, and they intend to come into the Darkworld and kidnap some of you, torture someone of your kind into telling them what they wish to hear. And then they will declare war against you."

Fenrick said nothing.

"I know that your father is important among your people. You've told me as much, before. Perhaps he could do something, to warn your race to take care, to hide for a time."

Still, Fenrick did not respond.

"Fenrick?" She pulled her shirt on, held it closed over her chest as she stepped closer to him. "Have I made you angry?"

He looked up then, sharply, and all the warmth he had shown her before this horrible night had returned to his face. "I'm sorry. Cerri, I'm sorry, I've been a brute. I should not have been talking to that girl on the Strip. It was stupid of me, especially when I know how much you care about me, and…how much I care about you."

She did not know why he did not run directly to his father, why he felt the need to say this to her now.

In truth, his apology hurt her all over again. But his admission of his feelings, to hear that he cared for her, quickly eclipsed her confusion and hurt.

"I should not have come looking for you in such a state," she blurted, wondering at the same time what she had to apologize for. But the elation at his confession filled her to bursting. "I should not have scared you."

He took her into his arms, tucked her head easily beneath his chin. "No. You were right in coming to me. And brave. And noble. Truly, I don't know anyone who would do such a thing, risk so much to come to my aid."

She did not think she had risked all that much. Nothing that she cared about losing, at any rate. "I cannot go back to the Palace. Not now. I cannot stand to be there, knowing the way my mother feels about your kind, and how hateful she is."

"We will worry on that later," he soothed, his hands smoothing over her wings through her shirt. "Now, we must go to my father. He must hear of this immediately."

She pulled back and nodded her agreement, and let him lead her farther down the tunnel. It occurred to her to mention his knife, tucked safely in her trousers, but the silence between them was so nice, companionable as they set off to save his people together. She did not want to spoil it.

* * *

"He has allowed you access to the creature?"

Ayla smirked to herself at Cedric's question. "If you had not disappeared so suddenly last night, you would have been able to watch Flidais in action against the Ambassador. She was quite impressive."

Behind her, Cedric's footsteps halted. "Flidais dealt with him?"

His ego was wounded. Good. "If you had been here, the task would have fallen to you. But you were not. And Flidais proved herself just as effective."

Perhaps this would curb his ridiculous urge to disappear without warning or explanation. Flidais was no threat to Cedric, and he well knew it, but his pride would not tolerate important jobs falling to someone of a lesser station.

Perhaps he no longer cares, she nagged at herself. He had been distant, it was true, but she could not believe that he no longer cared what happened in Court.

He followed her to a room near the guards' barracks. They had separated the poor, maimed creature from Bauchan's retinue, though Ayla thought it might have been more to Bauchan's comfort than the creature's.

"You are keeping him here?" Cedric sniffed, looked up at the low ceiling. "You could not find a place for him in the dungeon?"

"I wanted to keep him as far from Bauchan as possible. I thought perhaps it would do him some good and influence what he would tell us." She nodded to the guard who waited outside, and he moved toward the door reluctantly, as if frightened to open it.

"Oh, Morrigan's acorns," Cedric cursed, pushing the guard out of his way. He opened the door onto a room that was not, as Ayla was sure he expected, a prison cell. It was furnished as nicely as the rooms where Bauchan was being kept, with a brick hearth and oven for heat, a cabinet stocked with bread and a cistern of clean water. A rough bed frame, like the ones the guards slept on, covered with soft materials for comfort, stood against the far wall, and the creature sat, motionless, on a stool in the center of the room.

His hood covered most of the deformities. Ayla thanked the Goddess for that. She did not know if she could have forced herself into the room if his scars were on full display. As she and Cedric approached, the thing's head tilted, like a bird taking an interest in something on the ground, but it made no other move.

Cedric looked to her, as if she should speak, and when she did not, he gave a heavy sigh. "Please rise, the Queene has come to see you."

The pitiful thing stumbled to its feet and swayed there a moment before attempting a clumsy bow. The jerky movements reminded Ayla of the puppets in the shows she'd seen on the Strip as a child. She swallowed. "You may be seated, if you are more comfortable."

The creature sat, seemed to stare quizzically at the two visitors despite the hood over its head.

Cedric again observed him in silence, rubbing his jaw. "Can you speak?" he asked finally, and the creature shook his head. Then, uncertain, nodded. And shook its head.

It could have been daft. But Ayla thought otherwise. "Is it painful to speak? Do you prefer not to?"

The creature nodded twice.

"There is no need to speak, then," she assured him. "I wished to speak with you, alone, and away from Bauchan. That is why you have been brought here. Is this place comfortable?"

He made a shrug that seemed to say, "As comfortable as any other place."

"You must tell us if you wish to be moved. After this conversation, if you wished, you could be returned to the Upworld, or back to Ambassador Bauchan's cell." When the creature made no indication of preferring either, she continued. "We wished to know more about your…well, about your deformity. How you came by it."

"Namely, we wish to know if you were injured by the creatures known as the Waterhorses. Were you?"

Cedric leaned against the closed door and folded his arms across his chest.

The maimed Faery hesitated. He nodded slowly, then stopped.

Ayla looked to Cedric. It seemed the creature wished to tell them something, but could not. "Can it write, do you suppose?"

The creature nodded vigorously and held out its hands.

"I will go and find some parchment," Cedric said, turning to the door.

"No!" Ayla could not stomach the thought of being alone with the thing, and her fear was so great that she could ignore her shame. "No. Send the guard to do it."

Cedric's expression suggested he thought she was being absurd, but he did not argue. He addressed the creature with some impatience. "Stay here. We will return when we have what we need."

He opened the door and motioned for Ayla to follow him. "Paper, and pen," he snapped at the guard waiting outside, who hurried to do as he bid. Once the door was closed, Cedric smoothed his antennae against his head. "Do you think there is anything he can tell us, truly, that we do not already know?"

Something in his manner was agitated, and Ayla did not like it. Cedric was usually so calm. It was her place to be agitated, not his, and she felt as though they were doing a dance to which she had not yet learned all the steps. "I think," she began carefully, "that he can tell us whether or not these Waterhorses are a threat to us, now. Who knows how long this pitiful thing has lived this way. I would be absolutely sure before I did anything rash," Ayla reminded him, as he had advised her so many times. "Do you not think that caution is best?"

He opened his mouth to say something, and only got as far as "I—" before the guard jogged back, a ripped notebook in one hand and a broken blue pen in the other. Ayla took the instruments from the guard, then handed them to Cedric, thinking ahead to who would finally touch them.

"Is this all you could find?" he growled at the guard, frowning down at the scraps in his hands.

The guard beamed as if unaware of Cedric's mood. "Found them on our excursion into the Darkworld, when were looking for—" he broke off, remembered he was in the presence of the Queene, and bowed. "They had some mortal writing on them, and I found them curious, so I kept them. I hope I have not offended, Your Majesty."

"As long as it is a *curiosity* about the mortal world, and nothing more." She turned away, took a fortifying breath, and pushed the door open again.

The creature stood, began to bow, but Ayla bade him sit down. He did, and reached for the edge of the hood that covered his face.

When his countenance was revealed, Ayla did not shrink away. She had seen a great many horrors worse than this in the Darkworld, during her time as an Assassin. But when she remembered that this was a Faery, or had once been, her stomach went weak again.

Cedric's face was grim as he approached, the writing implements held out before him. "Here. Please tell us what you wish about these Waterhorses, and what happened to you. Leave no important detail out. We will wait for as long as it takes you."

And they did wait. An hour passed as the creature scratched down the words, painfully slowly, on the paper. He often paused, and a few times Ayla wondered if he had finished, but the pen still hovered thoughtfully over the page.

When he finally handed it back to Cedric, there appeared to be little written on it. But what was written there made Cedric frown. "The Queene and I will discuss this in private," he told the pitiful Faery. "Is there anything else that we can do for you?"

It—*he,* Malachi would have reminded her, had he been there—twisted his head to the side slowly, once, twice, then opened its horrible, scarred mouth. The sound that came from its mangled lips was less a voice than a rattle, but the words were unmistakable.

"Kill…me."

Ayla looked to Cedric, but it was clear that neither

of them had the answer. She realized her hand was at her throat, fingering the collar of her robe in a nervous thrum, and she forced it away. She nodded to Cedric, and then in the direction of the Faery.

"It…will be done," Cedric promised gravely, and they left the pitiable thing alone in its room. Outside of the door, Cedric spoke to the guard, imparting instructions, no doubt, on how to deal with the disposal. Ayla did not wish to hear it; she was only glad that it would be done.

"What did the paper say?" she asked Cedric when they had walked far enough away from the guard and the horrible room. "Is there any new information? Shall I call the council?"

"Not yet," Cedric ground out, his jaw uncharacteristically tight.

"But what does it say?" She reached for the paper, but maddeningly knew she would not be able to decipher anything written there.

"I will tell you in private. I do not wish for anyone to overhear." So, they went to the council room, but Ayla did not send for Malachi and Flidais. She waited patiently for Cedric to lay out the paper he had folded again and again on their walk, and settled herself onto the most comfortable stool while he paced.

"I will read it to you straight out, without embellishment or correction. Only what he wrote in his own hand," Cedric said nervously.

"That would be best," she agreed, ready to scream at him to get on with it.

He cleared his throat, as though about to embark on a great oration, and smoothed the page flat on the tabletop. "'My name is Alfric, and I was born in the Upworld after the last Great War. I have lived on the Upworld all of my life.

"'I *was* maimed by the Waterhorses, but not as Bauchan would have you believe. My family lived peaceably with a family of mortals on a farm, my mother fulfilling the role of a *bean-tighe* while my father toiled as a Human in the fields outside. The mortals hid us again and again from Enforcers. They were believers in what they called the Old Way, and believed we were close to their Gods and Goddesses. They reveled in our magic, or what they believed was our magic, and we let them, because we were grateful to them.

"'On Samhain, the Waterhorses came for us. The mortals had stupidly left out offerings and called to spirits, and the Waterhorses heard this offer and came to claim it. It was the early light hours of the morning. My father fell first; they tore him to pieces with their claws and teeth while I hid behind a Hawthorne bush. They went to the house next, and I heard the mortals screaming, and my mother. I thought I was well hidden, so I stayed where I was, in the bush. But they found me, too, and did to me what they had done to my father and mother and the mortals.

"'But I lived. I do not know why I lived. They ate of my flesh while I still lived, and yet I did not die. They tore my skin and the foaming saliva that dripped from their jaws burned me. I did not want to live. I begged to die. But I did not.

"'I had only come into being twenty-five years earlier. I have lived, with the memories and the scars, with the horrible burning. I do not wish to live any longer.'"

The silence that fell over them was that of the inside of a tomb, or so Ayla imagined. But there was a relief, as well. Not only that this broken, tortured creature would not suffer a day longer, but that Bauchan's threat had been entirely without truth.

"That is good to know," she said, her tongue thick in her mouth. "Now, do we try Bauchan for treason, or simply send him back to his Queene with his tail between his legs?"

"We will do neither," Cedric said, very quietly. "The Waterhorses have indeed come."

Ayla snorted. "Yes, if we were to believe that they took their time getting here. The creature was twenty-five at his maiming, and born after the Great War. Not as old as you, but he could be far older than me. I doubt that the villains in his tragic story have spent this much time trying to find their way into the Dark-world."

"I do not know how much time it would take them," Cedric said, his voice still maddeningly quiet. "But I know they have come."

She made a noise of disgust. It was as if Cedric had been infected by Malachi's disquiet of late. "Do not overcomplicate this, Cedric. We have no reason to believe that the Waterhorses are coming. The only proof Bauchan has—"

"It is not Bauchan who has proof. It is I." Cedric paced before the table a few times, his hands rubbing his face as though he could bend the flesh there out of shape. "I must confess something to you, Your Majesty, that I did not wish to trouble you with."

There was a current in the air now, something sinister and anticipatory. It prickled Ayla's skin. "Best to have it out. Trouble me," she responded, but whatever it was that Cedric had to say would come in its own, maddening time.

"I have a mistress." He quickly amended that. "A mortal mistress. A Gypsy."

It was certainly not the confession Ayla expected. Cedric, who never seemed to care for the creatures at all, dallying with a mortal? If it had come from anyone else's lips, she would not have believed it.

"I..." she began, but there was nothing to say.

Cedric, however, had more to speak of. "The

Gypsies are leaving the Underground, fleeing to the Upworld to get away from the creatures who are stalking them. The creatures are the Waterhorses. They have come to the Underground and, as they are confining themselves to the Darkworld, I can only assume that they are there at the behest of the Elves, as Bauchan warns."

"You are certain of this? They are not…confused? Mistaking a lesser Demon or another creature—"

"No." He did not meet her eyes. "Their leader is a mortal woman who deals in magic. She has seen a vision of them."

"Their leader?" Another unexpected blow. "You have spoken with their leader?"

He did not deny it. That nearly made the insult of it worse.

So, he had spoken to the leader of these people. That was involvement far beyond a simple affair. It showed that he belonged, in some way, that he was accepted by them. That he had somewhere else he could go. That was most frightening of all.

Had he intended to tell her this? No, otherwise he would not have bothered with the charade of interrogating the misshapen Faery. If the creature's tale had been different, he would never have confessed.

"Thank you," Ayla said, her voice scraping out painfully. "I appreciate your honesty."

"Your Majesty, I must also confess—"

The door to the council room opened, and Malachi entered without knocking. He held Cerridwen's governess by one arm, and she dangled at his side, sniveling helplessly.

"She is gone," Malachi said, pushing the Faery to the floor. "And this creature will answer for it."

Nine

"Malachi!" Ayla stood, took a few steps toward Governess, and then seemed to realize that the Queene could not help a commoner off the floor.

For once, Malachi was grateful for her pretensions.

"What do you mean, she is gone?" Cedric did not ask Malachi, but the sniveling Faery on the floor. "I saw her only hours ago."

"She must have slipped away as we met with Bauchan," Ayla said, her voice hollow. "I should have let her stay."

Cedric shook his head. "No. I went to see her after we disbanded the council. She wanted to know what took place there, and I promised her I would tell her."

"Your promises to her now mean something?" Ayla snapped, suddenly all wrath and fire.

"I have never made a promise to your daughter,

Your Majesty," Cedric said coldly. "Any promise you may have made on my behalf is not mine to keep."

"Cerridwen is missing!" Malachi could not believe they would become consumed in petty arguments over betrothal at this moment. "She has been missing for some time, and this creature has not reported it to anyone! She has been slinking around the Palace, trying to leave, herself! She probably helped Cerridwen to escape!"

"No, Your Majesty, do not believe him, I beg you!" Governess crawled on her hands and knees toward Ayla to collapse to the floor, prostrate before her. "It is true, the Royal Heir is missing. But I had nothing to do with it."

The fury in Ayla's demeanor did not die, but redirected. "Then why would you run? Several times now, the Royal Heir has left the Palace without my consent. I say it is you who is responsible, else you would not flee!"

"I flee because I am frightened!" Governess climbed to her knees. "I have served you well, these past twenty years, and yet you would wish me to stay here, to be slaughtered by monsters?"

Ayla turned to Cedric. "What did you tell her?"

Malachi did not like to intervene in arguments between the Queene and her advisor. He tried to only speak out when one or both of them seemed to lose all grasp of logic. And that time seemed to have come.

"There were at least a hundred Courtiers present when Bauchan made his initial announcement. She could have heard this from any of them."

"I meant Cerridwen," Ayla roared, advancing on Cedric. "What did you tell Cerridwen, to make her run away?"

"Everything, my lady!" Still in terror for her life, the governess inched her way forward on her knees to interject. "I heard all. He told her of your plans to invade the Darkworld, to capture Elves! No wonder she was frightened—"

"Enough!" Ayla screamed. "Get this traitor out of my sight. Lock her in the dungeon, lest she contaminates anyone else with her fear. I will not allow a mass retreat before the battle even begins!"

As the governess wailed in terror, Malachi stepped forward to do Ayla's bidding. It was right, and sensible, of her to think of the effect such hysteria would have on her Court. But as he approached, she called out, "Not you, Malachi. I will need you to help find Cerridwen."

"I believe I may know where she has gone, Your Majesty," Cedric said quietly.

Ayla did not look at him as she spoke. "You are as good as a traitor yourself, Cedric. Take this one to the dungeon and be glad I do not order your incarceration, as well."

Without a word, Cedric hauled Governess to her

feet and pulled her toward the door. In his face, every ruthless emotion that Malachi knew the Faery to have warred for dominance. If Cedric were not such an honorable Faery, Ayla would have made a very powerful enemy with her words.

The door closed, leaving both of them in silence, a silence Malachi knew better than to break.

But knowing that something was foolish did not always prevent him from doing it. He shrugged his shoulders and said, "Perhaps he did know where Cerridwen was. If he was the last to see her, before she ran off."

"I do not believe he was the last to see her." Ayla did not react with the anger she had displayed before, the anger that Malachi had fully expected. She sounded tired and resigned, and utterly hopeless.

"Where do you suggest we begin looking for her, then?" He would not ask her why she had called Cedric a traitor, or why they had been so tense when he'd entered. Probably more fighting over the betrothal, and Malachi could not take Ayla's side in that.

Sighing, Ayla moved toward the door. "We'll look over her bedroom, first. If she is leaving permanently because of what Cedric told her, she will have taken things with her, I suspect. She is intelligent enough to do that."

"And if we find that nothing has been removed, then we can conclude that she will return on her own?" He followed Ayla into the corridor, where she waved off the guards who had automatically flanked her. That simple gesture moved something in Malachi; she still felt safe with him at her side, did not see the need for further protection.

Ayla did not answer his question, though, and they went to the royal chambers, straight to the door to Cerridwen's room. Malachi had not been inside since it had been called the royal nursery. In those early days, he'd visited his daughter, cradled her tiny body in his arms. As she'd grown, he'd still gone to see her, but not as often. It was too painful to follow protocol that kept him a safe distance from her at Court when all he wished to do was put her on his shoulder and proclaim that she was his. When the child had begun to question his presence, he cut himself off from her entirely.

Cutting off a limb would have seemed painless in comparison.

The royal nursery had been much tidier before it had become the chambers of the Royal Heir. How Ayla would be able to tell anything missing from the ill-organized collection in the antechamber, he had no idea.

But she did not bother with the antechamber. Instead, she went farther into the room, beyond a screen to where the Royal Heir should have slept the night before.

The wardrobe doors were open, the contents rifled through. But clothing remained. The bed had not been made, but it did not look slept in, either. It looked slept *on,* as though she had not intended to go to sleep at all. A trait she shared with her mother.

Ayla went to the wardrobe and pushed some of the dresses aside, then righted them. She opened drawers, and flung back the bedcovers. She looked around the room, then her shoulders sagged and she sank to the bed. "I cannot tell. She could be gone for a day, she could be gone for an hour."

There was a small writing desk. "Would she have left a note?"

"For me?" Ayla scoffed. "No, she knows I would not be able to read it. She has made it a point to mock me and my lack of intelligence."

Malachi lifted the edge of the bedclothes and stopped to peer beneath the bed. He retrieved a crumpled ball of paper and smoothed it. "Perhaps she tried to write you, and thought better of it. I will take these to Cedric, and have him read them to me."

"If he tells you the truth in them, I would be surprised." The bitterness that dripped from her tone was like acid.

Malachi pocketed the other pages and sat down beside her on the bed. He could have put his arms around her and insisted that they would find Cerridwen. He believed they would; to lose her forever was unthinkable. But he did not wish to reassure her and draw her away from the matter that, at the moment, was even more troubling to him than his absent daughter.

"May I ask why we now treat Cedric as a traitor? What has he done to lose your trust in the few hours since you saw him last?"

She did not answer at once. He knew Ayla well enough to know that she realized she had acted foolishly. But still, she would tell him, as penance. "He has a mistress. A mortal mistress."

"Oh?" Malachi did his best to appear surprised, but artifice was not in his nature. "I must confess, I knew that."

"And you did not tell me?" She was not angry. Just defeated and sad. "How much is kept secret from me in my own, most trusted circle?"

"Only that which should not truly affect you." Perhaps, there was some deception he was capable of. "You believe that he has betrayed you because he has a mistress…but he had no reason to stay pure for you, or for Cerridwen. Is that what you wished? To have him all for yourself?"

"No!" Her shock and disgust was genuine, but only because she did not know herself so well as he did. "No, I have never thought of Cedric that way. But these last few days, he has been increasingly absent when I've needed him. The kingdom is in crisis and he has put his own needs before the interests of his race."

"If you truly believed that, you would have thrown him into the dungeon alongside Governess." Malachi stood, gave a last glance around the room. "I do not fault you for being angry with him over this…deception. You have been honest with him about a great many things that you did not have to be. But consider, perhaps, that he has sacrificed twenty years of his life to be loyal to you, twenty years of service whenever you have asked for it. Would you truly deny him a life of his own?"

She said nothing.

"I will go to him and ask about these letters. I will consult you before proceeding further." He left her there, and did not expect her to follow him. She loathed being wrong. No, not being wrong; she did not like being told that she was wrong when it was something she was forced to admit.

He did not go to Cedric. That he had taken information from the council meeting and disseminated it to others did not sit well with Malachi. How could he not have realized the consequences of such an action? The Court was already in a panic. Word would spread like an uncontrollable fire through the Lightworld. Why encourage that?

He would find Flidais, and let her tell him what the letters meant. He would not mention the letters to Cedric. And he would bring his daughter home.

* * *

The Great Hall was a second home to Flidais. A first home, she admitted grudgingly. She spent more time there than in the small room allocated for her living arrangements in the Palace. It was simply easier to do her duties to the Queene if she was in the middle of the Court, with open eyes and ears.

It was also an easier way to make her living. If she were inaccessible to the Courtiers, she would not be able to accept their bribes. Corruption was far from an honorable profession, but there was no honor in poverty, either.

The recent news of the Elven threat had sent many Courtiers scurrying from the Palace, back to their homes in other parts of the Lightworld. Some were even cowardly enough to rent rooms on the Strip. Flidais carefully cataloged their names in her mind. She would not forget, and if they wished to return to Court, she would demand recompense before putting their names favorably before the Queene.

But their retreat had a decidedly bleak effect on Court life, and it was difficult for Flidais to ignore the smaller crowd, the less exuberant mood in the Great Hall. That mood dampened further when the doors opened to admit the Queene's favorite, her Darkling.

Everyone knew what he was. It was no secret that he was not Fae, and no secret that he shared the Queene's bed. But knowledge was not official confirmation, and it certainly was not acceptance. He was far from accepted at Court, as evidenced by the hush that fell over the room.

Malachi rarely came to the Great Hall, and never alone. Usually, he travelled at Cedric's side, or the Queene's, on the rare occasions she graced the Courtiers with her presence outside of a feast or formal audience. Now, he came into the room as though he owned the Palace, had every right to walk about in it. It was an attitude Flidais did not like to see him exhibit.

Less endearing still was the fact that he walked toward her. He wanted to speak to her. The idea made her skin crawl.

She forced her revulsion away and tried to appear, if not welcoming, then not horrified, either.

"Malachi, I am surprised to see you here. So rarely do you grace us with your company."

He made a noise in his throat, like an animal, as he rooted through a pocket of his robe. "I need you to read these for me. I cannot."

He thrust a packet of papers toward her, and she had little choice but to take them. He could not read, but expected her to perform the task for him without the cost of gratitude? That was truly an insult. She was not his servant. With an annoyed glance at his face, she unfolded the papers.

It took only a moment to scan the first one, and she

glared up at him sharply. "These are written in the Royal Heir's own hand. How did you get them?"

Her pronouncement drew curious stares, and two Faeries who had been standing close by edged slightly nearer.

"They were given to me, by the Queene." He did not lower his voice, but Flidais had no doubt he had noticed the subtle shift of attention in the room. "She does not have time to deal with such trivialities now, but she wishes to know what her daughter asks for in these letters. In truth, I think she gives me such a task to humiliate me, as she knows I cannot read them myself."

Queene Ayla could not, either, but he did a good job of covering it up. He'd also lost the Courtiers' attention. A menial task given by the Queene to her Consort was not interesting enough to gossip about.

"I have very little time for this," Flidais said coldly, nodding toward the papers in her hand. "But if you wish to follow me to my next appointment, I will read them over and tell you what they say."

As always, the Court could not know that the Royal Heir was missing. Especially now, with the mood so infused with doom and despair. Malachi followed her from the Great Hall, and she took several twists and turns before leading him back to the council room. He did not complain. Though he could not read the letters, he would understand the need for privacy and subter-fuge.

"What do they say?" he demanded, almost as soon as the door had closed behind them.

"I have not had time to read them all, yet, have I?" She laid the crumpled pages on the table and smoothed them. "They are all incomplete. She did not mean for anyone to read them, though she did when she began them. But the shortest says she is in love with an Elf…and that she will run away to the Dark-world to be with him. The longer takes a more politi-cal view, but the outcome is the same. She will run to the Elves and warn them of what is to happen…."

Flidais looked up at Malachi. "This is bad."

He said nothing. He stared down at the pages, his whole body as tense as an overtuned lute string. "You will say nothing of this to anyone. Do you under-stand?"

Orders? From a Darkling? And orders that made little sense, as well. "I must tell. This could endanger the Lightworld far worse than we realized. If she tells the Elves that we are to war with them, they could attack before we are ready. This will be disastrous. I must tell the Queene, or Cedric, at least, and let him tell her."

"No!" The animal power in the Darkling was frightening and disgusting, all at once. He pounded the table, and the whole piece jumped, as if it had touched one of the Human power wires. "I must have your word on this! I will go into the Darkworld and retrieve Cerridwen myself. But you will not tell the Queene, or Cedric. They will send soldiers after her, and that alone would spark a war. You must give me your word!"

Flidais considered. Her word still meant something, even when given to a Darkling, and she did not take such vows lightly. But she could not ignore the rash, unwise thing Malachi proposed. So, the presence of guards in the Darkworld could spark a war. So, too, could the word of a certain Darkling, whose motives could never be trusted, who remained a Darkling even after twenty years of service to the Queene. The Queene might trust him, but Flidais had not lived so long because she *trusted*.

Still, she rolled his words through her mind. She could not tell the Queene. She could not tell Cedric. "You have my word," she assured him, very slowly.

And she would not go back on that promise. But there was another who would like to hear, she was certain of it.

Ten

❧~❧~❧

Fenrick had never spoken to Cerridwen about his home. He had certainly never taken her there. So, every step closer to the Elven holding was a bit more frightening, a bit more exciting. She clasped his hand at her side, so tightly and without thinking that several times he had disentangled himself from her with a pained expression. She had apologized sheepishly and walked with her arms crossed for a time, but then always took his hand back, and he always let her.

"Do not fear," he assured her as they turned down another narrow tunnel. "Our races are different, that is true, but they will welcome your devotion. And my father will reward you handsomely for what you have come to tell him."

She smiled, her nerves still a riot in her. It was not a reward she sought, and she wished she could make him know that. But there would be time for that later. Now, she could concentrate only on keeping her heartbeat quiet in her chest, her lungs from gasping for breath.

It seemed they had been traveling for hours, but Fenrick did not stop to rest. They were farther into the Darkworld than Cerridwen had ever traveled, farther, she was certain, than her mother had ever traveled in her days as an Assassin.

Her mother. The thought brought a fresh wave of resolve to her. What would her mother think if she saw her daughter tromping through the Darkworld, over rough, sometimes sticky ground, through passages that smelled like damp and worse? Would she still see her as a child?

It was too likely to deny. Queene Ayla saw everyone as beneath her…she would also disapprove of Fenrick, that Cerridwen could be certain of. The Queene whose Consort was a mortal Darkling would think ill of an Elf? At least they were not mortal.

They traveled in silence for what must have been another hour, before Fenrick stopped suddenly and took her by the hands.

"When we arrive, you must not speak to anyone. They must believe you are my prisoner. Do not look into anyone's eyes, they will see it as an insult. Most of them hate Faeries, and I do not wish for them to have reason to quarrel with you. Let me speak, unless

I prompt you to, and all will be well." He spoke with a sudden passion that unnerved her, his yellow eyes glittering in the dark.

"Your prisoner?" She did not like the idea, and it made her turn her head to look back the way they came. As if she could escape. As if she wanted to.

"For your protection only, and only temporarily," he reassured, tugging her hands to start her walking again. "Come, it is not far."

He did not lie. Another turn brought them to a great, wide tunnel, almost as wide as the Strip. The Strip, though, was wide and well lit. The Elven holding seemed a mass of darkness, and though Cerridwen's eyes struggled to adjust, she could not make out distinct shapes beneath the dim torchlight high above their heads.

She pushed closer to Fenrick, grasped his arm, and heard his laughter. "You are not afraid of the dark?" he asked, incredulous.

Screwing up her courage, she let him go…but only to the length of her forearm. If she lost hold of him now, she would not find him again.

As they moved through what had, at first, seemed an empty, wide corridor, Cerridwen became aware of others around them. The hiss of sliding fabric and the sound of breath seemed closer in the dark than it might have in the light, and prickles stood out on her neck. She looked into the darkness at her side and saw yellow eyes, then kept her gaze fixed sharply forward.

They came to a door, which led to a much darker, narrow hall, and then, at the other end of that, blessed light. The room they entered was round and tall, the top open to the night sky above. Full moonlight shone down through a wire grate similar to the one over Sanctuary, but it was hanging torches that lit the room like sunlight, revealing the dripping black of the mildewed walls.

In the center of the room stood an Elf in a long, white coat that contrasted so thoroughly with his blue-black skin that for a moment Cerridwen could not see his face, so blinding was the color of his clothing. His hair was not as white as Fenrick's, but tinged with a slightly dirty yellow. When he smiled, his teeth were not as brightly silver, and his smile was not as kind.

"Fenrick, what is this you've brought me?" He said it as though Cerridwen were some bauble or trinket he was about to be gifted. She did not like it, but remembered Fenrick's warning.

"Father." Fenrick made a queer bow, dropping to one knee with his arms clasped across his chest, a hand on each shoulder. When he stood again, he stood stiffly, as if avoiding a sword point to his back. "I have brought a prisoner. The daughter of the Faery Queene."

Fenrick's father laughed and clapped his hands

slowly. The sound echoed from the walls like a headsman's ax falling. With an audible hiss, the Elf walked in a slow circle around Cerridwen, looking her over with undisguised lechery. "Queene Ayla's daughter? Prisoner? How did you do it?"

Fenrick looked straight ahead, ignored his father's disgusting display. All part of the act, Cerridwen assured herself. "A happy accident. I had been trying to seduce her, to no avail, for weeks. It was out of love that she confessed her secret identity to me."

He'd been trying to seduce her? That sent a happy thrill through her, despite the unpleasant situation. All of those signals she'd been sure she'd seen and heard had not been the product of her wishful imagination.

Then, casually, his father lifted a strand of Cerridwen's hair in his hand and sniffed it, making a face. "This creature? You would pick this pitiful thing for a dalliance? That is truly disappointing, son. I thought I'd taught you better than to stray from your own kind."

Dalliance? That made it seem so…filthy. She opened her mouth, as if to argue, and closed it again.

"Oh, it wishes to speak." As if he'd suddenly lost interest and patience with her, Fenrick's father walked away. "What could it tell me?"

"She has told me a great many things, Father," Fenrick said, his gaze drifting nervously to Cerridwen. "Perhaps you should ask her."

"I will ask her nothing." The older Elf turned, his eyes blazing orange with wrath. Then, his expression turned sickeningly sweet as he regarded his son. "But I do thank you. She will make an excellent trophy."

As Fenrick looked blankly at his father, two shapes moved in the shadows. Other Elves, Cerridwen assumed, but they were clothed in armor…proper, matching armor, not the remnants of bygone wars disguised by shoddy tabards. They were covered from head to toe in dull black metal, so skillfully camouflaged that they had been indistinguishable from the darkness in the room.

What were they doing? Cerridwen turned to Fenrick, saw that he still remained where he stood, that he did not try to reassure her. The guards grew ever closer, their metal boots clanking on the floor. They would throw her in a dungeon, or worse, perhaps. And Fenrick would not, she could see now, help her.

Though he had warned her against speaking out, and though he had intended to present her as a prisoner—had that been the ruse all along, to trick her into coming here?—she could not remain silent. Not at the cost of her life. "I am no trophy!"

The guards faltered in their step, and Fenrick's father, terrifying in his stature and strange ways, stared at her as though he'd just witnessed a lowly cockroach speak.

Still, she continued, praying she sounded more confident than she felt. "I have not come here as Fenrick's prisoner, but as an ally. I wish to join your side of the coming war against my mother's Court."

"An ally?" The Elf laughed, and it was not a sound of humor. "An ally? A Faery? You have seriously overestimated the importance your life holds to me."

"I can tell you of my mother's plans! Are those not important?" she felt Fenrick's angry gaze on her now, and a veil of confusion fell over her. Would he not now see her as brave? Would his father not realize how valuable her knowledge could be to him?

As if in answer, Fenrick's father came forward and grasped Cerridwen's wrists, crushing them until the sound of bones grinding was audible over the ringing of pain in her ears.

"The only sound I want to hear out of you are your cries for mercy as I kill you. I want your mother to hear them, as well." He let go of her so unexpectedly that she tumbled to the ground. She hadn't realized that her knees had buckled. "Cage her. Leave her relatively unmarked, for the time being. I want her somewhat whole when I face the Bitch Queene."

"Fenrick?" She looked up at him through a haze of tears. "Fenrick, will you not tell him? I am on your side."

But he said nothing, would not deign to look at her.

"Fenrick?" His name was a bitter whisper now. Something tore away inside her as she looked at him.

The older Elf sighed and approached his son. "You did well, son. But you should have cut out her tongue before bringing her here."

"Yes, father. Thank you, Your Majesty."

Fenrick did not answer her cries even as the guards dragged her away.

Elves were not difficult to come by in the Darkworld. Turn over a moldy rock and you could find one. Lift a sodden, moldering pile of rags, and there he would be.

Malachi stalked through the tunnels, sword drawn. Already, the blade shone crimson, and where it was not crimson, it was black. Two Demons who'd approached and a Human who had been foolish enough to try to steal from him had already seen to that. He did not put his blade away, for he had not yet found his quarry, and though he planned to take it alive, he would not risk being overcome himself before capturing it.

He would not tell Ayla what the letter had said, he decided. He could not tell her that Cerridwen had run off with a lover to the Darkworld, in order to avoid her betrothal. She would blame herself, though she would not admit it. But inside, her regret would grow in her like a canker.

No, he would not tell her she'd run off because of

the betrothal. But he certainly would not tell her that she'd run off intending to see her mother defeated at the hands of the Elves. That Cerridwen had been so cruel as to suggest such a thing gave Malachi a sick feeling in his guts. He had no idea what he would tell Ayla.

How could the girl be so stupid? So careless? How could she walk willingly in the Darkworld, knowing how dangerous it was? Knowing that it was an unfor-givable offense to her mother, to her entire race?

How could she be so like Ayla, and yet so different?

Ayla had been able to handle herself in the Dark-world. Not that it justified her reason for going there, which was exactly the same reason as Cerridwen used now. Love. A silly thing that the Fae weren't even supposed to feel, not like mortals. And yet, both mother and daughter had fallen victim to the whims of their emotions. Even Cedric must know something of love, willing as he was to turn his back on the Court and chase after a mortal.

Malachi understood love. It was dangerous, and made its sufferers do stupid things. Stupid things like prowling the Darkworld, spoiling for a fight. Like trying to rescue a child who loathed him, and who would loathe him more if she knew the truth of why he sought to help her. Love made people lie to those they loved, to keep them from being wounded.

In the dark of the tunnel ahead, he saw a flash of

yellow eyes. Though he had not stalked Elves in his time as a Death Angel, he had seen them, and had delivered many mortals to Aether after they'd fallen dead at an Elf's hands. He had seen them fight, and had seen them hunt. Now, he was being hunted.

He did not react. If the creature knew he had spotted it, it might lose interest or flee. He continued to walk, knowing a trap had been set, praying there were not so many of them that they would easily overtake him.

His footsteps became splashes as he ventured farther and the fetid water deepened, sloshing over his boots, seeping into the hem of his robe. It was a good trap…most mortals would be slowed trying to escape from water that restricted the movement of their legs. But most mortals would run, not fight. Relying on him to flee would be the Elf's first mistake.

The second would be assuming that a mortal would make for easy prey. Malachi was mortal in as much as he could be killed—and easily, compared to those races that considered themselves mortal. But not easy when compared to the mortal fools who made the Darkworld their home, the kind these Elves were intending to waylay. Those mortals would scream, panic, beg.

Malachi would force his opponents to do those things.

Judging from the sound of bodies breaking water,

there were four of them in the darkness. He looked around, feigned helplessness. They drew closer; this he could tell from instinct. All of the training he had received from Cedric, from Ayla, all of that would have aided him little had he not retained the preternatural senses he'd had as a Death Angel.

One Elf surfaced behind him, and the surprise on his face was delicious as Malachi's blade severed the creature's neck before it could even move to defend itself.

Another had witnessed the fall of its cohort, and called out in rage to his remaining fellows. Malachi didn't bother to listen to the shouted curses and threats. Two Elves stood to his left, the gleam of their curved blades evident even in the near-total darkness. The third hung back, appeared to be unarmed.

He would live, Malachi decided. It would be easier to kill the other two, rather than wrestle their weapons away from them.

They were bold, both rushing him at once, moving to flank him as he twisted in their direction. The one remaining on his left swung his blade, and Malachi dodged it, simultaneously locking his sword against the other Elf's scimitar. He pushed down, hard, ignoring the repeated swing of the left Elf, ducking out of the way of the blade at the last possible moments but never letting up pressure on the right Elf's weapon. The trapped sword shot from the creature's hand, hitting the water before he could recover it. Malachi made a quick swipe and the Elf's hand followed the weapon into the murky depth.

While his partner howled in rage and pain, the left Elf increased the pace of his frantic assault. Malachi smiled to himself. They had just realized that this would not be an easy kill. And they had realized it too late.

Then, it all went wrong somehow. Pain ripped through Malachi's chest, muscles seizing painfully on some invading, tearing pressure. He stared down, unbelieving, at the slender wood protruding from his chest.

In that moment, the left Elf landed a blow with his knife, deep into Malachi's shoulder. The blade stuck, but he was able to shove the Elf away to disarm him.

Another searing bolt shocked him as something pierced his thigh; he stumbled and fell to his knees in the water, and the maimed right Elf leaped onto his back. He struggled, but the creature held fast, weighing him down. Malachi took a huge breath before the Elf managed to shove his head below water.

The left Elf had recovered from his fall and waded to Malachi, gripping his arms and holding them at his sides. Malachi kicked out, trying to get his feet beneath him on the rough bottom of the tunnel, but the combined weight of the Elves holding him was too great.

His lungs, paralyzed in his chest, ached for breath.

His limbs burned for want of air. He closed his eyes, and let his body go limp.

It took them longer than he expected, almost too long, to realize that they'd successfully drowned him. They released him, and did not bother to recover their weapons…they were glad, he supposed, to be alive. They did not pick over his corpse for money; any spoils they had hoped for were abandoned in the relief of escape.

He waited until they had waded away a few paces. And then, he burst from the water.

One of them screamed. Malachi ended the sound with a squeeze of his fist around the Elf's throat. A quick shake, the way Humans killed chickens, and the whole of the black throat came away his hand. He plunged the struggling body beneath the water and planted one boot on its back while he grabbed the other creature. He held him easily with one fist tangled in the creature's long hair and reached to pull the knife that still protruded from his shoulder. When the blade was free, he wrenched the Elf's head back and plunged the knife to its hilt through the creature's exposed neck. A jet of blood streamed from the wound as he jerked the knife downward and pulled the Elf's struggling body up. The metal hit the powerful resistance of bone then, and with a renewed burst of strength cleaved through it, splitting the body from throat to stomach. Malachi threw the corpse aside and reached for the Elf still fighting at the bottom of the pool. He caught him by the hair, as well, pulling his head up, keeping his body pinned by the weight of Malachi's foot at the back of his knees, bowing his body outward, away from his captor. With one swift slice the head came free and the body drifted limply into the water.

An arrow pierced the water at Malachi's side, and he cursed. The last Elf, the one he'd intended to capture, still seemed intent on killing him. But now that Malachi knew what he faced, he had a far better chance of overcoming him.

The Elf fired another bolt. Malachi heard the catch of the bow giving way, the whistle of the projectile rending the air. He easily moved from its path. Another came, and another, all easy to avoid, until a cry of fear and a splash revealed that the Elf had dropped his weapon in flight.

"Do not run!" Malachi bellowed to the fleeing Elf. He still held the head of the dead one in his fist, and he dropped it to the water as he started for the terrified survivor.

Of course, the warning went unheeded. But the Elf's terror impeded his own escape. He stumbled, fell into the water flailing, gasped as he surfaced and stumbled again. The water was deeper here, to Malachi's waist, and it caught in his wings beneath his robe, tugging at them, drawing him back. It was not enough, though, to slow him in time for the Elf to escape. Malachi grasped the creature by its sodden garments and hauled it up to face him. Its feet no longer touched the bottom of the pool.

"You have caused me no small irritation," he snarled into the Elf's face. "But you will live. You will live long enough to tell my Queene that you have abducted her daughter, and that your people intend to war with the Faeries. And then, you might live out the rest of your days in a dark cell, occasionally tortured for my amusement."

The Elf opened its mouth and began to protest having knowledge of any of the charges Malachi had levied against him. That was to be expected, and Malachi did not have time to listen. He jerked the Elf forward and his skull into that of his bretheren. The body went limp in his hands.

Now, his wounds began to make themselves known, his muscles began to ache under the strain of activity they could no longer sustain. Ignoring the throbbing that took his breath away with every movement, he hefted the whole Elf over his shoulders, dropped the ruined head of the other, and slogged through the water, back the way he'd come, toward the Lightworld.

Eleven

It was not difficult to convince the guards that she was there to see Bauchan on official business. They recognized her, of course, as someone close to the Queene, and did not ask to see the elaborate documents that she had forged.

It was a shame, Flidais lamented as she was admitted to the rooms where Bauchan and his entourage were being held. The documents might have been her most convincing forgery yet. They were even better than the ones for Faery Lord Vervain, when he'd commissioned false intelligence reports to help instigate the Vampire uprising.

In the antechamber, members of Bauchan's retinue lounged on the pallets hastily constructed for their imprisonment. The alcove in the back, which should have been discreetly concealed with a curtain, was exposed, and Bauchan himself lay on the bed, his back to the room.

"I have come to speak to the Ambassador," she said, loudly enough that he could hear her.

He did not stir.

"Bauchan is resting," a bored voice replied. She could not tell who had spoken.

Drawing herself up to appear as tall as she could—though she was aware that was not very—she said, louder, "It is a matter of grave importance."

"So is his rest." The same, bored voice, and several mocking titters answered it.

It was not difficult to ignore. She'd had plenty of experience with the vapid Courtiers of Queene Ayla's Court, and, before that, with Queene Mabb's inner circle, who had been infinitely more obnoxious. Clearing her throat, she pronounced, "Then perhaps I should come back at a more convenient time. After the Waterhorses have overrun the Lightworld due to the rash actions of an incompetent Queene? When all the races of the Lightworld are suffering and blaming it on the Fae? Would that be more conducive to the Ambassador's rest?"

The figure on the bed slowly pulled himself into a half-sitting position, twisted, and rolled sleepy eyes toward Flidais.

She had gotten his attention, then. She allowed herself a smirk of triumph as she watched him unfold himself to stand. "Ah, Ambassador. I am pleased to see you looking so…well rested."

This time, the insipid snickering was on her side, and shameful as it was to realize, she was glad of it. Bauchan, however, was not. He stalked out of the alcove like a cornered animal looking for a target to strike, glaring at his entourage as he looked from side to side to take them in. "What would the handmaiden of our *gracious hostess* want with us, lowly prisoners that we are?"

"A moment of your time, nothing more." Flidais said this with the proper deference, careful not to insult Bauchan any further. She knew his type; if wounded too deeply, he would lash out unhelpfully, not caring what might fall. She could not afford that now.

"Well." He made a gesture with open arms, as if to display his helplessness. "You have me. I am not going anywhere, that is painfully certain. So, speak your piece."

"My piece?" As if she had carefully planned what she would say. In truth, she had, but she would not admit as much to him. "I have no carefully crafted statement. I merely come to strike a bargain with you."

"A bargain? Like the one your Queene struck with that poor, misshapen creature who traveled with us? Struck his head from his body, as I understand it."

There was bitterness in his tone that did not come from grief for the maimed Elf. He was as relieved to be rid of the sorry article as anyone. But it was something he could take umbrage to, Flidais knew, in order to appear less amenable to what she would offer. He would, of course, accept anything she gave him. He did not wish to stay in captivity, and even his pride would not allow him to remain behind these walls.

"An unfortunate misunderstanding, I assure you," she said by way of apology, and bowed slightly to him. "The wretched creature requested that mercy from my Queene. I can see how very deeply he is missed."

"Get on with it," Bauchan ordered, dropping all pretense. "What does your Queene wish to do with me?"

"My Queene would like nothing more than to leave you here to rot for the rest of your days." It was true, as far as Flidais could tell. "She is far too occupied with other matters to give even a thought to you."

That worried him. Flidais could see it in his eyes, and in the way his antennae buzzed against his matted hair. "Then why are you here?" he asked cautiously, as if he knew what would come.

She let him have it all out. "I do not believe my Queene is in her right mind. Several things have happened of late that distract her from the real terrors that the Fae, and all of the Lightworld, face. I do not wish to stay here to the bitter end—for that is what it will be. Bitter and cruel. Our kind are not used to tolerating cruelty. We are much better at dispensing it."

He smiled at this, and nodded. "And what cruel thing do you propose? Assassination? Revolt?"

"No, nothing of the sort!" she exclaimed quickly. His ruthless ambition shocked her. She had seen a hint of it before, when he'd stood before the Queene at his royal audience, but she had not thought it would run so deeply. "Your Queene did not send you here merely to warn us. She expects you to return with more followers, more admirers for her to revel in."

He opened his mouth as though he would cut her off; she stopped him with a raised hand and a shake of her head. "Do not deny it. I have served under two Queenes, and I know their way of thinking. If you displease this Queene Danae, you will lose your place in her Court. And I can tell, simply from looking at you, that you could not survive such exile."

"I do enjoy the better things that life at Court can offer me," he admitted slyly. The Faeries around them rewarded him with a few lazy giggles.

"Then let me help you keep them. I shall set you free—not this moment, of course, for this plan will take a bit more time—and you and yours will lead any of those wishing to abandon the Underground into the Upworld. You may present us to your Queene as faithful new Courtiers and servants, and reap those benefits you so look forward to."

Bauchan's lips twisted in a cruel, disbelieving smile. "You said this was a bargain. Are you certain that is the outcome you wish to receive, on your end? Give up your place close to your Queene to become another unimportant face to mine?"

"I wish to live." She shrugged. "It is as simple as that. Any who stay Underground are doomed, that much is clear from my Queene's handling of this matter. Trading luxury for life seems a fair exchange. But then, I know where true value lies. Do you?"

Bauchan's smile widened. "You have made an eloquent point, Flidais. No doubt you will charm Queene Danae as easily as you have charmed your own Queene." In a flash, he was upon her, crushing her shoulders under his hands, forcing her to her knees as she twisted, pained, in his grasp. "Do not think that she will fall for it so easily," he hissed close to her ear. "Do not think that she will not hear of this treachery from my own lips."

When he released her, he pushed her to the floor, and turned away. "We have an accord, then. You come to me when you believe the time is 'right.' But do not wait long. I may develop a sudden loyalty to Queene Ayla. I would hate to have to inform her of your transgression."

Biting the inside of her mouth so as not to let loose

with the string of curses she wished to hurl at him, Flidais picked herself up with as much dignity as she could manage. "Very well," she said, bowing with no small amount of mockery, though he did not face her. "Wait for my return. And do not do anything foolish, Bauchan. I would not wish for you to lose your head, as well. Your 'sudden loyalty' would not save you should I deny the charges you lay against me. And I would deny it. As I said before, I know enough to value my own life. And my Queene trusts me implicitly."

With that, she left him.

The silence in the council room weighed heavier by the minute. Cedric, sullen and cross with his Queene, sat dutifully at his place, but he did not speak. Flidais was unusually distracted, and the smallest noise of a drip of moisture or a scrape of a stool leg against the floor caused her to jump.

Ayla let out a long breath and drummed her fingers on the tabletop. "You do not have to wait here with me," she assured her advisors, again. She knew they would not answer; they had not said anything last time. But it broke the horrible silence.

They sat with her, she knew, because they feared she was not able to handle the horrible reality of a missing daughter and a missing Consort. The guards had scoured the Palace, and found no trace of Malachi. And Governess had not held any further answers about Cerridwen's disappearance, even after she had been further persuaded to speak.

Cedric had not yet apologized for his foolishness in letting Governess overhear the news he'd taken to Cerridwen, nor had he apologized for telling Cerridwen in the first place. The irritation crawled beneath Ayla's skin as she watched him. He did not meet her eyes, but it was not out of his usual deference. It was obstinacy; the fool actually believed he had some right to be angry with her, with his Queene!

She wanted to lash out at him, but it would do no good. He would realize his folly in his own time. Or, he would run away to the Darkworld and never return. At the moment, it was not something that would bother Ayla in the least.

She turned her attention to Flidais. Her crystalline eyes, usually so clear and attentive, gazed at the tabletop but saw something miles away.

"Flidais," Ayla began, and though her tone was gentle, the Faery jumped in her seat. "Something troubles you. You are not yourself."

"I am concerned at the disappearance of the Royal Heir and the Royal Consort, Your Majesty," she answered automatically. It was a pretty speech, with no substance behind it.

Ayla stretched her back, ignored the soreness of her wings, which had been bound too long. "This waiting grows tiresome, more tiresome, I think, when it is shared. I will retire to my chambers. If you wish to wait here all night, then you may."

She did not bid them good-night individually and hoped they felt her irritation as the reason for it. She moved for the door, but had only made it a few steps when it burst open from the outside.

When Malachi entered, her heart leaped with joy. When she spotted the bundle over his shoulders, it sank in terror. "Cerridwen? Did you find her?" She could barely form the words.

Malachi threw the body down, and a fall of white hair indicated that it was not her daughter. Ayla reached for a nearby stool and dropped onto it to support her shaking legs.

"He told me his people kidnapped Cerridwen." His gaze flickered to Flidais, and Ayla wondered at this, but Malachi continued. "When he wakes, he can tell you from his own mouth."

"Kidnapped?" Cedric sounded incredulous. "I do not mean to doubt your story, Malachi, but Governess said that Cerridwen had run off. And certainly an Elf would have been spotted lurking in the halls of the Palace."

"Perhaps they grabbed her from the Strip." The answer came a fraction too late, and Ayla wondered at that, too. "You did say you found her there before."

"An action taken against a member of the Lightworld on neutral ground would be cause for war, Malachi," Flidais said, as though cautioning him. "You are certain this is what happened?"

"I do not know. You'll have to ask this creature," he snapped, his voice seething with irritation. Then, he swayed on his feet, and Ayla looked closer at the dark stains on his robes.

There was too much blood on him to be only from the Elf he carried, and far too much to be only his and the Elf's combined. But a hole in his garment, and slash across the sleeve gave testimony to Malachi's contribution.

Ayla jolted to her feet and stepped over the creature on the floor. "You have been hurt." It was stupid and obvious, but nothing else would come past the sudden block of numbness that paralyzed her throat. Cedric was on his feet then, too, and Flidais. They helped Malachi to a stool, positioning him on it just as his legs gave way and tumbled him down.

"There were four of them. I killed the other three." He smiled, then winced as Ayla tugged the hole in the fabric over his chest wider. "We only needed one."

Probing her fingers inside the garment, Ayla located the wound easily by the broken shard of wood protruding from it. He'd snapped the arrow off close to the skin, but not close enough to hide it completely. "You fool! You could have been killed!"

He nodded, looking truly apologetic, but his words

were anything but an apology. "I had to do something. For Cerridwen's sake, if not your own."

"Flidais, go, get the healers," Cedric commanded stiffly. "Tell them to hurry to the Consort's chambers."

"It can wait," Malachi insisted, nodding to the Elf on the floor. "If he wakes, we will want to question him. And I wish to be there."

"What you wish is immaterial," Ayla snapped. "Cedric, call in the guards, have this thing removed to the dungeon. Then, help me move Malachi."

"I do not need your help," he protested, but the words were weak, at best.

"You cannot admit that you need our help. Pride is not the same as strength," she scolded as Cedric went out the door. When it closed behind him, she softened. "Why did you do this? I had no idea where you were. If you had been hurt—you *have* been hurt!—but if you could not get back to the Lightworld, if you had been—" Tears choked off her voice, and she stood, turning away from him. Too much was still in chaos to let herself fall apart now.

"She is my child, Ayla," Malachi said quietly. "And this is the only time I have truly been able to do anything for her. Do you know what that is like? To watch her grow without having a hand in it, to know that she is mine but that I can never touch her? Oh, she does not grow ill and needy like a mortal child, but I have seen her hurt, Ayla. I have seen her hurting and wanting her father, thinking that she could not have him because he is gone. And knowing that my silence is causing that hurt…" He let the words die. "I do not say this to guilt you, not now when you have so many other concerns pressing on you. But I thought that if I could find her, and save her, perhaps I could protect her the way I have never been allowed to. And I could protect you, as well."

Ayla wiped a tear from her cheek and nodded, but still she could not look at him. "I do not need your protection, Malachi. I do need you, but not because I am weak. I need you because I chose you, all those years ago. I love you. If you wish to protect me from anything, protect me from the pain of your death."

The door opened, and she quickly wiped her eyes, took a fortifying breath before whirling to face her guards. "That Elf is a prisoner. Secure him, and notify me immediately when he wakes."

After they had cleared the room of the loathsome creature's body, Cedric returned and, with Ayla on one side and him on the other, helped Malachi to his rooms. The healers waited there already. Ayla did not know, or care, if it shocked them to see the Queene doing so menial a task as helping an injured mortal, but they immediately took Malachi and hurried him to his bed, closing off the doors and leaving her alone with Cedric in the antechamber.

For a moment, she stared after them, uncertain of

what she should do. Malachi's care was out of her hands now that he rested with healers more experienced than she. Other matters demanded her attention: the situation with the Waterhorses, her missing daughter. But she could not take action on either, not until she had heard what the imprisoned Elf had to say. Her head ached, her body begged for rest, but she would not be able to sleep with so many crises surrounding her.

Cedric had taken a seat on an uncomfortable piece of Human furniture that Mabb had collected when she was Queene, a tall-backed chair with no room for wings, bound or unbound, to lay without being crushed. He adjusted a cushion behind his back, then tossed it to the floor with a noise of disgust.

She almost spoke, to tell him that he did not need to wait here. But it would do as much good as it had done before. So, she found a more comfortable spot, the long bench with the back that curved over one of the seat's rounded ends, and she laid on it the way she imagined it was designed to be used, propping herself up with cushions. The healers had begun their song, low and droning behind the door. All she could do now was wait.

"Do you believe him?" Cedric asked, after a long time had passed. So long, that she wondered at first what he meant by asking such a question.

Then, she remembered Malachi's hesitation before answering their questions in the council room, and Flidais's seeming suspicion. "Does he have a reason to lie?"

Cedric shrugged elegantly, as though the answer did not matter to him. "No, I would not say that he did. But his behavior was strange."

"He is wounded." That, certainly must have been the answer. Unless… "What was in the letters?"

"Letters?" A wrinkle of confusion marred Cedric's brow.

"The letters," Ayla repeated, sitting up. "The papers we found in Cerridwen's chambers. He brought them to you, to read."

Cedric shook his head. "I have not seen Malachi since before I took the governess to the dungeon."

The door to Malachi's bedchamber opened, and an apprentice healer exited. He did not look at his Queene or her advisor, did not offer any words of reassurance as he hurried to, and through, the outer door. Ayla and Cedric fell silent until he was gone, and until the door to Malachi's room closed again, shutting out the low hum of the healers' song.

"If he did not come to you, why would he go looking in the Darkworld for Cerridwen? I assumed he had found some clue in her letters…why would he think she had gone there?" She narrowed her eyes at her advisor. "Is there something else you need to tell me, something that you have told Malachi but not me?"

"No," Cedric answered quickly. "No. I do not know why he went to the Darkworld. Perhaps he thought the worst had occurred, and his premonition was right? Or perhaps he searched the Strip and did not find her, so he kept going? There could be a very simple explanation as to why he chose to go to the Darkworld, and only he can tell us the answer. Although…"

"Although?" This was not, Ayla thought irritably, the moment for suspense. Not when her daughter was missing, when Malachi was injured, when her hold on the kingdom was slipping from her grasp.

Cedric, however, did not intuit this. He seemed to be considering something very thoroughly before speaking, and the wait was maddening. Finally, he looked up and said, "Did you notice the strange way Flidais questioned him? The way she warned him of what the consequences of the Elves kidnapping Cerridwen could be?"

The unease of that moment had been swathed in surprise and concern, but it had not been totally disguised. Ayla nodded.

"Do you think…" Cedric stopped himself. "I am jumping at shadows that are not there."

His shadows had raised prickles on Ayla's skin, as well. "You do not believe that Flidais would…" She thought of Malachi taking the letters to her, though that seemed impossible. "Malachi does not like Flidais. Perhaps he would trust her, but I do not think she would trust him with anything of importance. She thinks he is…unworthy of his position. Because he is mortal."

"She thinks most of us are unworthy of our positions," Cedric said with a surprise note of sullenness. Then, as though he remembered himself, he said, "I had noticed, of course, the way she reacts to Malachi."

"Would she have been willing to read those letters to him, to help him without coming to me?" That sounded impossible. He'd gotten a guard, then, or a Courtier he could trust.

But there were no Courtiers he could trust, no guard that would not report back to her immediately, if he wished to keep his place.

The apprentice healer returned, bearing a stack of linens in his arms. Cedric stood in his path to stop him. "You. When they removed the Royal Consort's garments, did he have anything, any papers folded away in them?"

"I did not paw through the Royal Consort's garments," the apprentice said, gravely offended. He made to walk past Cedric, but was blocked again.

"I understand that I must have insulted you with my question. I apologize, for that was not my intent." Cedric smiled, and it looked kind, but Ayla saw the tension at the corners of his eyes. "As a favor to the Queene, bring me the Consort's robes."

The apprentice looked to Ayla, and she nodded, once, slowly. He bowed to her. "It will be done, Your Majesty." He tried to bow again and nearly dropped the folded linens out of nervousness.

"Go now, quickly then," Cedric said, as if to a child, before stepping out of the Faery's way.

It did not take the apprentice long to return. Ayla watched Cedric as he looked the papers over, his scowl deepening. But she waited, patient though it could have ended her life, as he read them in their entirety.

He folded the pages carefully and tucked them into his robes. He had opened his mouth to speak when the master healer came out of Malachi's bedchamber.

The Faery was old, possibly the oldest in the Light-world. Though he was immortal, he appeared aged, his face lined as a mortal's would be, gnarled like the bark of a very old tree. It was the healer's art that took such a toll, and every Fae knew it; the energy the healers gave to the invalids in their charge robbed them of their own life, left them with just enough to survive. This Faery was the best of the healers, able to maintain the balance for so long.

He bowed his silver head in respect, his movements slow and pained. "The Royal Consort fares well, Your Majesty," he began without preamble. "He sustained only minor wounds. Being mortal, our art alone will not heal him, but we have used mortal techniques to clean and bind his wounds."

"Thank you," Ayla said, numb to her core, her mind wrapped around those simple pages in Cedric's possession. "May we speak to him?"

The healer nodded. "He is alert, but he must rest, and let our healing settle over him. If there is nothing else…?"

If any one creature in the Lightworld could dismiss the Faery Queene, it would be this one, so Ayla mumbled, "Of course," and motioned to Cedric to pay the healer for his services.

From the time Cedric pressed a jeweled broach into the healer's palm, to the time it took the healers to file out and leave them truly alone, was only minutes; it felt like a lifetime.

"What was in those letters?" Ayla demanded, and Cedric hushed her, his worried gaze flying to the bed-chamber door.

"It will do him no good to worry him with this. You must remain calm when we see him. We do not know that Flidais told him the truth of what was in these missives."

A cold frost of fear came over Ayla. "You believe she lied to him? Why?"

Cedric came to sit beside her, fished the letters from his robes with trembling hands. "Because I do not believe that he would keep the truth from you."

He unfolded the papers and began, in a low voice, to read them to her. And with each passing word, her dread grew. Dread, and horror, and grief. Grief, that her own daughter could hate her so much. And horror that she would knowingly walk into the hands of her enemies.

Unknowingly, Ayla admitted to herself, wiping her eyes on the cuff of her sleeve. Cerridwen had always been kept in the dark about such matters, and that had been Ayla's choice. What a foolish one that seemed, now. She had, of course, warned her daughter that the Darkworld was a dangerous place, full of dangerous creatures. But she had done so with a Darkling in her own Palace…as if Cerridwen would not have noticed! Of course, she would not listen to her mother's advice, but follow her example. Ayla cursed herself a fool for ever believing otherwise.

"We must speak to Malachi and make sure that he knew what these letters said." Cedric spoke quietly, calmly, but Ayla could feel the anger in him, the suspicion.

"You believe Flidais…what? Wished to send Malachi into danger on purpose, to harm him?" Ayla almost laughed at that, but it seemed more likely, now. "To start a war?"

"I do not know, which is why we must ask him," Cedric repeated firmly.

They let themselves into the bedchamber and found Malachi as the healers had left him. He slept, his wings unbound and spread, his body propped on cushions. His chest was wrapped in the linen bandages, but no blood showed through. A bit of crimson stained the bandages on his arm, and an angry redness glowed around the edges of the wound, through the fabric. The healing, fighting the mortal cells, bending them to its will.

Ayla went to his side and sat carefully on the edge of the bed, not wishing to jostle him. She laid one hand on his collarbone, willed some of her own energy into him. Closing her eyes, she saw the tree of her life force, and the bubbles of peaceful blue that raced to him forced their way out of her body and into his.

"I knew you would not be able to resist meddling," he said, his voice shocking her into opening her eyes. He had not been fully asleep. "I am not dead, so why have the two of you come to mourn?"

"We were concerned about you. Your disappearance, your sudden reappearance…" Cedric stepped closer to the bed, his expression indeed as grave as a mourner's. "What prompted you to look for Cerridwen in the Darkworld?"

Malachi was not a fool. He looked from Cedric's face, to the discarded garments on the floor, and took a breath that appeared to pain him. "You have read the letters?"

"We did." The thought of what was in them brought fresh tears to Ayla's eyes, but she forced them away. "Why did you not tell me?"

He could not answer her before Cedric cut in, "What did Flidais tell you they said?"

"The truth, I assume." Malachi looked to Ayla. "That Cerridwen was angry with you, and that she ran away to the Darkworld to warn the Elves."

This time, the tears could not be stopped. "Why didn't you tell me?"

The reason was clear in his pitying expression. "I did not wish for this to cause you pain. I thought only to catch her, before she went too far. Then, I found those creatures, and they had no knowledge. They could not tell me where she was, and they tried to kill me. So, I brought one back, and hoped that, by telling you she had been kidnapped, we might bring her home without you knowing the truth." He grimaced. "It seemed a much more intelligent plan when I thought it up."

"Why didn't Flidais tell me?" The anger that flared in Ayla caused her antennae to buzz against her forehead. "She has a duty to me!"

"I agree." Cedric sounded as angry, if not more so. "You should have her locked up, and arrange a trial. What she has done is nothing short of treason."

"No," Malachi said, trying to sit up. He groaned and fell back to the pillows, his face a mask of pain. When it passed, he said again, "No. She did not tell you because I asked her not to. She knew my reasons, and I forced her to swear, threatened her. I know that once given, the word of a Faery is binding, even if given under protest. Do not harm Flidais for this."

A loud pounding broke the silence that followed Malachi's plea, and Cedric moved out of the bed-chamber. Ayla held one of Malachi's large hands in her own small ones, silent as they listened to the door in the antechamber open.

"An urgent message for the Queene," an unfamiliar voice rang out from the other room, and, with a look and a nod from Malachi, Ayla got to her feet and raced to the door.

A guard stood in the hall, and at the sight of him Ayla blurted, "You've found her?"

"The Royal Heir," Cedric clarified for the momentarily puzzled guard. When the Faery shook his head, Ayla's heart dropped.

"I come with urgent news. The Captain of the Guard wishes to inform you that Ambassador Bauchan and his retinue have escaped. A member of your council sent him orders for their release, written in Council Member Cedric's own hand, but he now believes them to be a forgery."

"They absolutely are!" Cedric roared. "Did he send someone after them?"

The guard nodded. "It was too late. Bauchan's party was seen leaving the Palace, headed toward Sanctuary. None of the sentries on duty questioned them, because Council Member Flidais accompanied them."

"She was taken hostage, then?" What had she been doing with him in the first place? Ayla wondered. "Did they demand a ransom?"

As if afraid to speak the news, the guard stumbled over his answer. "N-no, Your Majesty. The Captain of the Guard believes the orders were forged by Flidais, herself, as she was the one who delivered them into his hands."

Ayla staggered to the uncomfortable Human chair and sat down heavily. She needed to think, and she could not do that on her feet, not when the problem before her demanded so much energy.

"Thank you." Cedric moved to close the door as he spoke. "The Queen and I will speak on this and contact the Captain in haste."

The guard put his hand out to stop the door from closing. "He says it is urgent, Your Majesty," he called past Cedric. "He says that more Faeries are leaving through Sanctuary...and that the sentries are not able to hold all of them back."

That was the fear that had kept Ayla awake. Like a nightmare coming true, her only allies, her Court, were fleeing and leaving her to the Waterhorses.

She looked to Cedric, her body suddenly as hollow-feeling as her voice. "Well, then. It seems we are doomed."

Twelve

They put her in a cage. A cage, like an animal.

Her prison sat on a ledge that ran round the middle of the Elven great hall, the dark room she'd been so afraid of before. She had been right to be afraid; now that her eyes had adjusted to the gloom, she saw clearly what the Elven Court was like.

Long tables constructed of rough materials hosted piles of raw meat that the creatures picked over. It smelled horrible, rotten. Flies buzzed on every morsel, but they paid them no mind. Those not gorging themselves on their spoiled feast were playing games of dice, or worse, testing their bravery and strength by burning their flesh or plunging knives into each other. It was hot, and loud, with Elves shouting and laughing and fighting like drunken mortals on the Strip.

If their revels would have distracted them from the new prize in the hall, it would have been tolerable, but they had great fun spitting at her, poking their fingers and their daggers through the bars of her cage, pressing their faces against them and making lewd motions with their slimy pink tongues.

To think she would have gladly spent the rest of her days here, if someone had asked her yesterday. Now, she could only find solace that those days would not be long.

It seemed the night must be over, but Cerridwen had not slept. There was not room to lie down in her prison. She could curl up like an animal, but she did not wish to let her guard down in sleep, not when so many of them still wished to crowd in on her and threaten her. And still, their revels wore on.

Fenrick had not come to see her. He had not come to see if she had been treated well, had not come to defend her from his kin.

He was not *her* Fenrick, and she mourned for him now, hot tears stinging her eyes.

"Is the little beasty sad?" an Elf hissed, pressing close to the bars. His breath stank of mortal alcohol and rotted meat. "I can make her feel all better."

A few of the Elf's cohorts laughed rudely behind him. Cerridwen shrank as far into the cage as she could, until the bars at her back cut into her wings.

The Elf jabbed his dirty hand through the cage and made a few swipes, barely grazing her knees, and she yelped, jumping up involuntarily. She mashed her head against the top of the cage and crumpled, her palms clutched over her stinging scalp. The Elves laughed, and her tormentor gripped the bars, shook the whole of the cage until she was forced to brace herself or risk being injured further.

"Stop!" a voice called out, and she wished her heart had not leaped at the sound. Fenrick strode over, as cold and distant-looking as he had been before his father, and grabbed the Elf by the collar to pull him away. "Does this Faery belong to you?" he demanded, lifting the Elf off his feet.

"Of course she don't," the tormentor wheezed.

Another Elf called out, "Leave him, Fenrick, he was just having fun."

"Fun?" Fenrick tossed the Elf aside, into one of the tables. It toppled as the creature crashed through it, ruining a game of dice and eliciting angry calls from the Elves who'd been enjoying it.

"Fun," Fenrick repeated, louder, commanding the attention of the rest of the hall. "It is fun to destroy my father's property, then?"

No one answered, and several Elves looked down, as if ashamed.

"Fun, then, to meddle with this, a trophy of war

that my father prizes? To gobble down his food and drink, to take advantage of his hospitality while showing him no respect?" Fenrick paused, as if daring them to deny it. "Fun. Perhaps he should hear the names of those who have been engaging in such 'fun.'"

Again, no one spoke. It was, Cerridwen realized with a shock, as though they were afraid of Fenrick. Only a day before, she could never have imagined such a thing. But she felt it now, too. There was something powerful about him, commanding, and he was very frightening.

"Go. The hour is late, and we are nearly at war. What worthless soldiers you'll all be, drunk and gorged to pain." He made a noise of disgust, then, seeing that they were not yet on their feet, and roared, "Out!"

The Elves hurriedly gathered up their weapons and games and, Cerridwen noted with disgust, handfuls of rotten meat and moldering bread. They fled so quickly and noisily that their sudden absence caused a weird silence to descend, a silence that was almost louder than the commotion that had been there before.

Fenrick went to one of the tables and picked out a chunk of meat, which he brought to the cage. Cerridwen recoiled.

"Eat," he ordered. "You cannot starve yourself to death."

She crossed her arms over her chest and turned her face away from the offered food. Her stomach was empty, but the very thought of consuming what he gave her made her throat close up in protest.

"Have it your way," he said, tossing the meat to the floor. He wiped his hands on his trousers. "If I try to offer you comfort, and you reject it, then that is your own preference."

"Comfort?" Cerridwen heard the disbelief in her words. "Comfort? I am caged! I am a prisoner condemned to die! You promised me that all would be right, that you would look out for me."

"I promised you what I had to in order to bring you here," he said with a shrug. "You would have done the same thing, had you been more clever."

Tears burned her eyes. "I am clever." She sounded like a child, and she hated it. "But I am not cruel. That is what you are, Fenrick! You are cruel! You lied to me, you knew all the time—"

"Did you not lie as well?" He folded his arms over his chest and leaned against the edge of a table. "You wanted me to believe you were mortal. And a common thief, at that. You knew of the animosity between my father and the Faeries, because I spoke to you of it. Did you think you would, what, impress me? Make me love you if you came to me in spite of the fact that we are enemies?"

She had, and that cut her more deeply than any

blade could. "You lied to me, as well. You behaved as though you really—"

"Loved you?" He laughed. "Yes, I know. It's a part of the game, Cerridwen. I wanted something from you, the same as I want from all Human girls. I had to behave a certain way to get it. You're young, and you didn't understand it then, but do you understand it now? Have I at least taught you something of value?"

He honestly believed that he offered her valuable advice, and it sickened her. He believed that his deception, his cruelty was…what, a *favor* to her? She wanted to spit in his face, then feared what would occur if she did. Instead, she glowered silently at him.

"Perhaps, if you hadn't been so naive, you wouldn't be here today," he informed her sagely. "Think on that, while you're waiting to die."

"Why?" She laughed, heard the bitterness in it, and recognized the sound from somewhere. "Some good it will do me, to have learned my lesson only to die."

"At least you will have learned it. Some people never broaden their horizons, never look beyond their narrow beliefs. Consider yourself lucky." He examined his fingernails, the sharp silver things that glinted in the dim light.

"Pardon me if I do not thank you for the enlightenment," Cerridwen spat, working herself into a more comfortable position. With her back resting against the side of the cage, she could bend her knees and almost be comfortable. "If I sleep, will your kin take the opportunity to further torment me? Or will I be left alone?"

He chuckled, obviously pleased with himself. "After my warning? I doubt any of them will even look at you. And if they do, I will see to them personally."

"Well, forgive me if I do not trust you to keep me safe. Your record of promises kept is very poor." She closed her eyes, because she did not want him to see that she was about to cry.

How could she have not seen this in him before? The callousness, the deception? Her mother had believed her a child…and she'd proven her right.

"You are angry." He sniffed, the annoyance in the sound echoing in the empty hall.

"I believe that is my right," she said, willing her tears away long enough to pierce him with her glare.

He did not argue. He spun on his heel, left the hall. Left her alone, in the dark, cavernous space.

Alone, she could dare to make herself more comfortable, and to sleep. It would not be a sound sleep; she needed to be aware when the monsters returned. She slid down to the floor of the cage and tried to curl into a ball, but something pricked her leg beneath her clothes.

The knife! Her hands shaking, Cerridwen reached into the waist of her trousers. The curved blade had grown warm against her flesh, and she had not thought of it since she had first met with Fenrick on the Strip. But it was there.

Disbelief and trepidation mingled in her as she looked out at the darkness of the hall. There were no guards, that she could see, not a single Elf left in the place. Still, she trembled as she pulled the blade free, the last hope she had to protect herself from what was to come.

If she could protect herself, she admitted ruefully. She had never needed to engage in physical combat before in her life, had never even been trained in case of an emergency. She was more likely to harm herself than another person with the weapon.

The thought brought fresh tears to her eyes, and she swiped them away angrily. She could beat herself down with her fears, or she could take whatever chance came to her and fight, until death, to save herself.

And then, another thought occurred to her. She might not have to fight at all. She gripped the handle of the knife tight in her fist and twisted to face the front of the cage. Though the blade was curved and wide, it tapered to a long, slender point, almost needlelike at the tip. She poked it carefully through the bars, then, thinking better of it—if she dropped it, all would truly be lost—she reached through the bars and fished for the lock that held the cage closed.

It did not budge, at first. The lock held the door of her prison closed by securing a heavy chain, and though it creaked and groaned, there was not slack enough to bring the lock into the cage with her. She tugged and strained and, with a sob of frustration, kicked at the door with the little movement she could achieve in the cramped space. Miraculously, the heavy links of the chain slid over themselves, released from whatever kink had held them back. The lock did not come close enough to enter the cage, but now she could twist it to its side and reveal the keyhole at the bottom. With one hand wrapped around the bars to hold the lock in place, she used the other to work the tip of the knife into the lock.

It was tedious work, but not work Cerridwen was unfamiliar with. Picking locks was a necessary skill for a Royal Heir who often grew bored and wished to leave the Palace without permission. This was a mortal lock, too, far easier than the complicated wooden tumblers crafted and enchanted by Faery magic that she'd encountered in the Palace. She had to go carefully, though. If the knife broke against the resistance of the lock, if a piece were left inside, obscuring the hole, her chance would be lost.

She did not know how long she worked. Crouched

over, her back began to sting, demanding to be stretched. Her feet grew numb as she sat on her legs, and the bars at the bottom of the cage cut into her knees. But finally, the mechanisms of the lock gave way with a click that was far too loud in the empty room. Cerridwen recoiled at the sound, certain it would bring a host of Elves to investigate, but, stupidly, they had left their prisoner alone.

She tucked the knife back into its hiding place and moved more carefully, now that she knew it was there. The lock slipped from the coils of the chain, and she began to unthread the heavy links when a thought stopped her.

There were doors all around the hall, but she did not remember which one they had entered from. She could not remember which ones the Elves used as exits—if they were exits. And in her journey to this place, she'd paid more attention to Fenrick than she had to the places they'd turned, which tunnels they'd taken. Even if she escaped from this room, she might venture deeper into the Darkworld, rather than out of it. And if she became lost, well, the chances of them finding her and recapturing her would be greater.

Reluctantly, she replaced the chain and slipped the lock through it. Then, thinking better of it, she closed the lock around a single link of the chain and tucked the unsecured end back into the coils. With one glance, they would not be able to tell that anything was amiss. But, when the time was right, she would be able to spring herself free.

She settled back, her body tired, her brain churning, and pretended to sleep.

They moved their council into Malachi's sick room. It was the only way, Ayla had realized, that they could keep him at rest, though he would get little of it.

Guards came in and out of the antechamber, mobilized by Cedric's orders. Ayla stayed at Malachi's side, but her thoughts were far away.

At first, they had tried to set up a barricade, had sent guards to block the entrance to Sanctuary and threaten death to any who attempted to leave. Bauchan and his retinue had left the way they had come, through holes in the metal grate high above the trees of Sanctuary. Two guards were sent with tools to patch the gaps; they slipped through and followed Bauchan. As had some of the guards who'd been sent to keep others from leaving.

Now, wave after wave of Faery deserted the Lightworld. Deserted *her*.

Cedric came into the room, his expression grim. "It is not good news, Your Majesty."

"Ayla. Please, just…call me by my name," she told him wearily. Titles and protocol only reminded her how truly alone she was in this.

"Then it is not good news, Ayla." There was no

humor in his voice, though the repetition should have been comical. "We've lost many guards."

"How many?" Malachi asked, as if a number could change anything.

"More than half. And the Court is…gone. There are Faeries outside of the Palace who will stay, because they do not believe the threat of the Water-horses. We've managed to enlist a few of those into a militia, but they are poorly trained."

"What of the Guilds? Have they gone, as well?" The question had to force past the icy, tight fist gripping her chest.

Cedric shook his head. "No, thankfully, they remain loyal."

"That is good news, then," Ayla said, forcing a smile as Malachi squeezed her hand.

"Better than we should hope for, in any case." Cedric paced stiffly to the hearth and leaned against the mantel. "But you must remember that the Guilds trained in weaponry—the Assassins, the Thieves, the Weaponscrafters—they are not trained to fight as the guards fight, nor can they properly organize a militia and give orders that will be effective. We have no one capable of that, at present."

"Yes, we do," Malachi said, sounding outraged at the insinuation. "I have already spoken to Ayla about this. It will be my responsibility."

"And I do not doubt that, were you in better condition, whole and healthy, you would be able to do so," Cedric explained patiently. "But you are not able to lead troops, let alone fight."

This seemed to subdue Malachi, but Ayla knew that this was temporary. There would be an argument. There would be many arguments until she relented and let him limp off into battle.

She had no energy for such a fight, now. "What are we to do, then? Wait, until we are overrun by the Waterhorses, and hope that our clumsy fighters will rally to save us?"

"A bleak prospect, I know." Some animation returned to Cedric as he turned back to face them. "But not how it must play out. You see, there was an unintentional benefit to Malachi's attempted deception."

"The Elf," Malachi said, as if he suddenly understood what Cedric had begun.

Irritated at her fatigue and inability to catch on as readily, she waved a hand at the both of them. "The Elf, yes. We have an Elf. Has anyone spoken to him, yet?"

"No," Cedric admitted. "But we will not need to, not yet. I propose that, instead of waiting until the Elves send the Waterhorses to do their bidding, we use the Elf to our advantage. Make him lead us into the Darkworld, to their stronghold, and launch an attack there."

"That will start a war," she said uncertainly. "Is that

not exactly what we wished to avoid?"

"It was what Flidais wished to avoid," Malachi said, his voice a growl. "I see no reason to follow the advice of a traitor."

"It was not only Flidais," Cedric admitted. "But we are beyond wondering whether or not the Elves have reason to war against us. The Waterhorses have been seen in the Darkworld. Cerridwen has gone to warn the Elves that we plan to attack. The latter alone will prompt action. As they already believe we will come after them, we should do it, and before much time passes, before they truly expect it."

Ayla considered a moment. "We have a reduced number of soldiers," she mused aloud. "But we still have the Guilds." True, they did not know how to fight in an organized manner, but they did know how to sneak about, how to strike without being seen. "We could use the skills of the Guild-trained fighters, in conjunction with the guards."

"Use the latter to create a diversion, while the former attack in more unconventional ways," Malachi finished, his face alight at the idea. "The guards they will expect. But Assassins, lurking in the shadows..."

Cedric nodded. "Exactly. The Elf we have prisoner can lead us there, and then we can strike at them before they come anywhere near the Lightworld."

"What about the Waterhorses?" Ayla did not like

to cast a pall over the only idea of merit that they'd managed to construct so far, but to leave that threat out of their plans would spell disaster.

Cedric thought on it for a moment. "I do not believe that the Elves would be stupid enough to let the Waterhorses roam free, if they had summoned them. The creatures can turn without warning and kill even those who command them. If the Elves are the ones controlling the Waterhorses, and we have no guarantee that this is actually so, they will have them locked up somewhere, or they are more foolish than any immortal creature should be. We will simply have to strike quickly, before they can be released, and pray that it is indeed the Elves who command them, so that we do not come upon them by chance in the Darkworld."

It was the best they could hope for, Ayla realized, and though she did not like the element of chance that ruled the outcome of their plan, she would force herself to accept it.

But one aspect remained undiscussed, and that was one she would not leave to chance. "And what of Cerridwen? If her plan is to fight against us, with the Elves…what will you do then?"

Cedric did not answer, so Malachi did, angrily. "We will bring her home. If she fights against us, we will subdue her—without harm—and we will bring her home."

"Is that true, Cedric?" It was a fine speech for Malachi to give, but he was in no position to offer his aid. He could not fight in his present condition, and they could not afford to wait for him to heal. If he was not there, he could not assure Cerridwen's safety.

"And what if she does not wish to return?" He said it as if she had a choice in the matter, as if he valued her wishes. "If she wants to stay and fight and die with the Elves?"

"You place too much trust on her judgment." Ayla sniffed. "If I cannot charge you with the task of returning my daughter safely to me, then I will find someone else to do it."

There was no one else she could trust, and Cedric knew that. That was how she knew he would promise her, and fulfill his promise.

He nodded in defeat. "If I must bind her and drag her all the way, I will return her to you unharmed."

"Do I have your word?" She could have simply left it, but she needed to hear this reassurance. Not that he would bring Cerridwen back unharmed—she knew he would do that—but that he would give his word, despite the lies he'd been telling her for so long. She needed a *geis* hanging over his head, to prove the seriousness of his commitment. The threat of death, should he fail, not to spur him toward his goal, but so that he would know she had lost her faith in him.

"You have my word," he promised solemnly.

Ayla cleared her throat and straightened her back, returning to a more conversational tone. As if she had not just discussed going to war, as if she had not just forced a once trusted friend to make a *geis* to her. "If we are to undertake such a task, we must meet with the Guild Masters. I will speak with the Thieves. They are my most ardent supporters. You can see to the Assassins, as you led them well for so many years, and the Weaponscrafters, since the two Guilds work so closely together. We should gather all involved for the royal audience tonight."

"A wise decision," Cedric said with a bow of his head. "But I must beg a small indulgence."

"Go on," Ayla prompted.

Hesitantly, Cedric began, "You know of my involvement with the Gypsies in the Darkworld. I wish to see that they are safe, so that my mind can be easy and I can turn my full concentration toward our battle."

"You cannot turn your full concentration toward the survival of your race in the Underground, otherwise?" She did not mean to sound so angry, she was certain. But the words had already been uttered.

Cedric did not respond. He waited. As if he did not need to explain his request. And truly, he did not. Who was she, to demand he put his duties first, when under his command in the Assassins' Guild, she had broken her *geis* without consequence? It was twenty years past, but no doubt still fresh in his memory.

"Will you return?" Malachi asked, breaking the silence. "I do not doubt your feelings for this Human mistress, but it is unfair to ask us to trust you on a topic you've already lied about."

"I can accept your distrust, Malachi, and Ayla's. But I could not devote my thoughts entirely to our cause if I feared my mortal friends were in danger." He spread his hands helplessly, as if content to offer this explanation as his only plea.

Ayla sighed. "Go. If you do not return, we are in the same predicament as now, and I do not believe you will desert us. But return before the evening audience."

"Thank you." Cedric bowed. "With your permission, I will leave at once."

"After you talk to the Guilds, of course," Malachi said, flicking a glance to Ayla. "I have no doubt that you could persuade them to hear you out, Ayla, but while you were one of them, you have not been for twenty years, and you weren't a Guild member for long. They trust him. He is the one who should go."

"You are right, Malachi," Cedric conceded. "I will go to them immediately, and hasten my departure from there." He bowed and went to the door, stopping before he exited. "I will return in time for the evening audience, but please, Your Majesty, take care until then. We do not know who else in the Palace may have turned traitor, or who else might try to flee."

A chill ran up Ayla's spine. "I will be careful," she told him. She turned to Malachi and tried to conjure a smile, something to reassure him.

But he was not the one who needed reassuring, and the feeling of doom that haunted her had not diminished. It had blossomed.

Thirteen

❧⟳⟳❧

The Strip was not as thick with traffic as usual, Cedric noted as he moved through the thinned crowd. But the inns and shelters had all taken in their signs, indicating that they were full. More creatures had thronged to the neutral zone, but they kept to their own lodgings, rode out the storm where it was safe. It was not unusual, and the level of activity on the Strip was a good indication of the activities going on in the worlds of Light and Dark.

More troubling to Cedric was the absence of the Gypsy market stalls that usually cluttered the Strip, no matter what occurred. They viewed themselves as apart from, rather than a part of, the Underground, and seemed to operate under the assumption that so long as they were not involved in any intrigues, the conse-quences of such would not affect them. Their little shops—some no more than blankets spread on the ground to display their wares—were often the only things still present on the Strip during times of unease.

Now, they, too, were gone. Whether anyone else noticed, Cedric could not say for sure. But it pricked at him as he moved toward the Darkworld path that would lead him to the Gypsy camp.

Perhaps their absence on the Strip meant they had all gone; he panicked at the thought. They had said to go west, after them. But he could not follow them now, and if they had left some time ago, or if he was detained, he might never catch up to them.

To calm himself, he remembered the chaos of the folding camp, the seeming lack of any plan to flee in an organized fashion. They could not possibly have picked up and left already. Maybe the Gypsies on the Strip had realized that which the other creatures huddled there either did not know, or wish to acknowledge: that the Waterhorses would not care which spaces were neutral in the Underground, and that they would cut a bloody swath wherever they strayed. Those in the inns were as dead as the soldiers who would fight.

It had rained in the Upworld, and heavily. The Darkworld echoed with the sounds of storm drains emptying into the tunnels below, the walls were slick with moisture. The ground was stained with seeping wetness, which deepened into puddles as he walked, then banded together to form one long, shallow stream down the center of the tunnel, continually widening and deepening until it splashed over his boots. He ducked the first few overhead drips he passed, then gave up trying; he did not wish to stumble and strike his head on the curved concrete walls simply because he feared a bit of rainwater.

He no longer needed the map to find his way, but the way did seem more sinister and unfamiliar, covered in water. A few times, he wondered if he'd taken a wrong turn or passed by a tunnel he should have come upon already. By its very presence, the water had changed things. It made him uneasy, and he hastened his steps.

The familiar scent of smoke did not rise up and greet him as he drew closer to the encampment. Instead, something else was on the air, the stale smell of long-dead fires and something sickly sweet.

He ran.

The tunnels were dark. The flickering shadows were the cool white echoes of light on water, not the chaotic imprint left by the orange-red glow of fire. They had left, he realized in dismay. He slowed his progress through the knee-deep water, made his way to the mouth of the cave, which was dark, but for the sunlight streaming from the opening in the rock ceiling.

Though the water was deeper in the cavern, and

choked with debris, it was not impossible to make out the shapes of the cinderblock cubicles that still stood. The paths toward the central fire pit were clear, as well, marked out as unbroken, serpentine stretches that pooled beneath the beam of sunlight.

He turned away and started back for the Lightworld, cursing himself for making such a promise to Ayla. He should have been free to fly after the mortals, to be quit of the Underground entirely. But he could not break his oath. She had known that, and it was why she had forced it on him.

Something between a whisper and the flutter of dried leaves caught his ear, sent a spark of doom through him that he could not ignore. He knew that sound, and his ears strained for it again in the darkness. Ahead of him, blocking his way, it became louder, the sliding of a corpse's winding sheet…a mournful wind…the slithering of dark and festering things in a grave…

A Wraith.

He took a few steps backward, unwilling to turn away from the sound, though he did not wish to see the creature come into view out of the darkness. Wraiths were notorious even on the Astral; slinking through the darkest fears of mortals and immortals alike, feeding on the life and energy of all they could touch, they twisted their victims into copycat shadows, which would, in turn, feast on others and corrupt them as well. Even the dead were not safe, and here, in the Underground, especially in the Darkworld, the Wraiths found that type of defenseless victim easy prey.

He could not go forward and risk capturing the creature's attention. He knew no other way out of the Gypsy encampment, save for the hole into the Upworld, and if the Wraith gave chase, it could easily follow him there. But why had it come to the Gypsy camp in the first place? It was empty. All the mortals were gone.

When the creature noticed this, it was certain to move on. Though he had not much time, and had sworn to return for the evening audience, he had no other choice. He plunged back down the tunnel, moving as quietly as he could through the standing water, and splashed down into the lake that had once been the Gypsy city.

There were plenty of places to hide, he realized as he pushed his way through the chest-deep water. It would be easy enough to hide from the Wraith and let it pass him by, then leave the way it had entered. He checked over his shoulder, saw no trace of the creature, though the sounds of its approach echoed closer and closer. Something bumped his leg in the water, and he jumped, then cursed himself for it. He was, or at least had been, a warrior. A tap on the leg should not have been enough to terrify him into panic.

Drawing closer to one of the concrete buildings, he slipped inside. There was not much room, and he barked his shins against something—a table? A bed?—below the water, but it gave him something to climb up on, and he did, moving back the blue tarp that served as the ceiling. From his vantage point, he could see the mouth of the tunnel he'd come from. He waited, the horrible sounds growing nearer and nearer, louder, lapping over each other as they approached. Finally, a flicker of white at the source of the tunnel, and five wraiths slid into view.

Their appearance alone was enough to disturb him. At first glance, they resembled wisps of white smoke in the dark air. But the longer he looked at them— though he knew he should look away—the more solid they appeared. A curling tendril became a skeletal arm and slid smoothly back into nothing a second later. A rictus grin on the roiling coil that revealed a face blended into the air. Cedric's antennae flattened to his forehead; his body tensed; his wings itched for flight. But they had gotten wet, and he was a creature of air…if he unfolded them now, they might be too sodden to lift him from the ground.

That there were so many was a concern, as well. Wraiths were solitary, consumed only by their need to devour and destroy. It was possible that these creatures did not realize they traveled in a pack, so great was their drive that they would ignore anything that was not a source of life or energy. What had drawn them all to this place, then? A horrible chill went through Cedric at the thought that it might have been *him*—that they had followed him there.

The five forms broke off from the tunnel mouth, slipping silently above the surface of the water, dipping below it without disturbing the surface. They scanned the area, heads swinging side to side like reptilian predators. They would draw closer, he realized, but he could not look away, even to run.

And then, strangely, they did not come nearer. They found something of interest, swarmed about it, screeched like metal on stone among each other, and four jetted away, smoky bodies writhing horribly as they sought out other prey.

While they were distracted, he could flee.

He let the tarp slide down silently, and eased himself into the water.

In the darkness of the little building, beneath the surface of the water, a face. A face made pale in death shone up like a beacon of blue, eyes open wide and unseeing.

In his shock, Cedric lost his balance, fell, splashed into the water completely before he could stop himself. He struggled away from the mortal body, the sickly, bloated thing that seemed to catch on him and drag him down further. It took a great effort to remember to stand, to remember that the water was not a deep abyss.

When he surfaced, he heard them. Their greedy voices raised to a pitch of excitement, the sound of a hangman's rope twisting in the wind as it bore its heinous load. They were coming for him.

He waded out of the cubicle, horribly aware of the bump and slide of more corpses below the surface of the water. He saw the Wraiths approaching and sprinted, futile against the weight of the water and its terrible contents. He had to make it to drier ground, where his movement was less restricted.

Nothing hindered the Wraiths, however, and they came closer and closer, grew louder. The cold chill of their presence intensified behind him and then, suddenly, lessened. He dared to look over his shoulder and saw that they had stopped in their pursuit. The energy left behind by the death of the mortals was too tempting. They would not leave it behind.

Cedric did not know why he had not sensed the angry, red energy of so many deaths. What he had mistaken for his own unease, his own fear that the Gypsies had fled without him, had been something far more serious.

They had not left.

Something in him clawed upward, trying to escape through his mouth. A scream, he thought, but when it erupted, it was a strangled cry, nothing more.

He waded past more bodies floating in the water, bodies that he had, no doubt, pushed aside callously, as though they were mere objects.

And they would have been, to him, if he had not known these people. If they had not fascinated him, if he had not wished to become a part of them. If a Gypsy girl had not lured him into an obsessive tryst, into giving up all that he knew.

Another sob choked him. He subdued it, to lessen the attraction of the Wraiths that still feasted behind him. Did they feast on Dika? Steal her energy, which had always seemed so sparkling and bright, even when she was angry with him? Did she float in his mass sea grave?

The thought nearly brought him to his knees as he climbed up into the tunnel. He turned back, aching to go to her, to find her or not find her, to know whether she had escaped whatever had befallen them.

To know what had befallen them. He stared helplessly down into the Gypsy encampment, or what remained of it, and shifted into his other sight. The Wraiths still did not pursue him, but they stood out as black voids in his vision. The death energy, preserved in the dying moments of the unfortunate mortals, glowed angry red, pulsing. The part of them they thought of as their souls, their consciousness, as Malachi had explained it to him once, was gone, ushered away to some waiting vessel until they could be returned to their One God. If that was what they believed. Cedric realized bitterly that he had never asked Dika what she believed in, or if she believed in anything at all.

With his vision occupied by the other, he touched the surface of the water. Water connected, absorbed, and the death energy filtered into him, not as violent as if he'd touched it directly. It washed through him, revealing pictures that were, if disjointed, somehow fluid and beautiful in their progression. Waterhorses, black and scaly and terrible. Yet oddly graceful. They cut a swath through the still-dry camp, laid waste to everything. The strong, able-bodied men could not protect the women and the children. They were killed for food for the ravenous creatures. At first. But once those appetites were sated, they killed for sport.

It would have disgusted him, but he was so overcome with the water's memory, which neither condoned nor condemned the actions that had taken place in the space it now occupied, that he could do no more than watch. The creatures killed all; not one mortal survived. And in the final picture the water gave him, the creatures seized Dika, tore her apart before his eyes, then tossed her broken carcass atop that of her grandmother's, the Dya. And as the water, rain from above, descended merrily onto the grisly scene and the Waterhorses retreated, the Dya's proclamation rang out, mocking, in Cedric's ear.

He will be faithful to you for as long as you live.

When he forced himself out of the other, into the cold, stark reality of the tunnel he crouched in, the Dya's voice still echoed off the walls. The Wraiths heard it as well, for they paused in their feeding, looking for the cause of the disturbance.

His eyes burning with tears unshed, his chest filled to bursting with sobs he could not release, Cedric ran down the tunnel, back to the Lightworld.

"What are you doing?"

Malachi ignored her question and continued the arduous task of binding his wings. "Have you seen my ring? The large one that you gave me last year?"

"Your ring?" He did not have to look at her face to know that her brow crumpled with confusion. He could hear the matching emotion in her voice. "What ring?"

"The one made of silver, with the large blue stone. The Dragons sent it as part of the gift they bestowed on you for quelling the Troll rebellion." He winced as he reached behind his back to change the wide linen band from hand to hand. He frowned down at it and smoothed a wrinkle that would, if left unchecked, later cause a deep red welt in his flesh.

She came to his side, took the binding, and pulled it across his chest, helping him though she did not yet realize it. "What do you want with that?"

"I want to wear it," he said simply, raising his arms so she could more easily maneuver around his back. "I think it impresses them."

With a frustrated growl, Ayla made another pass

with the binding and tucked it a bit roughly beneath itself. "Impresses who? Malachi, what are you talking about?"

"The Courtiers. The ones who are still left, anyway. And the Guild members. I think I should look as imposing as I can, should I not? Hand me my blue robes."

This command she did not follow. "You do not need to appear imposing for anyone. The audience is being held in the throne room, not your bedchamber."

Now, she was seeing his plan, though she had not expressly forbid him from attending, yet. He eased himself to his feet, and she put out a hand to help steady him, then jerked it back.

"You cannot go, Malachi! You are not healed." She stamped her foot, and he found it difficult not to laugh at her.

"If I do not go, I cannot see who I will be organizing into the militia." Before she could protest, he added, "You promised me, Ayla."

"That was before you were injured!" She followed him to the chest that held his clothing, and sat upon it, arms folded across her chest. "You are not going."

"I will go. In this state, if I must," he said, gesturing to his nakedness.

"That will impress them, no doubt," she grumbled, and she moved aside, for she knew he would make good on his promise.

He moved slowly, still aching from his wounds, and located the blue robe in the chest. It was the color Ayla favored on him, and so he would wear it tonight. She seemed unable to deny him much when she found him physically attractive.

He tried to remember if it had been easier when he was young, but it seemed that in Ayla's eyes, he had not changed. Or, perhaps the Human half of her caused her to function as the Humans did, their feelings of love not fading simply because age took its toll on their bodies.

"Malachi…" Her voice was a plaintive whisper that stung him to the core. "Please. I do not wish to see something happen to you. I cannot be in this world without you, knowing that there may never be a time when we would see each other again on the Astral. If you die, and if things return to the way they were before—"

"I would be with you." His chest hurt, and not from the wound there. He slid the fabric over his shoulders and limped to the bed to sit beside her.

Tears shone in her eyes, and one spilled, sparkling in the light, down her pale cheek. She made no move to brush it away, as she would have were she angry.

He put his arms around her, ignoring the pain that still lingered in his flesh. "You know I will die one day. You cannot prevent that."

"I do not wish to hasten it," she muttered angrily,

but she did not pull away from him. "You cannot know what will happen after your death. You were a Death Angel, yes, and you watched many mortals die. But you do not know what it means to die, to be the one dying."

"And you do?" He forced a laugh to hide his own fear. "You are correct. I do not know what will happen to the mortal part of me that is my soul once I pass on. But I have spoken to Cedric about your realm, the Astral. He remembers a time when mortal souls roamed there as freely as they roamed in Heaven when I was created. Even were Heaven to be restored, I cannot imagine that my soul would be welcomed there. Not when I have fallen."

She leaned back from him, her eyes as wide as the full moon she had never seen. "I have such a horrible dread, Malachi. It has gripped me from the moment the Ambassador came into the throne room, and nothing has yet to dissuade me that this—the war, Cerridwen's disappearance, Flidais's betrayal—is not some tipping point. There is doom over this place, like a shroud over the dead. Do not tell me that you cannot feel it, because I know you can! Otherwise, you would not have gone to such lengths to disguise those letters from me, to keep me from knowing the truth of what Cerridwen has done. You did those things because you wished to deny that which is becoming clearer with every passing moment. Our death approaches, Malachi."

He did not like to hear her speak in such a way, not when every word she spoke seemed to lay bare the fears he'd been struggling against. "Cerridwen will be fine," he said, knowing it was not the issue. "We will bring her back."

"It is not Cerridwen I fear for!" She covered her face and laughed hopelessly. "What a thing for a mother to say. But I say it because I do not believe that she is in danger. The horror I feel has nothing to do with her, as if fate is unaware that all those around her are doomed. I have no doubt that she will survive whatever trap she has laid for herself. I only hope that I will see her again, before this dark cloud strikes us down."

The certainty in her voice was too bleak. No words came to him to argue against her, though, as if the very blackness that she feared had robbed him of his hope as well. "You will not die. And I will not. And if we die, what then? Do you not believe that the dead reunite with one another after?"

"You cannot know what happens for certain!" Her hands dropped to her lap, her shoulders sagged. "And there is the other place, the one you told me of, where you would be separated from the divine, tortured for eternity. I do not wish for you to go there!"

"I do not wish to go there, either." He had seen Hell before, in the days after the first fall, when it had opened like a festering sore and tainted all those angels who'd stupidly followed their new God into the flame.

"What, then?" Ayla's tears crept into her voice on a wave of hysteria that broke as she struggled to speak. "What is left for me but to keep you safe for as long as I can? I cannot bear the thought of you suffering for eternity. You are mortal, and have no understanding of how very long that will be."

"I have not always been mortal," he reminded her, though he knew she had not truly forgotten.

"Why, then, do you insist on leaving me for that bleak world? Why do you…cling to your beliefs in one God, one cruel God who wishes only to punish you?" She stood, paced as though she meant to imprint the floor with her steps in her anger.

This was not a new sentiment she expressed. For a time, after the tragedies and trials of their meeting, after he had left her and then returned to her in the Lightworld, they had argued often about his devotion. He'd thought at first that her lack of understanding had been because of her race. How could an immortal creature look to the divine, when they had no real chance of ever confronting it? But as they argued, tirelessly at times, he found that she was not mocking his belief out of immortal superiority, but that she truly could not understand the concept of one God, and only one.

And she could not understand how he continued

to worship a God that had abandoned him, just as her Gods had so clearly abandoned her people.

She'd confessed that to him, tearfully, one night, recounting the charge given to her by one of her Goddesses in a dream. While she'd lain in seclusion in the dungeon, imprisoned by her own mate, she'd had a vision, and that vision had shaken her to the core. And when she'd nearly died fighting against Garret, that Goddess had come to her then, too. But never again.

"She has left me, and all of us, to our devices," Ayla had raged in bitterness. "She has used me, and now that she no longer needs me, she will not call on me again."

He had not tried to explain to her the unselfish nature of the One God. He had not wished to tell her that the Gods and Goddesses she so craved seemed far more mortal and fallible than the One God he had served. It would not have comforted her then, just as another argument would not comfort her now.

"I have never known the fate of another Fallen," he said patiently. "But I have faith. As you should have faith in me, when I tell you that I will return to you, no matter what should occur."

She closed her eyes, seemingly too weary to continue with him in this fight that neither could win and both were too stubborn to concede. With a motion so quick and subtle that he would not have recognized it for what it was had he not spent the past twenty years at her side, she wiped away a tear. "Come to the audience, if you must. But I have not yet decided to let you train the militia."

She did not offer to help him dress. That was her last effort to leave him behind, as she walked out of the room. But he would manage, and she knew that.

Just as she knew that, no matter what decree she might make in the matter, he would lead the militia into battle.

Fourteen

❧⬥❧

The members of the Guilds had already convened in the throne room. Malachi had gone ahead of her, to sit beside her throne. Usually, he would stand behind her, to her left, to display to the Court that he was not her Consort in an official capacity, that he was no Darkworld threat insidiously worming his way into the politics of the Lightworld. Tonight, though, his strength was not great enough to stand, and her strength was not great enough to embark on this task alone. Tonight, she and her remaining council would represent a single monarch, and the few Faeries who remained loyal to their Queene would feel the combined strength.

Cedric, though, was a worry. He had not returned yet, and Ayla was adamant that she would not appear without him. If the Guilds believed that Cedric, the most loyal of all Faeries to his Queene, had fled, there would be nothing to keep them there.

That was what she told herself, while another part of her raged that it was not true. Had she not been a good and fair ruler to her kingdom? And was she not in a way pardoning those who fled by doubting her ability to inspire loyalty in the very Court she ruled?

No, those worthless creatures who had fled had done so not because she had failed them, but because they had failed her. She drew herself up taller and forced energy from the center of her tree of life outward, to calm her shaking limbs. It served only to start up a shaking of a new kind, an eagerness that trembled in her limbs and brought giddy hope to her, despite the words she'd confessed to Malachi in his bedchamber.

Doom might await her, but she would not rush into its arms with self-doubt and self-pity.

She swung the door open and strode into her throne room, and was instantly taken aback at how empty it seemed. Usually, guards would have kept out anyone who had arrived late, simply because they would not fit inside. Courtiers should have lined both sides of the center aisle, jostling each other to get a better view, and to make their way to the front that their petitions could be heard.

Instead, the meager handfuls of Guild members— no more than a hundred—stood in a motley half circle around the front of the dais. Many of them had never been privy to a royal audience, had never even been in the throne room.

Ayla remembered those days, when the Palace was her home, but she had seen only the barracks and Guild halls. When the gap between her world and the world of the Court seemed insurmountable. And it hadn't mattered, for she had never aspired beyond the life of an Assassin.

So, how to address them? "You honor me with your presence," would have been appropriate, perhaps, but would they believe it? She would not have, in their position. "I stand before you, not as your Queene, but as a fellow Guild member?" No, that was far too lofty.

She stood on the dais—even sitting on her throne seemed too ceremonial—spread her hands and said, "I am frightened."

There was no audible reaction from the Guild members, but they shifted surreptitious glances toward each other.

"I am frightened," she continued, "because we stand on the eve of battle with our enemies, and they have more strength and power than our guards. We are faced with a horrible choice—to flee in dishonor and become slaves to an Upworld Queene, or to face the Elves and the creatures they have called forth as their warriors: the Waterhorses."

This brought a few ill-tempered mutters, but she pressed on. "Yes, it is the Waterhorses that we knew to fear on the Astral plane." She did not know this, not from experience, but she would not remind them that the Underground was all she had known. No doubt some of them held this in common with her, but she would not remind the elders of the group that she had not only less life experience, but had less experience as an Assassin, than them.

"An Ambassador from the Upworld came to us with this warning, but he did not seem genuine. Whatever his motives might have been then, they are no more clear to us now. He urged us to flee, and we did not. A mistake, in the eyes of some. But we will not be driven from the safety of our homes by bullies from the Darkworld.

"Are these creatures—*monsters* that the Elves have bribed with the promise of Faery flesh—are they fearsome? Yes. And fierce warriors, capable of crippling and maiming even immortals, such as ourselves. But fearsome as they might be, is the prospect of living on the surface, cowering from Human oppression, no less terrifying?

"We are caught between two unwelcome prospects. We can choose to flee our home here in the Lightworld, risk capture and slavery at the hands of those Humans who put us here in the first place, or we can fight the traitor enemy who seeks to obliterate our race entirely, though we once lived together in peace.

"To flee, nothing is required of you. You can choose to live in the Upworld, perhaps live there without ever encountering the Human Enforcers who would kill you or send you back into exile." Ayla paused, knowing this to be the critical moment. If they chose to leave, she would have nothing. Still, better to make the option available and appeal to their honor, rather than have them march, forced, into a battle they could not believe in. "But it would be another kind of exile, and you would live forever knowing that you are in constant danger of discovery and capture.

"I will tell you what I choose. I choose to fight. To stay here, in the Underground, until my last breath, no matter if it comes tomorrow or two thousand years from now. Perhaps it will never come. But I would rather risk death than live a million lifetimes at the mercy of the Humans, thought of as a coward by another race of Fae.

"If you stay, and you fight, you will play an integral part in winning back our Kingdom. The glory will not go only to the guards, as it has in the past. I recognize your strengths in a way that my predecessor never did. She saw you as capable only of work too lowly for her guards. I know, because I was one of you. And I know, because I belonged to your ranks while Mabb was Queene. Perhaps I have not been as eager to include you in our past military exploits—I apologize for that slight. It was not intended. I value your skills much too highly to see them wasted in a battle that could easily be won by the guard. But these are different circumstances, and your special skills are needed now."

The throne-room doors opened, admitting Cedric. Irritation, at being interrupted, and at his lateness, spiked in her, and she almost lost her temper and asked him to leave. But the words died on her tongue as he came closer and she saw the state of him. The filth that clung to his robes and hair, and the fact that he had not taken the time to fix his appearance before coming to the audience, were distressing enough. But it was his face that froze the anger in her, compressed it into a pinpoint of worry. His eyes were rimmed red, his face swollen. He did not look up at her, nor did he look at any of the Assassins he passed on the way to the dais. His every movement seemed wreathed in sorrow, and he hung his head as though the weight of his sadness prevented him from lifting it.

"Cedric," she said, forcing herself to keep an even tone. She would not show the Assassins that she found anything amiss in his manner. Proceed as planned, that was the most sensible way. "I was just about to tell them of their role in the fight against the Elves, if they should choose to fight for us. Perhaps you would be more suited to explain it."

He looked up at her then, helpless emotions warring in his eyes. He would do his duty as she commanded it, but he would not be able to conceal his pain.

"With Your Majesty's permission," Malachi interjected, standing smoothly, as though he had not been so recently wounded, "I would like to address them to that point. After all, I will be the one leading them, will I not?"

It was an ugly thing for him to do, trapping her between his will and Cedric's distress. But she could scold him for it later, make it clear to him that he would not be fighting. "Yes, of course," she said, stepping back, letting him know with her easy compliance that he had made a mistake.

He knew it. He smirked. She swallowed her rage and motioned to Cedric to follow her as she stepped down from the back of the dais, to one of the alcoves concealed there by a tapestry. "Cedric, Gods, what has happened?" she hissed, once they were concealed by the heavy tapestry.

He struggled to speak; with every second that passed, the dread grew, until finally he held forth with an answer almost too simple for the long, difficult wait: "They are dead. All of them."

"All of…" Ayla's mind raced. "The Humans? All of the mortals in the Darkworld?"

He shook his head, still unable to look her in the eye. "No. The Gypsies. They are all dead. Even..."

He could not say the name, and Ayla's arms came up to encircle his shoulders. Cedric remained stiff in her arms, though, and did not break down as she feared he might. She heard Malachi, still addressing the Guild members from the dais, and relaxed. He would hold them in his thrall long enough for Cedric to compose himself and return.

She stepped back. "I am sorry to hear about your... woman. Was it an attack by the Elves?"

"It was the Waterhorses." The disgust in his voice raised his volume, but he remembered, at least, where they stood, and lowered it again. "But as the Waterhorses are here by command of the Elves, I hold them culpable."

"As do I." She did not care for Humans, but she could not accept such an act of violence. "It is despicable, that the Elves have sullied the Underground by bringing them here."

"They sent them off to feed, I have no doubt," Cedric seethed. It was, Ayla realized, likely the first opportunity he'd had to voice his anger. "As if the Gypsy camp was merely a trough of slops. And they did not just feed. They continued to kill for pleasure. The men, the women, the children..."

A chill gripped Ayla, and she spoke quickly to chase it away. "Could there have been any survivors?"

"None that I saw evidence of." He paused, his breath held in tight as he struggled to keep back the tears that shone in his eyes. A moment passed and he continued. "There were Wraiths there, feeding on the death energy, but still, I managed to catch glimpses. It seemed to happen so fast that it was unlikely anyone could have escaped. And Humans are strange…they seem to doubt their mortality. They will fight until death, and when that death comes, it surprises them."

Ayla thought about Malachi, about his willingness to go into battle, possibly at the cost of his life. Perhaps he was more Human than she had thought. Perhaps he was more Human than even she was.

"Did you see how many there were? The Waterhorses, I mean? Where you able to discern a number?" She did not wish to be callous about his loss, but there were other matters pressing down on them, and he would understand this.

He shook his head in despair. "I did not. I could not. There were more than ten, more than twenty. Beyond that, I cannot say how many the Elves have enslaved. But they were able to decimate this camp, Ayla. Hundreds of people, in mere seconds. This does not bode well for our small force."

"Well, then, we shall have to strike the Elves down before they can release their scourge upon *us*." She sounded more confident than she was. Outside,

Malachi's address to the Guilds winded down; Ayla peered out of the tapestry and chewed her lip.

"I must go out," she told Cedric, giving his arm a squeeze. "Stay here, until you are…able to speak. If you cannot speak to the Guilds, then stay here until they are dismissed. But we have much to talk about."

"I am ready now," he said, and the shaft of light that entered the alcove from the edge of the tapestry illuminated his face, hard as stone once again. "Lead on."

He followed her out to the dais, and she felt his every step behind her as though his sadness chased her, tried to drag her down with him. She squared her shoulders and stood back while Malachi finished his proposal to the crowd.

When he finished, he nodded to her, shot a worried glance toward Cedric, and went back to his chair. Ayla faced the Guild members. "So, what say you, then? Will you fight?"

"When?" a voice rang out from somewhere in their midst.

Cedric stepped forward, any trace of his grief and anger erased as if by magic, though his ruined clothes still testified to some ordeal he had faced. "Tomorrow night. One full day for training, though you will not need much. Then, we will march. We wish to strike down the Elves before they can think to loose the Waterhorses on us."

A rumble of dissatisfaction came up from them, then, and Ayla raised her voice to be heard over it. "What do you balk at? A day of training, that you do not truly need, to hone skills you already have? If this is the case, you can march on the Elven quarter now. Or, do you protest at being asked to go into battle with so little preparation? You, Assassins, who engage in fights far fiercer than any an Elf could put up, forced to think two, three moves ahead while in the heat of combat? You, Weaponscrafters, who know the art of the weapons you make far better than any who will ever wield them, in order to make them stronger, more deadly? You, Thieves, who are more adept at cunning and trickery than the shadows themselves? I do not believe that a one of you could not face an entire army of Elves this very night."

There was no reply. The Guild members stared up at her, something akin to shame on each face.

"Go," Cedric said, gesturing to the door. "Rest yourselves and report to the Great Hall in the morning, rather than to your respective Guild halls."

"Will they return?" Ayla asked quietly as she watched them file out of the throne room.

Cedric nodded grimly. "They will return. We are doomed."

She waited until he had prepared for bed before going to him. She could not stand to see the pained way he would move, or the trouble he would have caring for himself.

She could not stand to see it, because she knew that despite whatever pleading she could do, despite threats and forbidding him going, he would do as he pleased, and likely die in the fight.

For days now, she had feared it longer than that, she had feared his eventual death, but had comforted herself with the knowledge that the time was far off.

Now it was so close, a certainty in her mind. And she would not fight it.

All things came in their season, he'd told her. And that was a sentiment inspired by his God. Ayla had rarely asked him about the strange God he worshipped, and acted purposefully distant when he'd chosen to share. Now she felt a pang of guilt; she should not have been so selfish. But he—his God, perhaps—had been correct. All things did come to pass in their season, and the summer of Malachi's life was now over.

She could keep him a while longer. Forbid him from fighting her war, lock him in the dungeon until the danger had passed. Force him to travel Upworld with her guard, where he could easily pass for Human and never be suspected otherwise.

She could keep him until he died in his bed, gray and withered limbs of a dead tree. Or, she could let him have this glorious death, and remember him forever as he was.

He lay in his bed, propped up on the cushions, the posture making his injuries bearable. The healer had been back and wrapped the wounds on Malachi's chest and arm in new bandages, which stood out stark white against his dark honey skin. His eyes opened when she entered the room; he did not smile at her.

"You have come to forbid me from fighting." His jaw was set as steel. "I will not listen."

"I know you will not." She walked toward him slowly, giving him time to understand, to let the anger die in him.

"Then why do you bother?" He had planned for this confrontation, and now that it was being taken from him, he did not like it.

She looked down to hide her smile. "I do not." When she looked up at him again, her throat closed, the tree of her life force choked with an emotion like thorny ivy. "I have come to let you go."

He rolled his eyes toward the ceiling, made a growling noise in his chest. "You have come to say goodbye?"

"Yes." There was no sense in denying it. "I believe that this is the last time we will spend alone together, and I do not wish to waste it bickering over something we both know you will do whether I forbid it or not."

"And no matter how I argue otherwise you would

not believe that I will be fine." He let out a heavy sigh. "Ayla, I have gone to battle a hundred times. I fought in the Great Fall. That should count for something."

She pulled back the bedclothes and slid in beside him. He made room for her, despite his foul temper.

"If you believe I am going to die," he prodded, "then why are you so calm? Do you not care about me after all?"

"I care to remember you as a kind mortal, not an infuriating Demon." She could not help her smile, though he hid his well. "I do not know where this peace has come from. Perhaps it is because I will not be surprised by our doom, that I have come to accept it."

When he did not answer her, she lapsed into silence. Then, as if spurred on by a question he had not asked, she continued, "I have told you of my time in the dungeon, what I experienced there? And what was revealed to me when Garret struck me down in our duel above Sanctuary?"

He made a noise that could have been an indication to continue, and so she chose to interpret it as such. "The Goddess told me that it would not be myself that brought the change that would save my race, but that it would be Cerridwen, though I did not know her by name then."

"Cerridwen is a...she is with the Elves." He carefully avoided calling her a traitor. "Do you believe she will care about the fate of your race if she allies herself with your enemies?"

"We have not always been enemies. Perhaps there is a reason that only fate knows for why she has turned away from us." The darkness crept back over her, and though she fought it, she could not help adding, "Perhaps I am to blame and I have befouled the plans of the Gods with some mistake I have made."

"I do not believe that," Malachi said impatiently.

Ayla shook off the gloom that had descended, as if the matter of life and death—their lives, their deaths—that they now discussed was nothing more than a trivial conversation between two mates as they settled into bed. "No matter. There is a plan in all of this, and I accepted that when I accepted my throne. I did not see it then, but I do now—if I am alive, our daughter cannot fulfill her destiny."

He raised an eyebrow in wan skepticism.

"Do not look at me that way," she huffed defensively. "I do not say this because I am already defeated in my mind. I say it because it is true. As long as I live, Cerridwen is merely the Royal Heir. How is she to lead her race out of Human bondage if she is not their leader?"

It was Malachi's turn for darkness. "Perhaps the same way her mother did. Perhaps her allegiance with the Elves will have the same results as your allegiance with me. She might think to kill you and claim the throne."

That thought had not occurred to her, and something in her chest tore imagining it. Her own child would wish to strike her down? Never.

But she had killed her own mate, had she not? The one person who'd shown her any preference, any true attention?

"I will not compare myself to Garret," she said, to Malachi and to herself, to stop that irrational thinking. "And you should not, either. Am I as cruel as he? Remember—" she ran her hand down his stomach, over the tight, puckered scars there "—how he tortured you? Do you think I could do such a thing to our child?"

He hissed and caught her hand. "This is another kind of torture, altogether." The flash of humor in his eyes was too brief, replaced too soon by something else. "I think that if Cerridwen wished you dead, you would willingly die for her."

"As would you," Ayla noted, laying a hand gently over the bandage at his chest. "Our season is passing, Malachi. Can you not feel it?"

He covered her hand with his own. "I can."

Tears sprung to her eyes, and that disappointed her. She did not wish to feel sadness at this moment. She gave them a chance to subside. "I do not fear. You say that we will not be parted—I believe you. You have fought through worse than death to reach me before."

"And I would do it again." He tipped her face up to his, covered her mouth with his.

There was nothing more that needed to be said. He would die. And she did not know how long she would live without him. She might rally from her grief and live for many years. It seemed more likely that she would fade away with the sadness of his passing. But she feared the separation of death less, now that she was certain she would follow.

The training was long, and difficult. Not physically, but for Malachi, having to explain to them the nuances of battle they had not been taught before was difficult. Asking them to fight according to a plan, rather than to their independent impulses, was much more difficult a task than he had expected. And the Weaponscrafters, who could fight, but did not, as a rule, had their own troubles adjusting. But it had turned out all right in the end, by his estimation, and it seemed that even Cedric had been pleased with the results.

"I am impressed," he'd said, though his voice had lacked the animation Malachi was used to hearing in it. Ayla had told Malachi how Cedric had lost his woman, and the thought of that loss fairly burned Malachi when he looked at him. He prayed the sorrow would not hinder the skill he knew that Cedric possessed.

They had left the Great Hall together, just as tables were set up for the night's dining. "I will rejoin you at the feast," Malachi had told Cedric. "Tell Ayla not to worry, that I will return. I have something I must see to myself."

He'd left Cedric before he could be questioned, and kept his head down as he'd left the Palace. He did not know the way, exactly, by heart; Ayla did not often go, herself, and she was even less inclined to take him. But he followed the symbols marked high on the tunnel walls, and at last, he came to Sanctuary.

He had been there once, maybe twice before, and the sight of it, looming green and peaceful beyond the crumbling brick archway, stopped him.

This place was sacred. It pulsed with an energy of the divine that even he could feel, though it did not originate with his God. He had lived among the Faeries, but not for long, when compared to the length of their lives. And they did not accept him—what of their Gods and Goddesses?

He did not wish to show disrespect, but as he had not disclosed his intentions tonight with anyone else, he had not thought to question whether his trespass in this holy place would cause offense.

Slowly, cautiously, he slipped off his shoes, watching the gaping green mouth for any sign of Faeries inside. But there were none, it seemed; they had all fled through the holes in the metal grates that normally seemed like the bars of a cage, not as a venue of escape. He picked his way carefully down the ruined stairs that, a long, long time ago, had carried Humans down to their underground trains. How strange that now the place was overrun by the nature they destroyed for their convenience.

The air here was warmer, and sticky-wet, owing to the trees and grass that were vacant from the rest of the Underground. It was a pleasant feeling, despite Malachi's unease and the pervasive feeling of being somewhere he should not. He stepped onto the lush green carpet, followed the worn-in path the led into the trees. Something in the canopy overhead rustled; Ayla had told him of the signs she'd received here, and he wondered if such a sign might appear to him now, to warn him away. But nothing revealed itself, and if the presence he felt all around him did not wish him to be there, it did not seem intent on showing him.

The path split, diverging off into clusters of growth so thick that Malachi wondered how anyone, Faery or not, could pass through, into clearings, into arched, canopied tunnels of green that mocked the Underground world surrounding Sanctuary in bleakness. But Malachi sought one place, the place where he had been before, with Ayla.

In the days after her coronation, after the furor had died down over the outcome of the duel between Garret and the new Queene—the Court had not wholly supported her then—she had kept him a secret. They had not appeared together at royal audiences. She had not allowed him to leave her chambers, for the most part. But she had, through the use of hidden passages in the Palace, led him out late in the night, and brought him to Sanctuary.

He remembered the heady feeling of it, being invited into a place so special to her. She had stripped off her Court garments and flown, high above the trees, delighting in the freedom she did not have, had never had, because the captivity that had defined her life as a poor Guild member had simply changed to a new, more regal form. He'd stood on the grass, wings carefully concealed, and watched her, not in envy, but in gratitude to fate that he had lived to be with her. And at that moment, it had seemed like eternity was before them.

After she'd tired of flying and returned to him, she'd led him to the pool in the center of the green haven, and she'd told him of the duel, and of her visions, and of the signs she had received that had comforted her while she had thought she was dying. And they had immersed themselves in the surprisingly clean water, and made love, and slept, and woke and spoke at length about the times that would follow: the birth of their child, the trials of being a Queene and her Consort, of war and responsibility, and all of those things that would intrude upon them.

That night had seemed to last forever, an eternity by itself, and yet it seemed so short a time now, on the brink of their impending separation.

So, it seemed to him that it was a magical place and he would find no better to conduct his intended ritual.

The water gurgled a welcome to him as he entered the clearing, talking in the way that water always seemed to. In the past, he had never understood it, but in the twenty years he'd lived among the Faeries, he'd learned some of the strange dialect. He crept cautiously into the space, regarding it as though it were the most holy cathedral, and knelt down.

It took a long time to find the words. He had thought of what to say, how to be poetic and prayerful, as he'd walked here. But now, with the grass beneath his knees and the leaves rustling overhead, it sounded false.

"I do not know how to address you," he admitted out loud, his stomach jumping at the shockingly loud echo of his voice in the space. He took a deep breath and continued. "I do not know if you are here. Ayla says that you are. She has faith. And I do not know where else you might go.

"You appeared to her. You showed her signs. And now I ask you to show me a sign. I am mortal. I will die tonight. It is a certainty, if I believe what she tells me. And though I was bound to the One God, I have lived too long away from him. I have fallen. I no longer know him. But I wish to know you."

A strange emotion gripped him as the words left him, akin to relief. He felt hot tears on his cheeks, heard the ragged sobs of his breath torn from his chest. He lay on the ground, stretched out in a pose that had once meant supplication, but now only seemed an invitation, a call to the Earth beneath him to envelop him, body and soul.

"I wish to know you, so that I might not be lost after death. I want to walk with Ayla again. I want to see my daughter when order is returned to your Astral plane. I do not ask for immortality. I simply wish for a sign. I must know you are there! That something awaits me, something other than Hell and eternal torment!"

The cool of the grass pricking his face and the gentle bubbling of the water were the only answers he received. As he lay, motionless but for his racking sobs, they soothed him. In the still and quiet, the fear that had driven him here seemed almost foolish. It melted from him, mingling with his tears on the grass, pulling away from him a bit at a time, until he was not sure how long he had lain there, or what had compelled him to prostrate himself in this way to begin with.

He sat up, brushed the soil from his garments, and looked around Sanctuary. Nothing had changed. And yet, everything had. There had been no sign, nothing unusual, like the appearance of Ayla's Goddess. But the world looked new to him, and he felt a pang at the thought of leaving it.

Still, he forced himself to stand, to fix his appearance, and to walk away from the peaceful, timeless spring, back to the reality that seemed so far removed from where he stood. He found the path away from the clearing and turned back. In the trees, something moved, something that was almost a face formed in the leaves.

When Malachi blinked, it was gone.

Fifteen

❧◦⟨○⟩◦❧

They gathered in the throne room, transformed from individual fighters into a force that, at least on the surface, appeared organized and battle ready.

The moment had arrived. Ayla stood on the dais, looked over the Faeries who would go and fight for her, for their race. Her envious gaze sought out each bow, each blade. No matter how dire, she wished to fight with them. Always, she wished to follow her guards off to battle. It stung doubly that she recognized some of these faces from the ranks of the Assassins' Guild. If she were not Queene, perhaps she would be a part of the fight now.

Two guards brought the Elf prisoner to the throne room. He was gagged, so that he could not alert his foul kin to their presence.

Ayla stepped down from the dais, her fists clenched

in the folds of her robes. The creature was frightened. *He should be,* she thought with wicked satisfaction.

The guards had not been gentle with him. The grotesque yellow of one eye shone out beside its twin, too swollen to open. Deep red blossoms mottled the black of his skin, as if his face had been filled to bursting with pulped flesh and festering blood.

Ayla looked into the face of the enemy, and she lashed out, striking him. "You will lead my men to your king's Palace. You will show them the way to gain entrance, and warn them of any traps or guards along the path. If you do this, they will kill you. If you think to warn the others of your kind, to make yourself our downfall, you will learn exactly how long immortality can be when confined to the hands of my most skilled torturers!" Her hand smarted from the slap she'd given him, and her threat still rang from the bare walls. Her small army awaited their orders, tense in the growing anticipation of battle.

Malachi stood among them, a few steps from Cedric at the front of the dais.

"We wait for your command, Your Majesty," Cedric prompted. He stood like a toy soldier, empty and mechanical. Perhaps the loss of his Human was too much to bear, after all, and he wished to join her in death. It was not something Ayla wished to dwell on now.

She went to Malachi. There was no appropriate

action for this occasion, no way to tell him goodbye in front of the troops he would command. So, she raised up on the tips of her toes and kissed his cheek.

Is is the last time I will see you, she told him with her eyes, and something in his refuted her with gentle mocking. She nearly laughed at the absurdity of the moment.

Goodbye could not last forever. She nodded to the drummer, the Court musician who led them not only in feasting and dance, but into battle, and he struck up a rhythm like a death tattoo accompanying prisoners to the scaffold. Still, she shouted over it with confidence and true conviction in her voice, "For the Lightworld! And for all Fae!"

They marched to the drummer's call, out the throne-room doors, leaving her with the only guards who could be spared: a force of six who immediately surrounded her, obscuring her view of the troops, protecting her with their bodies as if attack were imminent. She pushed one aside to catch sight of Malachi; he did not look back. When the doors shut, closing her in, and the sound of the drumbeat faded, all that was left was the waiting, in her throne room that felt all too much like a burial cairn.

The passage of time was impossible to mark from Cerridwen's place in the lightless hall. The Elves had returned, waking her after what had seemed a very short time. But their intent had not been the raucous feasting and debauchery of the night before. It was as if a new group of Elves had appeared in their place, clean and serious and ready to go about the business of their war.

They were shockingly free with the information they mumbled and shouted in front of her. Perhaps they thought she was not a threat to their campaign, caged as she was. Perhaps it was because she lay in her cage unmoving, pretending to sleep, so that they would take no notice of her. But the end result was the same: She knew now, without a doubt, that what Bauchan had said at Court was true. The Elves of the Underground held the reins of the Waterhorses, and they planned to loose them on the Lightworld.

After a long while, their council had fallen into easy chatter. Heaps of food—the rotting meat and other disgusting fare she had seen before—were set out on the tables, and the gaming and carousing had resumed. She was forced to sit up then, and keep a watchful eye. If any of them noticed her cage was unlocked, they could reach her easily. She wished to be on her guard.

The lock still dangled ineffectively from the links of the chain holding the cage door shut. It took all of her will not to stare at it. Not that it would have mattered; they paid little attention to her. Perhaps they had taken Fenrick's warning to heart, after all.

It seemed hours passed, but Cerridwen could not be certain. She had always been impatient and easily bored; it could have been minutes that felt like hours to her. But suddenly, a hush fell over the hall, and she rose up on her knees, clutching the bars of her cage— carefully, so as not to disturb the chain—straining to see through the darkness.

It was maddening, that these creatures did not need light to see. In the near total blackness, all Cerridwen could make out were the shapes of the Elves, glints of tarnished silver where their hair caught the light. She could see that each body was still, though, and all attention was focused on the other side of the hall.

Then, a voice that she remembered so clearly rang out through the space, and the flesh on her neck and arms puckered at the sound.

"Are you…enjoying yourselves?" The Elves did not respond to their leader's question. "I do so hope you are. For this is but a taste of the celebration we shall have tomorrow, after the Faeries, those pitiful, winged insects who dare call themselves Fae, are scourged from the Underground, and we are given back our rightful place in the Lightworld."

It could never happen, Cerridwen realized with satisfaction. The Trolls and Dragons hated them, the Pixies were allied with no one. The various other races held no quarters of their own, had no real governance or authority with which to welcome the Elves back. What game did he play against his own race, she wondered, that he would lie to them so?

The Elves cheered this, but it was controlled, as if they knew there would be more to follow.

"Tomorrow, while the sickening, indulgent Court of the Bitch Queene still lies in their slumber, we shall attack. Without mercy, as she attacked us. This so-called 'Assassin,' this murderer, this loathsome creature who slunk through our Darkworld territory, blindly carrying out orders on behalf of her predecessor, Mabb, the Queene of Madness! Shall we suffer her to live?"

Cries of refusal rose from the Elven horde. Cerridwen shook her head, at once disturbed by his rage and filled with pity toward him. To think that he'd harbored this anger for twenty-four years. Longer than her mother had been Queene. But the death of his brother could not have been the only thing fueling his rage. He'd hated Mabb, that much was certain, as she had cast him out of the Lightworld. Cerridwen had not paid much attention to the history lessons Governess had given her, but she had known that, at least.

"No, we shall not!" their leader continued. "We shall not allow this half-breed Queene and her mongrel race to dominate the Underground!"

Another chorus of cheers from the slavering crowd.

"We will repay her for the Elven blood the Fae have shed! In the morning, we shall march to her borders, we shall call her out of her Palace, and we shall let her see our might! We will let her watch her daughter, the slut princess who dared to seek refuge among us, die by this very blade!"

Something glittered in the torchlight, and the rest of the horde unsheathed their weapons, as well, brandishing them high.

"Until then," the leader shouted over them, "I say, feast!"

Cerridwen shrank back into the corner of her cage, as far as it would allow. She would not die tomorrow. Her mind was made up on that score. But she had little time to plan an escape, and lacked the information she would need to carry herself safely back to the Lightworld.

She touched the blade concealed under her clothing, and waited.

"They knew we were coming," Malachi said, his mouth set in a tight line upon seeing the Strip deserted. Shops were boarded up, carts and stalls hastily fortified against trouble.

Cedric nodded. "They knew. But there was no way to disguise our approach."

"The Elves will know."

Cedric said nothing. If the Elves did know, then the

element of surprise would be lost. But he'd been a warrior far too long to rely on something so far from his control. If anyone had set out on this mission with the expectation that they would not encounter the Waterhorses, that their attack would definitely be concealed and all would go according to plan, well, they were fools.

They trooped across the Strip, held a moment while Cedric conferred with the prisoner.

Before what had happened to Dika and her people, before he had seen the carnage there, he had pitied the creature Malachi had brought back from the Darkworld. Now, he cared far less for the vile thing, simply for its association with the Elven race.

Two guards held his bonds, a rope looped around his neck, another around his wrists at his back. His ankles were tethered with a loop left slack between, so that his every step was shuffling. Cedric reached for the gag in the Elf's mouth and tore it free. "Which tunnel?"

He waited a moment to let the creature speak, to recover the ability after being so long stifled. But he said nothing, rolling his eyes toward the ceiling of the Strip.

It took only the connection of Cedric's fist to bring the creature to his knees. A handful of silver-white hair hauled him back up.

"Which tunnel?" Cedric asked again in the same,

calm tone, though his anger roiled like a boiling cauldron inside of him.

"To the west," the creature sputtered, a bubble of dark red blood coming to his lips. "The west, by the stall with the tavern marker above it."

"Gag him," Cedric ordered the two guards, then motioned to the troops behind him. "Carry on," he ordered, turning to lead them.

A yelp alerted him, and he turned in time to see the Elf struggle free from the guards. Still bound, he did not go far. But he screamed and flailed, his gaze fixed on a point somewhere ahead. A dark shape broke from the shadow of a merchant's cart, and raced toward the Darkworld tunnels.

"A runner," Malachi called, stepping aside from the group. "I need an archer."

"Archer," a Faery responded, jogging forward from the center of the group. Her bow was already drawn, and she disappeared down the tunnel after the Elf.

The guards had subdued the prisoner, and Cedric faced him now. "Do you not recall what my Queene warned you of?" His shout echoed through the eerie quiet of the Strip. "Did she not warn you that the consequence of such an action would be great pain?"

The Elf stared coldly back, his yellow eyes looking not at Cedric, but through him.

His rage got the better of him. Before he could calm it, his hands were around the creature's throat, grasping the knotted rope that wound around his neck. He steered the creature to the nearest object—a sturdy-looking stall constructed of cinderblock, where a painted wooden sign proclaimed the various prices and kinds of breads available within—and slammed the Elf's head forward once, twice and a third time, until he dropped limp to the ground.

When he stepped back, he felt the combined stare of all the Guild members and guards behind him. He did not look up, but pretended to adjust the strap of his scabbard as he returned to his place at the head of the column.

"That was foolish," Malachi said, no real reproach in his tone. "Now, we'll have to carry him."

"And hope he wakes before we need him again," Cedric agreed with dismay. How could he have been so stupid, to let his temper best him so?

The image of Dika, floating blue and cold in the flood, great scarlet gashes marring her skin, flashed through his memory. That was how. And it was not stupid of him.

"I need a runner," he called out, and when one presented himself, he instructed, "Catch up with the archer. If she has not already killed the Elf that has gone ahead of us, catch up with him. See where he goes, and kill him when you believe his path has sufficiently indicated his destination."

The runner embarked on his mission with haste;

Faeries could all be unusually fast if they put their minds to it, but runners in the guard were especially so. They barely saw him leave.

"In case the other doesn't wake," Cedric explained to Malachi with an apologetic shrug.

Malachi did not respond. He raised his hand and made a fist to signal to the drummer to silence his beat. "Forward, in silence," he commanded.

And with a few steps, the Faery army entered the Darkworld.

News of the attack had spread through the Court, as they had planned that it might. Ayla had been prepared for this, but she had not been prepared for the effects of it. Within an hour of the soldiers departing for the Darkworld, the Palace was inundated with the Faeries who had not fled for the surface.

When they had discussed it, Ayla, Cedric and Malachi had been certain that news of impending war with the Elves would send more Faeries fleeing for the promise of safety in the Upworld. But it seemed they felt safer instead in the walls of the Palace.

They were not, Ayla recognized with some dismay. With only six guards left behind, there was no way to secure them all within the sprawling Palace compound. She sent two guards to the gates to organize the refugees, many of whom had brought all of their meager possessions with them in packs and bundles.

They crowded into the Great Hall, and the noise of their presence emanated through the corridors of the Palace, all the way to Ayla's throne room. It was both a comfort and a terror.

"What am I to do with all of them, if the Water-horses do come?" she asked herself, and only when one of the guards came to attention and bade her repeat her order did she realize she'd spoken out loud. "It's nothing," she said, waving her hand. "I was merely thinking. Perhaps another pair of you should go to the Great Hall and try to keep as much order there as possible. With so many in so small a space, and in such fear, there is bound to be a need for your presence."

"Your pardon, Your Majesty," one of the guards began, bowing, "but how would we protect you?"

"There is but one of me. Two guards will be more than enough to keep me safe." All four should go, she knew, but they would balk further at leaving her completely unprotected.

When they had gone, she addressed the other two. "I am tired. I wish to go to my chambers and lie down. You may stand watch as you see fit, outside the doors, but do not hover over me." She stood and walked toward the door to her chambers, then paused. "One of you should go to the dungeons. Any prisoners therein are not a threat to us anymore. Let them go, on the condition they must leave the Faery Quarter, and escort them out of the Palace."

"Yes, Your Majesty," one of them said, but his words were cut short by the scraping open of the throne-room doors.

Immediately, both guards drew their swords, stepping back to shield their Queene with their bodies. For her own part, Ayla reached for the daggers concealed in her sleeves, but she left them as they were. If it were an Elven horde, or the Waterhorses, they would have already heard the screams of the Faeries in the Great Hall and been warned.

The figure who entered wore a long cloak of rough, brown cloth. It halted at the sight of the guards and held up two small hands. Then, slowly, to show it was not reaching for a weapon, it pulled down its hood.

Relief flooded through Ayla, replaced at once by rage. She teetered between ordering the intruder killed and making her guards stand down. She chose the latter.

Flidais stayed still in her place, though the guards had sheathed their swords. Her hair was wet and matted, her face streaked with dirt. Her large eyes were rimmed red, with tears or exhaustion, Ayla did not care which.

"What are you doing here?" she demanded, striding past her guards. She felt as though she might strike Flidais but could not say for certain whether she would, until the errant Fae came to a halt in front of her. She lashed out, and Flidais did not shrink from the blow. "How dare you come back!" Ayla screamed, fisting her hands in her sleeves so that she would not be tempted to strike her again. "Do you have any idea what you have done?"

"I did what I believed was right," Flidais said, her voice maddeningly pitiful. "I heard this morning of your plans. I wish I had known. I had no idea—"

"You had no idea that your actions would *destroy* us?" Ayla leaned closer to her former advisor's face, her voice dropping to a deadly whisper. "Tell me why I should believe that, when you were always the first with a solution for any problem? Did you not believe yourself the most brilliant of Mabb's council? Did you not believe yourself the most brilliant of mine? Tell me!"

Now, Flidais showed emotion. She quivered beneath the folds of her brown cloak, looked down at her feet. "I was frightened."

Ayla raised her hand, but stopped it before it could fly again. This was theatrics, all of it, on Flidais's part. She was not afraid, and she did not return now to apologize. She was truly intelligent, there was no denying that, and wholly Fae. Anything she did, she did to benefit herself.

"If you were frightened then," Ayla whispered menacingly, "you should be doubly so now."

She strode away, calling, "Guards! Take this one to the Great Hall and secure her there. Do not let her escape."

"Please!" Flidais called, still pathetic, still playacting. "I came here to help!"

"To help?" Ayla turned to face her again. "How would you help? How would you correct all of the things you have done to destroy this kingdom?"

"I cannot…undo those things I have done." The tears in her voice, the way she kept her gaze fixed firmly on her clasped hands, all of it was a show. "But I can help those that are left behind. Upworld, there is a boat, to the east. Bauchan and his party are traveling to it. Humans own it and operate it, but they will smuggle us away and keep us safe from the Enforcers, until we reach the land of Queene Danae."

And there it was. She had not returned out of guilt. She had returned in a last, futile attempt to gain the rival Queene more followers.

Ayla would not play along. "How long have you been in contact with Queene Danae?"

Flidais's head snapped up, her eyes flashing anger for a moment. She could school the emotion from her face, but not from her antennae, which flared red. "What do you imply?"

"You were the one who told me of contact with Ambassador Bauchan. Thinking back on it, you never told me how he contacted you. Or when." Ayla circled her, looked her up and down. The throat. The spine. The wings. A catalog of ways to cause pain. Thinking about hurting her was all that kept her from actually killing her former advisor.

"I tell you the truth when I say that I did not have

any contact with Lord Bauchan before learning of his intention to visit us here." Flidais met Ayla's eyes as her Queene came to face her again.

It was a rare talent in a mortal to be able to lie while looking into a victim's eyes, but not for the Fae. Still, Ayla believed that Flidais had not known Bauchan. "But you did know Danae."

Flidais did not argue. "I did what I thought was best for my race. I did not believe that Garret would be a good leader. Mabb, most certainly, had declined in her responsibilities, so it was better that she died. I helped put you on the throne in the hopes that you would be better. Instead, you flaunted your love of all things Human. Allowed a Darkling to live within the Palace walls. You are no more a Queene than I am a Dragon, *Your Majesty.*"

The mocking would have hurt Ayla five, perhaps ten years before. Now, all she felt was amusement that the best Flidais could do when faced with failure was to hurl childish insults. "Guards! Take her. See that she does not leave the Palace."

"You would sacrifice all of those Faeries who have flocked to you for help?" Flidais laughed as the guards each gripped one of her arms. "You are a vain, selfish fool!"

"I will sacrifice no one, Flidais." Ayla crossed her arms, allowed herself a smug half smile. "You've told me of a boat to the east. If the Waterhorses bear down upon us, we will go to it, and I will lead my subjects there, to much fanfare. But you will not be on that boat, and neither will Bauchan and his retinue. Do you have the money to outbid me to the Humans? For I have all the treasures Mabb collected, and more from my own reign. But the Waterhorses will not come to us. I say this with certainty. As we speak, my forces slay the Elves of the Darkworld. They will not have the breath in their bodies to summon their monsters."

As she watched the guards drag Flidais from the throne room, she prayed her words would not hold false.

"We followed him this far, but I was running out of wind, and I had to kill him before he went farther," the archer explained. It wasn't an apology, just a simple statement of her limitations.

"Good work." Malachi clapped her on the back. "We're close now."

"How do you know?" Cedric asked, in a low voice, as if he did not wish to remind the others that a Darkling walked with them.

Malachi did trouble himself at the thought of offending them. "Because this is an area I was rarely dispatched to. It has been twenty years, and twenty mortal years, at that. I do not recall where we are with clarity, but we are not in an area populated by mortals."

The runner, who'd been sent ahead with orders to be stealthy and alert, splashed up the tunnel toward them. The water had receded some, but there was still enough to wet the bottom of Malachi's boots. The sound of the runner's footsteps echoed like bright thunderclaps in the tunnel.

"If they did not know we were coming before, they surely do now," Malachi mused aloud to Cedric.

The Faery gave a humorless chuckle. "He is trained to be swift, not intelligent."

"What say you?" Malachi called when the runner came near.

"The Elven stronghold is ahead." The Faery leaned over and placed his long, thin hands on his bare, knobbed knees.

Cedric's hand went to his sword. "You are certain?"

The runner nodded, gasped for breath. "I saw Elves milling about near a doorway…and the doorway was guarded. I could not make out what they said, but there were so many…if it is not their fortress, it is at least a nest of them." Immortal creature though he might be, he was tired from a long run.

"How far?" Malachi asked. If they did not reach the Elves soon…

"Not far." The Faery's breathing began to slow. "I had to flee quickly, because I believed they saw me. And though none followed, I wished to get the information to you as quickly as possible."

"You have done well," Malachi reassured him. Then, turning to the soldiers behind him, he called, "The Elven fortress is ahead! Assassins and Thieves, you will go ahead. The rest of us will follow, and we rely on you to keep up your part of the plan!"

Malachi stood by Cedric's side and watched them go. "When we go in, friend, I will not be coming back out."

Cedric snorted a derisive sound. "It will not behoove us to become fatalistic, Malachi."

"Ayla has…received a sign." Signs held much weight with the Fae, and so Malachi was not surprised that Cedric did not argue further. "As I am to die, I wish to do so defending my daughter. My Cerridwen. Return her to her mother. Even if she strikes me down by her own hand, keep her safe, Cedric."

"I have already given my word to Ayla," he replied, staring straight ahead, though the Assassins and Thieves had vanished into the darkness.

"I know you have," Malachi responded patiently. "Now, give your word to me."

And he would not move from where he stood until the Faery did.

Some time had passed. How much, Cerridwen was not sure. She'd drifted to sleep, against her own better judgment. Snapping awake, her hand went immediately to the knife concealed in her clothes.

Something hushed her, close by. She squinted in the darkness, saw only the shapes of Elves slumbering on tabletops and the dirty floor.

"Stay where you are," a voice, the same that had hissed at her for quiet, whispered now.

"Who's there?" she asked, gripping the front of the cage. "I can't see you."

"Shh!" it insisted, a bit louder. An Elf at a table close by muttered in his sleep. "Look up."

Cerridwen tilted her head back, saw the shape of something in the darkness above her, and recognized wings.

And then, a door to the Great Hall opened, and a screaming horde descended upon the Elves.

Sixteen

❧⚬❧⚬❧

The Elves came to life still drunk from their beer, still sluggish from their rotten feast. Cerridwen shrank back in her cage, watched with horrified fascination as the Faery crouched atop her cage lunged and grabbed the nearest Elf, sinking a short sword vertically into the creature's chest. An arcing torrent of blood stood out black against the murky torchlight, and the creature fell.

"We need more light!" a voice called out, a Faery voice from the cadence, and someone lit a table on fire. Covered as it was with sticky liquor and made from dried-up wood, the thing went up like a great torch itself, illuminating more of the space.

And, oh, the wondrous horrors that light revealed. A Faery fell, shrieking, as an Elven scimitar cut the legs from beneath him. An Elf was pinned to a door by two long daggers through the shoulders, and with the deft use of a torch was transformed into writhing, screaming flame himself.

Cerridwen had never seen battle. She'd heard the poetic stories of it, but found now that those stories, with their muddy wording—the heroes always dueled, or clashed, or fought to the death—none of that had prepared her for the truly glorious sight of war.

The blood of both sides gleamed like liquid garnet scattered across the floor. The greedy concrete soaked it up, creating tiny puddles in each pock and crevice, bejeweling itself in death. The smell...the smell of all the blood and fire and foul, unwashed stench of the Elves drove the energy in her to a fevered pitch. Her hands clenched so tightly on the knife she now ached to use.

"Keep your gaze to the doors," someone called out, and she saw that it was Cedric, blood streaking his pale hair as he and the other Faeries fought their way to the center of the room. And he was right to give such an order, as one door, then another, opened, letting in more Elves, these not affected by surprise, not in the same way that the others had been.

In the center of the room, most of the Faeries were surrounded. But Cerridwen saw ahead, in her mind's eye, that this served a purpose. They could fight as one unit, and defend each other, and not worry that an opponent would strike them down from behind.

A scream close to her cage startled her. No one on the ground, she looked up and saw a Faery, his wings unbound, carrying an Elf up to the top of the hall. At its height, he dropped the creature, and it fell with a sickening crack to the floor. The bones splintered, showed shocking white where they burst through skin and garments, but the thing was not dead. The Faery folded his wings and fell, driving his feet hard into the creature's skull, obliterating it, blowing it apart as easily as though it were a soap bubble. But soap bubbles rarely sent such a shocking starburst of blood and thick pulp spraying over the concrete. It was oddly satisfying, and still it made her sick.

At the end of the hall, she saw Malachi. Her mother's Consort? He had fought in many battles before, she was certain, but he was old now, withering up as mortals did. She watched him dispatch two Elves readily, though, grasping one by the hair and driving a dagger into the side of its skull, striking the other down bloodlessly, grabbing its head and twisting it sharply to the side as it struggled with a Faery.

The Faery, who had been locked in futile combat with the Elf, holding its wrists in an attempt to keep it from plunging a sword into his belly, nodded at Malachi with something Cerridwen thought could be admiration—but why admire a mortal? A Darkling, at that?

And while she mused, still paralyzed by the sight of her first true battle, an Elf suddenly gripped the cage. "Want to go for a ride, missy?" he cooed. The smell of his breath indicated that he was either too drunk to realize or care that he was in danger, that violence raged all around him. He shook the bars, and the chain began to slip free. "What in Hades?" he muttered, confused at what he saw as the links came loose easily in his hands.

The drunken veil lifted as his eyes met hers, though the cruel, lecherous intent of before returned. He smiled, displaying rotted gray teeth that jutted like broken pebbles at odd intervals in his black gums. "Pretty birdy's got out of her cage."

She flattened herself against the bars behind her and drew her knees back as far as she could before thrusting her feet forward. The chain slipped loose the rest of the way, the door sprang open, and the Elf received a face full of iron before falling back in agony.

Rocked by the force of her kick, the cage teetered over the ledge it had been placed on and fell. Cerridwen tumbled inside like a discarded doll. Her breath whooshed from her lungs as she collided first with the top, then the rear bars of her prison. Mercifully, though, the cage landed with the door unobstructed. Dizzy from the fall, she pulled herself through the open hole now over her head. The Elf had recovered

enough to spring at her, and she tripped, sprawling on
the filthy, bloodstained ground. He caught her by the
hair, jerked her to her knees. She saw the flash of a
blade from the corner of her eye and knew his intent.
She fumbled for the knife in her trousers, but she saw,
as if through a portal to the very near future, how it
would play out. Even if she pulled the weapon free,
his blade would slit her throat before she could raise
her hand. Still, she tried, unable to stop the lightning-
fast motion in progress.

Something interrupted the fall of the Elf's blade. He
released his hold on her, screaming, and she turned to
see him clutching his face, blood streaming from a
slash across his eyes. The Faery who had been her de-
liverer had blinded his opponent, and now she leaped
onto his back, plunged her dagger straight down,
behind his collarbone. She spun the body as it fell, put
a foot on the creature's shoulder and kicked it free
from her blade. She wicked the blood off with a quick
shake, her incredulous gaze on Cerridwen. But she
said nothing, opened her wings and sprang back into
the fray.

Cerridwen scrambled to her feet, pulled the dagger
free just as a hand fell on her shoulder. She spun, saw
the white of the creature's hair, and rammed the blade
home into its throat. It took more force than she had
expected, the shock of flesh splitting by her own hand
reverberating up her arm painfully. She gripped the

knife harder, pushed with all her might. Someone screamed in rage, a chilling, amazing sound, and she realized it came from her. She pulled the knife back, let the creature fall to his death on the floor.

Beside her, a Faery in flight was struck down by a Human weapon that rent the air with loud cracks. The Elf holding the weapon unleashed a torrent of projectiles that flew too fast for the eye to see. Cerridwen dropped to the ground and rolled behind an overturned table, listened as the unseen force's noise drowned out the sounds of battle. Though it did not go on for very long, it left both Faeries and Elves on the ground, riddled with bleeding wounds, some with limbs severed messily.

"You fool!" a voice cut through the screams of the dying and the sounds of those still fighting. "You'll kill our own!"

Fenrick. She pulled herself up to peer over the edge of the table. He wrestled the weapon from the Elf who had wielded it, threw it against the wall. It discharged another loud crack, then fell harmlessly to the ground. Then, spying the empty cage, Fenrick looked around the hall, panicked and less composed than she'd ever seen him.

There would be a penalty, Cerridwen realized, for her disappearance.

An Elf shrieked behind her, and she turned to see it fall, neatly halved by Cedric's twin blades. Her mother's advisor glared down at her. "Get yourself somewhere safe. We cannot protect you here."

As if she needed his protection. The power of her first kill vibrated through her, inflamed her. It was only encouraged by the sights and smells of the battle around her. The scent of burning flesh was the most exotic perfume, the screams of the dying the best music she'd ever heard. She watched in fascination as a Faery brought down a huge cudgel upon an Elf's head, smashing it, hammering it into the creature's torso. A Faery's head flew cleanly from its neck, leaving the body on his feet for a long moment before it crumpled.

The violence was more intoxicating than the strongest wine. She reveled in it, was drunk on it.

So drunk that she forgot about Fenrick, and that made it so easy for him to find her. He grabbed the collar of her shirt and used it to haul her off the ground, the fabric choking her, she clawing at it, but she could not unfasten the buttons without letting go of her weapon. He placed another hand at the small of her back, found the waist of her trousers, and she saw herself flying through the air before he threw her. She landed in the pile of bodies the Human weapon had cut down, sliding over sticky blood and spilled vitals. Still, she held the knife, had managed to stay alert so as to not fall on it.

Fenrick stalked toward her, kicking bodies and

smaller pieces aside on his way to her. "We wished to present you alive to your mother, but you will be as fit a prize dead, I think," he growled, and he reached to his belt for the sword that hung there.

She had not been trained in weapons, but Cerridwen knew that the dagger would do her little good against that. She slipped it into her waistband and scrambled over the floor. The weapons of dead Elves and Faeries lay scattered where they fell, but which one to steal? There was an ax here, a spear there. She could crawl to a sword, but he would be more skilled, she was certain.

She gripped the ax and scurried to her feet. It was heavy; it dragged her arms to the ground. She lifted it, knowing it was too late to change her mind.

Fenrick lunged at her, his sword held in one hand, a loose, easy posture that suggested he was as comfortable fighting as she was inexperienced at it. But he did not know of her newfound talent, her ability to see beyond the immediate. She saw the trajectory of the blade and stepped aside easily. Her body knew the space around her, though she did not give it conscious thought, her feet knew to avoid obstacles she could not see.

Unperturbed by his miss—surely, he believed it but luck on her part—he came at her again, striking out with the sword. This time, she brought up the ax, and their blades met with a force that shocked Cerridwen's bones.

Surprised rage lit Fenrick's eyes, and she could not help but laugh, though she knew it would only serve to fuel him in their skirmish. Truly, he must have believed her weak. Weak in body, weak in spirit, weak enough for him to take all he wished from her without complaint. He'd expected her to cower, she realized now. When he'd brought her here, she had been meant to cower. And she had, for a while. But he had gotten nothing he'd worked for from her. He had not taken her body, and he had not been able to break her to his will and use her in his father's campaign against the Fae. Even now, as he tried to kill her, she opposed him.

He had thought her weak. And that gave her the rage she needed to drive strength into her arms, which ached under the weight of the ax. She shoved, hard. His blade slipped as he fell back, and he stumbled. Before he could right himself, she swung the ax. Her blow was clumsily aimed, and did not catch him. She cursed herself, gave herself over to the stream of images that she'd ignored when she'd taken action of her own accord. He would regain his footing, and he did. And he would rush at her with the sword, to drive it into her middle. She brought the ax head down as a shield, and he redirected, raising his blade over his head. She met that blow, as well, and their steel clashed briefly before he dropped his arms, intending to cut her from the side. She matched him, her weapon whirling in looped arcs to meet his attacks at his every turn.

And then, pain. Nothing had struck her, but her leg faltered, crumpled beneath her. She fell to one knee, unable to stand any longer, her arms shaking with strain.

No! It was not supposed to be this way! She could still see in her mind all the ways she could have defeated him. Now, he stood above her, frozen in disbelief as she was. She looked down, saw the wet that stained her trousers, the blood she had not realized was her own, flowing from the perfectly round hole in her calf.

Fenrick raised his sword, and she tracked his motion with despair. He lifted the sword high, with both hands, as if intending to cleave her head from her neck. She closed her eyes and saw the intent, and saw how she could stop it.

Time felt slow as she moved. She opened her eyes. The blade still fell. Her hand moved—so fast it was as if she had not commanded it to do so—to the knife at her waist, and she pulled it free. The blade still fell. And she lunged forward, catching him in the stomach before he could stop the downward motion of his arms to defend himself.

Someone shouted her name, but Cerridwen could not see who. She saw only Fenrick's face, his yellow eyes wide with disbelief as the sword swerved left and fell from his hand to clatter to the ground. Cerridwen forced her arm upward, widening the wound until it would cut no further. She wrenched it free, her gaze still intent on his face. He stared at her as if unable to comprehend what she'd done, unable to grasp the reality of what had just happened. A stream of dark blood rolled from his mouth, and he looked down to where his hands clutched at his wound.

It took only a moment for him to die, but time seemed slow again, in a different manner, and that moment was a lifetime.

And then, as he fell, eyes rolling back into his head, the world resumed its normal pace, and the voice shouting for her was in her ear. Huge hands, not Faery hands, gripped her shoulders, pulled her to her feet.

"Cerridwen, are you all right?" It was Malachi, and though she nodded, he did not let her go. "We must get you to safety."

"The Elves," she protested as he supported her, helped her limp across the fallen bodies.

"We are doing fine, they can spare me," he insisted. "Right now, we must get you home to your mother."

The thought made her sick to her stomach, but not in the way it would have two days before. She had left her mother's Palace with hatred in her heart, and learned that her hatred had been misplaced. Though her mother would not know the reason for her absence, how could she face her and not know herself to be the worst type of traitor?

"It will be all right. She will forgive you," Malachi said, as though he'd been able to read her thoughts. And it did not matter to her then that he was a Darkling, that he had disgusted her before. Now, she wanted only to let him lead her from this place and keep her safe. She leaned against him and forced her leg to work, despite the agony that jolted through her with every step.

But Malachi went suddenly rigid beside her, staggered sideways. She kept her balance though it pained her, and then she saw it. A sword point protruding from his body beneath his ribs. The Elf that had struck him pulled the blade free the way it had entered—straight down, through the juncture of his shoulder and neck. It had plowed a jagged path through him, and he fell without a sound.

Cerridwen screamed, and the scream went on and on, fueled by her pain and fatigue. She crumpled beside him, aware of the Elf behind her, aware that there was nothing she could do to protect herself. She clutched helplessly at Malachi's clothing, crushing it in her fists as she wailed.

But the Elf's next strike never came. Cedric leaped, seemingly out of the flames of another burning table, hacking fiercely with a broken sword as he shouted his rage. He hit the creature once, brought him down, and again, and again, carving away at the shrieking body with each blow, driving the Elf to the ground in a spray of blood that wetted the front of the Faery's already gore-crusted garments.

"Cedric!" Cerridwen screamed, when it seemed he would not stop until the Elf was nothing but sand.

He stood, wiped his forearm over the blood that coated his face like a horrible mask, and stared down at Malachi's body, an unreadable expression on his face. He knelt, turned Malachi's body over, saw the blood that flowed from the wound, and howled.

Malachi's eyes flickered beneath their lids, opened weakly.

"He is alive!" Cerridwen cried, gripping Cedric's arm. "We must take him to a healer."

"I must take you to your mother," Cedric said, as though far away from the chaos around them. "Can you walk?"

"We can take him!" She shook his sleeve. "Please, we must take him!"

"No." The word was a whisper from Malachi's pale lips.

"I swore my oath to your mother that I would return you safe," Cedric said in that same, mechanical voice. "You must come with me."

Her limbs trembled with fatigue, but she forced herself to her feet. She ignored the pain in her body as she reached for Malachi's arms, intending to drag him. She saw the pain it caused him, and she sobbed in frustration.

"Leave him." Cedric stood and moved as if to grab her.

She stepped out of his reach. "We will take him!" Even her voice hurt as it scraped from her throat. Malachi had been wounded protecting her. She should not have been there in the first place. If he died, it would be her fault. "We will take him or I will not go!"

The loud, insistent whine of metal screeching against metal suddenly cut through the air in the hall, and the combatants on both sides halted in their fight.

"The Waterhorses!" someone screamed, and Cerridwen froze.

She did not have to argue further that they should take Malachi. Cedric stooped and lifted the fallen mortal's large body, a feat that seemed impossible. "Run!" Cedric shouted at her, and she turned, helpless. She did not know which door would lead them out.

Cedric grabbed her arm and tugged her nearly off her feet. "Run, or die here!"

A rusted metal door, one that Cerridwen had not been able to see from her place in the cage, cranked down on huge, creaking gears.

And behind that door were the Waterhorses.

Seventeen

❧❧❧

Black in the torchlight, they shone with iridescent blues and greens, as they began to move, like oil rainbows on dirty water. The thick, scaly plates that covered their bodies moved like a suit of armor, but they were not unbalanced and clumsy as a Human in a suit. They moved as though made of fluid, rolled like quicksilver as they advanced into the hall, steam roiling from their flared nostrils, surveying the battle with their hungry red eyes.

And Cedric plunged through the fray, directly toward the Waterhorses, the Darkling over his shoulders. Cerridwen followed; she had no choice, as his hand still clamped firmly over her wrist. It was then that she realized the monsters stood between them and their escape, and her vision narrowed to a pinprick of terror focused only on the door that both Elves and Faeries fled from.

The Waterhorses, seemingly unconcerned that some of their prey escaped, tore into those who had the misfortune of coming within reach. They made horrible, shrieking noises as they buried their gleaming claws and dripping teeth into their victims. A sound almost like laugher, and the door seemed impossibly far away. Each step seemed to bring them no closer, and she cried out in despair. Still, Cedric held fast to her, Malachi balanced over his shoulders and held there with one arm, as they charged forward.

They were nearly there, just steps away, when Cedric pushed her down and dropped Malachi beside her. She struggled to stand, body trembling in hysterical anger. They had nearly made it! Why did he stop her now?

Cedric ducked, and something flashed over his head. The wind of it brushed Cerridwen's face. With a roar, Cedric pulled a knife from his boot and lunged at the darkness. Only when the clawed hands closed over his arms could Cerridwen make out what he fought. One of the Waterhorses.

Two other Fae, covered in blood and gore from the fight, rushed to aid Cedric against the beast. One gripped an Elven spear and leveled it at the creature. "No!" Cedric shouted, far too late. The Faery drove the spear into the monster's side, and it tossed Cedric aside, slashing with its claws as he fell. Cerridwen screamed and scrambled backward, a thousand, selfish fears flying through her mind. What could happen to her in the Darkworld, with these creatures running loose? Would she ever make it back to her mother without his help? Silently, she urged him to stand up, and to her relief, he did, springing to his feet, weapon in hand.

The creature gripped the spear in its side and pulled it free with an unearthly scream, releasing a torrent of slick, green blood. The smell was foul, even above the stink of death around them, and Cerridwen covered her nose. As the Faery scrambled for his weapon, the Waterhorse caught him with its claws, jamming the shining talons through his neck and lifting him off the ground. The wings at the Faery's back beat frantically as he tried to free himself. The Waterhorse drew his arm back and swung in a wide arc; the Faery's body spun one direction, his unattached head in another.

Cedric lunged at the creature again. He had been intent on the violence of the fight before. Now, facing this creature, he seemed the very spirit of disconsolate rage.

"Cedric, no!" Cerridwen screamed, crawling forward, as if she could stop him from attacking the beast. The damage was already done. The creature slashed out at him again, and he jumped back. It grabbed for him, and he evaded. But he could not seem to land a blow to destroy it.

Neither could the other Faery, who swung at it with

his blade and cursed. "Get the Royal Heir and flee," he shouted. "Do it, or you might not have another chance!"

Something held Cedric back. Cerridwen saw it written on his face. Some desire to utterly destroy this creature, a willingness to die fighting it, so long as he did not give in. And pain. It pained him to turn from the fight.

"Please," she called to him, not frantic, not in terror. "Please, Cedric, let's go."

He turned and stared, as if seeing her there for the first time. His gaze dropped to Malachi, and he seemed to remember, as if waking from a dream, why he stood there.

The creature struck him. The blades of its claws sank through his arm, and he shouted, bringing his knife down to chop the monster's hand from its arm.

"Go!" the other Faery urged him, and this time, he heeded the warning. He jumped back, pulled the horrible claws from his arm as the creature stalked forward again. The Faery blocked the way, and Cedric grabbed Malachi, pulling him over his shoulders with a hiss of pain.

Cerridwen shot to her feet and, heedless of the burning in her ankle, ran to the door.

"Do not look back," Cedric called to her over the sound of the Faery's dying screams, but she would not have dreamed of it.

Then, they were out the door, whipping through the darkness of the tunnel. She stumbled over a fallen body, and now it was not exciting, it was terrifying. She screamed and struggled to her feet. The danger was behind them; the Waterhorses did not follow. But Cedric did not stop running, and neither did she.

He seemed to know the way in the darkness. She wondered if she could close her eyes and let her body keep running, to escape for a moment the fear that pounded through her limbs. She tried it, and caromed off the wall of the narrow tunnel. Her shirt tore, the hot pain of scraped skin radiating up her arm. Her leg ached; though she was driven on by fear, she could not go much farther. "I am wounded," she told him, and it sounded almost casual, something she would have said to him in passing at a feast. "I cannot run much farther."

He cursed the Gods, and she heard the weariness in his voice. He halted, just for a moment, and looked around them. Then, he charged ahead, to an intersection in the tunnels. They turned, went a few steps, and Cedric dropped to his knees. He groaned as he let Malachi's weight fall from his shoulders.

"Is he dead?" Cerridwen whispered as she watched the body meet the ground like a broken doll.

"Quiet," Cedric said gruffly, much louder than Cerridwen had been. "Do you want them to find us?" Then, lower, he told her, "No, he is not dead. But I fear he will be, before we make it back to the Palace."

Cerridwen ignored this. If Malachi died, it would be one more horror that she had seen, that she had caused. And she could not think of that now. There would be time for reflection later, but now it would only make her tired. As it was, she was not sure she would escape the Darkworld. The sudden weariness that plagued her, helped along by the searing ache from her wound, weighed her down like a stone; the thought of moving again made her want to weep.

"Where are you hurt?" Cedric asked, crouching beside her. She moved her leg toward him, and he took her foot in his hand. With his other hand, he threw something into the air. A ball of energy, she realized, impressed at this feat that she'd only seen utilized a few times in her life. The energy gave off a soft, yellow glow that weakly fought off the cold darkness.

"Will they follow us?" she asked. She did not have to tell him who she meant.

Cedric nodded, his gaze intent on her leg as he pushed the leg of her trousers up, toward her knee. "They are unleashed now, and they will seek out their target, if the Elves still have the power to give them one. If not, they will kill indiscriminately, rampage through the Underground until there is nothing left."

His fingers found the wound and he turned her leg, almost too roughly. They hissed in unison, she with pain, he with dismay.

"This was made by a Human weapon, far more destructive than any of ours," he said, as though pronouncing a death sentence. "I cannot heal this myself. The healer will need to use mortal surgery to take the weapon out. See here, it remains in your flesh."

He prodded at the hole, and she squeezed her eyes shut, cried out. "I do not wish to look!"

"You will not be able to travel with this injury. The spirit of battle kept you up this long, but it will not last." He considered. Then, with a dismayed sigh, he placed his hand over the wound, closed his eyes.

A veil of light fell over Cerridwen's vision, and she gasped. The tunnels around her stood out stark white. The spot of energy that illuminated the tunnel around her pulsed far brighter than it would have to her eyes. This was the other sight, that her mother had spoken of but Cerridwen had never seen. She looked down at her body, saw the energy within her, the shape of a tree with branches and roots spreading through her limbs, and it pulsed benign green, except for where the wound sent evil red energy coursing into her. She saw Cedric's energy, a tree like her own, pulsing stronger and stronger, as if building up more energy than it could contain. Sparks of it glided over the branches that twined into the hand covering her wound. And when the sparks found the end of their path, they jumped into her flesh, onto her own energy stream, and she jumped. The branches of her tree of life trembled, and she realized it was because she trembled, her body caught in the grasp of some great surge that she wished would stop and yet never cease, all at once.

With each spark of energy that she absorbed, the insidious red dimmed. The pain was far away now, but still present, an evil thing lurking in the muddy brown that colored that root.

Cedric removed his hand, and the other sight drifted away. She tried to hold on to it, but she could not; it slipped away like a dream upon waking. Now, the tunnel appeared as it had before, and she stared at Cedric, suddenly overcome by the strange intimacy of receiving his energy. She looked away.

"I must see to Malachi now," Cedric said, dropping her leg. "Do not stand on this. You will have to fly." He paused. "You know how to fly?"

She had never seen with the other sight until now, and she looked more mortal than Fae, but his implication bristled her. "Of course I can fly!"

While Cedric knelt over Malachi, Cerridwen slipped her shirt self-consciously from her shoulders, freeing the black, feathered mass of her wings. She flared them open, felt the ligaments stretch gratefully, and brought herself up from the ground, then back down, once, twice. The wind from her motions ruffled wisps of Cedric's bloodstained hair, and, not wishing to disturb him as he examined Malachi, she folded her wings. She twisted the sleeves of the shirt around her neck, letting the rest of the garment hang like an apron to cover herself, then limped to sit beside Malachi's body.

"His wounds are too great." Cedric reached for the neck of Malachi's robe, jerked the material apart. "Do you still have your knife?"

She did, she realized with some satisfaction, and she readily handed it over to him. He slid the blade beneath the fabric covering Malachi's chest and ripped it upward.

A bandage already encircled the mortal's chest, and fresh, red blood stained it, streaked the skin below it. "He was already injured? Yet he went into battle?" Cerridwen shook her head. "Are all mortals so foolish?"

Cedric tore away the sleeve that covered the nearly severed arm. Cerridwen flinched at the sight of the wound. She'd seen gore and death today, but not affecting someone she knew. It had not truly touched her, then. It had intoxicated her, like wine. But this deep, red-black crevice that marred Malachi's body, opening his shoulder, digging through skin and muscle and bone, nearly to his waist, sobered her. Her throat closed, she grew dizzy.

Cedric pulled the torn, stained robe down, uncovering Malachi's torso completely. And then, her head still swimming, Cerridwen saw them: wings. Black, feathered wings, so similar to her own, but for rust-marred patches of metal that peeked out from between the feathers.

She shot to her feet, mindless of the pain and Cedric's warning not to test her injury. She leaned against the wall of the tunnel, shaking far more than she had when accepting Cedric's energy. She looked away, looked back. They would not disappear.

Black, feathered wings.

Cedric looked up at her, his expression grim. "Not foolish," he answered her quietly.

She opened her mouth to speak, heard the echo of a shriek she had not produced somewhere far down the tunnel.

Cedric stood, lifted Malachi onto his back once more. "It is not safe for us here," he said, emotionless. "Keep moving."

He waved his hand, and the illumination died, leaving them in darkness. But even still, she could see the gleaming black feathers in her memory.

Eighteen

Something inside of her had gone cold.

Malachi died, even as Ayla waited for him to return. Hope, she had learned, could be denied, but never truly banished. And she had felt the blow that struck him down, and hope had cruelly deserted her.

She sat on the edge of her bed, stared at the walls. Because she had expected this, known the outcome, she could not conjure tears. Or, perhaps, she could not make those tears come because she knew she would be out of her own pain soon enough.

Closing her eyes, she saw him as she'd first seen him. The paper-white skin, the glassy black eyes staring at her without pity. He had not been Malachi then, not the one she'd known. He'd been some other creature, a thing to be feared, a thing bent on destroying her.

Would that creature be proud that it had finally achieved its goal? That she was destroyed, as plainly as if she'd let him tear her to pieces in that tunnel? It had taken nothing but time.

And love. How cruel was that emotion, that it could make one feel so much, with so little power in return? To love was to have a dagger at your throat, and the whims of fate clenched the hilt in their fist.

Now, they had plunged in the blade, as surely as the one that had split Malachi. He still lived; she could feel that with a power that did not come from the Fae part of her. It came from the Human in her, that she had given far too little credit to in her lifetime. Humans felt more deeply than Faeries. Perhaps it was a credit to them, perhaps not. But with that feeling came a knowing that was supernatural, and she was grateful for it. She did not have to wait for news of his death, news that might never come, that might leave her able to doubt.

Yesterday, she had feared this inevitability. Now that events had begun to unfold, beyond her control, she was at peace.

Though her body was weary, she did not sleep. There would be sleep after, or, at least, time to rest. All she feared now was the unknown that would come after her death. Would she return to the Astral, though it could not be accessed from this plane any longer? Would her form change, or would she carry on, the same as always?

Or, would there be nothing but black emptiness ahead of her? That, she could not comprehend. She at least had the intelligence to realize that.

But even if she willed her mood to become darker, she could not believe that end awaited her. She had seen a Goddess, had been given proof that more waited.

She thought of Garret, whom she'd dispatched twenty years before. Would he wait for her on the other side, revenge in mind?

She stood, paced to banish the evil ghost. Now was not the time to fear death, but embrace it. And she was ready. If only death would not be so long in the coming.

It was selfish, she knew, to will her death prematurely. Whatever might come to destroy her could also destroy her subjects as they cowered in the Great Hall, and she did not wish for them to be harmed. Ultimately, if the plan worked, the Elves would be dead and the Waterhorses banished. The Lightworld would be safe, though she would not be. Her end loomed before her without escape.

How would it come? If their plan failed, she had no doubt that all of the Faeries would be slaughtered, and her with them. If the warriors returned victorious, she would die some other way. By Cerridwen's hand, as Cedric had suggested? That, she could not bear. From loneliness and despair, once Malachi was gone? That seemed far too painful.

She looked to the vanity, where she had sat the night before her duel with Garret. Mabb's ghost had appeared to her, then, and showed her the poisoned blades she could use to avenge her murder. They were still there, cleaned of Garret's blood and returned to their deadly jar. Ayla had told no one of them, save Cedric and Malachi, and they had remained, so untouched that a thick, sticky veil of dust coated their handles.

She went to the vanity and seated herself before the tarnished mirror, and this time, the ghost that visited her was her own. She knew what she would do, if the time came. She would die, and remove herself from the path of her daughter's destiny, but she would not allow the fates to dictate how. Gripping the dagger's filthy handle, she lifted it out of the jar. The blade dripped with poison, clean and polished despite the dust that had settled over the rest of the weapon. Ayla reached for a gown she'd thrown to the floor in haste and used the skirt to dry the poison and brush the dirt away. The handle gleamed, the blade was dry, but still deadly. She coiled her hair onto the back of her head and carefully jabbed the knife through it, then carefully cleaned and inserted the other dagger in the same fashion. It was heavy, the combined weight of her hair and the knives, but the weight was as reassuring as the thought of what those weapons would easily do to her, the way they would effortlessly fulfill her destiny.

"I am ready," she whispered to the mirror. "I am ready."

A loud knock at the door startled her; as if death itself would have the courtesy to knock. She almost laughed at herself, but the door to her bed chamber was already opening, and she stood to receive the guard who entered.

"What is it?" she demanded, not caring for the way he had entered without waiting for admittance. It was their duty to protect her, but it was not her duty to let them walk over her. "I trust it is important, or else you would not barge into my chambers."

"A runner, Your Majesty. Fresh from the battle. He has urgent news."

This was not something she had been prepared for. Of course, news would come, it would have to. But so soon? She smoothed her skirt with shaking hands. "I will come."

She followed the guard, her breath an immovable force in her chest. All at once, she wished to race to the Throne Room, and yet race back to her bed, to pull the blankets over herself and stave off certainty for another night.

Fickle hope had returned to her, and she did not wish to see it flee again.

The runner cowered before the dais. His wings were unbound, and smeared with soot and blood. He trembled as he knelt, his dirty arms and bare legs scored with cuts and scrapes. When the door slammed closed behind her, he trembled even more at its echo.

"Rise," she told him gently as she ascended the steps. She sat in her throne, because she feared whatever news he brought her would take her knees from under her.

He climbed to his feet, revealing the whole of his burned and torn clothes. "Your M-Majesty," he stammered. Shocked from battle, Ayla recognized. He would never recover; they never did. The pity she felt overwhelmed her, and her fingernails dug into her palms as she willed herself not to stand and comfort him.

"You have brought me a message of great importance," she said, after a silence in which she took long, deep breaths. "Tell me, how do we fare in the Darkworld?"

"It is a slaughter, Your Majesty." His words came out on choked sobs. "M-many Elves were killed. They did n-not expect us."

She relaxed a little at this, felt the evil hope swelling in her. She tried to evict it, but it had already set itself up in the trunk of her tree of life, infested itself like a scourge of beetles. "Get him some water, and a blanket," she ordered the guard.

When he moved to do her bidding, the runner cried out. "They did not expect us! But they were ready for us!" His wide eyes showed shocking white in his smudged face. "They are coming!"

Ayla leaned forward, gripping the arms of her throne. "The Elves?"

The runner shook his head, struggled to speak against the stammer that had possessed him. Finally, it burst out with horrible clarity: "The Waterhorses!"

Ayla's gaze snapped to her guard. He looked back. Both of them stared for the space of a heartbeat, expecting the other to do something, for someone must do something if those terrible monsters were coming for them.

Then, Ayla realized that only she could do something, for everyone else would follow her command. So, she gave the only order she could think of. "Move everyone to Sanctuary. Now."

The guard took a few steps back, almost uncertain, then turned and raced from the throne room. Ayla came down from the dais, where the runner still swayed and trembled like a dead vine in the autumn wind.

"Come," she told him gently. "Come with me, it will be all right."

The runner would never run again; his steps were slowed to the shuffle of an aged mortal's. As they made their way to the Great Hall, her guards returned to her, all six with grim faces.

"Is the hole above Sanctuary covered over?" She had given the order, but was not sure if it had been done. One of the guards nodded. "Can it be uncovered with little trouble?"

"Counselor Flidais made it back through," one of them pointed out.

"Good." Her mind raced. She did not wish to send all of her subjects fleeing to the Upworld, not just yet. There was still an army that fought in her name, and she would not desert them. "We will move to Sanctuary. If the Waterhorses find us there, at least we will be able to escape the way the others did. But I want no mention of the creatures. I will address my subjects in the Great Hall. You will station yourselves at intervals to guide them to Sanctuary and ensure their protection. It will not be easy to cover so large an area without the benefit of extra men, but I do have faith that you will manage."

"What about him?" one of the guards asked, gesturing to the runner. "If they see him, in the state he's in, it might cause a panic."

"That is a good thought," Ayla admitted. "Take him with you. See him on his way to Sanctuary, and make sure he arrives there safely."

"Which one of us will escort you?" another guard asked.

"No one. When every last Faery has been evacuated from the Palace, I will follow them. You may then follow me, and guard my passage, if it will put your mind at ease."

When none of them spoke or moved, she added, "It will be all right. I have faith in your abilities, as you must have faith in mine."

"Right," one of them said, marking himself out as unofficial leader of their ranks. "The Queene has given us an order."

"Go," she urged them, prying the runner's clutching hand from her arm. "Go, and see that he is safe."

Then, she turned to the doors of the Great Hall.

How would she tell them, so that they would not fear? She silently begged the deities that they believed had deserted them to let her find the right words, the right manner with which to address them. Then, she pulled the doors open and entered.

At first, they did not notice her, and for a moment she could take in their numbers, the vast sea of them. Some huddled over the possessions they'd brought with them. Others wandered, empty-handed, gaping in awe at the sights of the Palace they had never before seen. Faery children played chasing games, hopping off their feet to fly over the heads of the adult Faeries, who swatted at them in annoyance. The children did not realize how dire the situation was. The adults did, without realizing exactly why.

She squared her shoulders, projected her energy into the room, so that each head turned toward her. Some of the Faeries had the presence of mind to bow; she wished they had not. In situations of extreme calamity, she did not like to be reminded that it was her duty to help, that she was the one who had all the power, and therefore, all the blame.

"Rise," she commanded, speaking louder than necessary. The hall was dead silent. "I thank you all for coming here. To know that, in times of great need, you rely on my counsel and protection is an honor I am not due."

She caught sight of Flidais, bound and gagged and tossed carelessly on the floor, and looked away quickly. "By now, I am sure you have heard that our brave guards, Assassins, Thieves and Weaponscrafters have embarked on a task far more dangerous than we would ever have imagined encountering. They have marched into the Darkworld, and engaged the Elves in battle."

Of course, this rumor would have reached them. Now that it was confirmed, murmurs rippled through the assembly. She gave them only a moment, not wishing for them to mature into a chorus of voices that she would not be able to overcome. "I have received news that was very pleasing to me. Our army was able to take the Elves off their guard, storm their fortress, and are currently engaged in a battle they are winning."

It was not exactly the truth. But they did not need the truth. The truth would only lead them to make poor decisions, and she could not let what might be her last act as Queene cause chaos and ruin.

"Still, I fear for them," she continued. "They fight an enemy whose numbers we do not know, whose allies may be many. I feel it is our solemn duty to send our petitions to the Gods, to beg for help and protection for every Faery who fights, at this very moment, against this terror." She paused, waiting for a reaction. There was none. "That is why I charge each and every one of you to go with me to Sanctuary. There, you may concentrate your energy on our current predicament, and take advantage of all the comforts that Sanctuary can offer. Food from the trees, fresh water, clean, soft grass to bed down in. I do not believe it will be safe for you to return to your homes before we know that the Elven threat has been diminished."

They did not move. It became apparent to her, then, that she would have to explain it more fully. These were not Courtiers, but peasants unaccustomed to being ordered this way and that. "So, if you would please, take up your bundles and follow me…"

This spurred them to action. As one great tide, they lifted their bundles, gathered their children, and advanced toward the doors.

"You, hold this door," she instructed a male Faery standing close by. She took another solitary Faery from the crowd that had pushed its way forward, and instructed him similarly. Then, she led the mass, becoming the head of a huge, seething serpent that would wind its way through the Palace. She let them follow her until they reached the first guard, then gave him the task of leading them on to the next.

"When you reach the next guard, work your way back to the end, see that no one is left behind," she told him, marveling at how very little direction the crowd required as it moved along the corridor. She flattened herself against the wall and watched as they streamed past her, some of them bowing or curtsying as they passed. She nodded to all of them, told them it would all be all right, commended them for their kindness in caring so thoroughly for their brothers in arms.

Then, when the last one had passed, she went back to the Great Hall. The two who had held the doors had left, and when Ayla entered, she found only Flidais, lying, bound, glaring up at her.

Ayla gripped the ropes that held her former advisor's wrists and hauled her to her feet. "Walk with me, *friend*," Ayla said, venom dripping from the word, "and you will tell me all that you know about this boat in the east."

The tunnels in this part of the Darkworld were wide, and could hide any multitude of horrors.

They had been trudging on in the darkness, Cerridwen alternately beating her wings to keep herself aloft and, when that grew too tiring, limping on her injured leg. She did not speak.

He knew it had been a shock to her, to see the proof that her father was not Garret, as she had always been told, but Malachi, the Darkling, a mortal for whom she had never hidden her revulsion. Cedric felt a mean sort of happiness at that knowledge. How it must twist the knife in her, to know that the mortal she'd hated so much was her father.

And yet, still he pitied her. How could he not? Even after he'd heard her praise her dead "father" time and again, to the pain of her mother and, yes, to Malachi as well, even after the times she had denounced her mother's involvement with her "unnatural" Consort, Cedric did not believe that this was the way she should have found out. To learn that he was her father, and to know that he would soon die, with no chance for her to make amends with him if she wished to, that was almost too cruel.

Almost.

She had caused this. Because of her bizarre fascination with the Elves, her naive desire to become one of them…all children rebelled against their parents, Gods knew that. But to start a war, and to end so many lives? Was there not some part of her that had known this would happen? She was not stupid, though her diminished role at Court had fooled many into believing that she was.

His shoulders ached under their burden. Cedric shifted into the other sight, saw that Malachi was alive, if barely. He could not expend any more energy to heal him, not do that and still manage to carry him. He trudged on.

He did not know the way exactly, but he relied on his inner compass to guide him. Finding the way into the Darkworld was difficult. Finding a way out would not be. He only hoped they would make it to the Strip and back to the Palace before the Water-horses did.

He did not mention this fear to Cerridwen.

Again, her foolishness—no, her utter stupidity—rankled at him. He heard her wings close, heard the gasp of barely subdued pain as she stepped onto her injured ankle, and he almost stopped, almost turned to her to shake her and demand answers. But he did not. Instead, he simply asked, "Why?"

She did not answer. He wondered if she did not understand what he asked—no, she would understand. She would be thinking of it, herself.

They came to a place in the tunnel where a low concrete shelf, marked out with remnants of yellow and black stripes made by Humans to warn them of some danger that had long since vanished from the Underground, and Cedric lay Malachi there, slumped beside him.

"Won't they catch up to us if we stop now?" Cerridwen asked, but she sat, anyway.

Cedric shook his head, could not look at her. The energy of the battle had left him, too, and it had left him angry and defeated. "They will spend too much time killing those that flee in their immediate path.

And when they reach the Strip, they will kill everyone there. We have some time. Not much."

They fell into silence, listening to a far-off drip of water that echoed through the tunnels.

"Why?" he asked her again, and this time, he did look at her.

She crouched, her wings being too long for her to sit while they were unbound. He'd seen Malachi do this a thousand times, it seemed, and the posture sent a shard of sorrow through him. But Malachi had rarely looked *so* sad as Cerridwen did now, with her arms wrapped around her knees and her chin resting on them, eyes directed miserably to the floor. "Even if I tell you, it will not be enough."

Her self-pity erased any he'd had for her, and he snapped, "You could try. Malachi is dying. You are injured. A horde of monsters bears down upon the Lightworld even as we sit here. For the love of the Gods, why would you put yourself, your mother, all of us in such a position?"

His words seemed to hammer her further into herself, and it felt good. For a moment. Then he saw the tears shining on her face, and he remembered that he was not the only one who had been through an ordeal. "Please," he tried again. "I simply wish to know why you wanted to turn against your own race. Why you thought betraying your mother would—"

"Nothing I can say will justify what I did," she

interrupted. When she looked up at him, it was with hate-filled eyes. "I cannot give you some magical answer that will wipe away all that has happened. I knew that by going to the Elves, I put the Lightworld in danger. I knew it. And now you want to know the reason? Will the reason undo what I have done?"

This was not the girl who had thrown public tantrums at Court, who had defied her mother on so many petty issues that it had become expected for her to act contrary to the wishes of anyone in authority. In the past, Cerridwen would have been all to eager to give him an answer, and that answer would have been an argument to persuade him that she did not truly deserve punishment for her actions, that she was a helpless pawn to the whims of others who controlled her. Perhaps that was what Cedric had been looking for, all along; a reason to hate her, to erase the sympathy he had for her by listening to her contrived explanation of how nothing was her fault, that she was not responsible for anything that had befallen her this day.

Now, he was relieved that she would not give it to him.

"I was a stupid child," she continued. "I thought that Fenrick…I thought that an Elf loved me. Stupid, really. He didn't know I was who I was. And I thought to warn him about my mother's plans against the Elves."

"The plans that I informed you of." That had been foolishness, on his part. He should have known better than to trust her, when her own mother had not.

"You had no way of knowing what I would do. All anyone expected of me was to sit in the Palace and wait for my mother to die. If she ever did. And I do not say that because I wish for her to die. But did you really believe I would understand how important the information was that you told me?"

"No, I did not." He'd overestimated her there.

She rested her head on her arms again, closed her eyes as if too tired to continue on. "I have learned my lesson. I know that is small comfort, considering all I have caused. But I have learned something, at least."

"It is small comfort," Cedric agreed. "But it is comfort, nonetheless." And then, though he could not believe it himself, he said, "This would have happened whether or not you had run off. Your actions merely brought it about sooner. The results would have likely been the same."

How could he just excuse her? That was not his way. He should have wanted to see her tortured for eternity for what she had done. If she had been anyone else—no, that was not true, for there was no one he could think of at Court who grated on him more than she—he would have twisted the knife of her pain until it caused a wound that would never heal. The loss of his friend, who lay dying just inches from him, that was enough to make him want revenge.

But then, he knew he could never hurt her as much as she hurt herself. It was a bit unfair, really. But it was true.

He stood and lifted Malachi onto his shoulders, his every motion causing his body to protest.

"Come on," he said, offering Cerridwen a hand up. She got to her feet and limped a few steps into the center of the tunnel. He turned away from her. He could not stand to see her pain, not now.

"Keep moving."

Nineteen

Pain.

He had felt pain before. Not like this.

"It will be all right. She will forgive you," he'd said, and he'd looked at his daughter. And despite what she'd done, despite the foolishness of her actions and the hurt she had caused her mother, he had been proud of her. She'd survived imprisonment, had fought in the battle when she should have run screaming away. Her hair, that same flame-orange as Ayla's, hung in a matted tangle around her shoulders, her face was streaked with soot and blood. She'd looked so much like her mother, but she'd reminded him of himself.

Then, the pain.

The crushing blow of a blade striking his shoulder, the flesh and bone putting up resistance, agonizing resistance under the weight and power that bore down on them, but ultimately splitting, rending, what should have been relief turned to sheer agony in a second's time.

And how long was the second, as the edge drove farther and farther, separated more flesh, more bone, cut through him easily and yet with so much pressure, so much pain. He could not make a sound. He could not fall to escape the thing that burrowed through him, bruising, tearing, cutting.

It was a second, and a lifetime. The weapon that had become a part of him withdrew, and then he could do nothing but fall, the whole of his world. He heard Cerridwen scream, knew that he must protect her, and the knowing was another pain, for he could not. He felt her weight atop him; she'd thrown herself over his body. That extra weight added a warm spike to the pain, to the hot blood that cooled so quickly on his skin. It was a gift, to feel her slight body thrown over his, and his only regret was that the first time his daughter had embraced him should be the moment of his death, and hers, too.

Then the pain took him, washed over his mind with a red-hot veil, and he listened for the sound of wings, dreaded them. But they did not come, and he could no longer think.

He did not wake, not his eyes, but his mind did, and he knew he was moving. Not under his own power.

He heard the grunting breath of someone running, felt each step in the pain that jolted through him. But the pain was somewhere else, somewhere beside him. Though he could feel it, it did not consume him. He could not see where he was, but he heard an occasional voice. Cedric, he thought, and Cerridwen?

That was good, that she was not dead.

Eventually, the jostling stopped, and he fell, though hands tried to support him, and hit something hard as though he were a discarded sack. The cold crept into his skin, leached through his clothes, to where he was wet with his own blood and perspiration.

He listened for wings. He did not wish to hear them.

He remembered another time when he lay like this, in the dark, in pain, waiting for them. His once-brethren Angels had come for him swiftly then. He had seen how they shined…he did not shine that way himself anymore. And he had felt hatred and despair for the first time. Hatred and despair because of that Faery, whose name he did not know, did not wish to know. His only wish had been for revenge, even as he'd pleaded for forgiveness from the shining creatures he'd once worked beside in service to the Almighty.

The pain then had been unbearable, as they'd lashed at his wings, left him a humbled shell. It had been much worse then, because he had never felt it before. He'd never felt this pain before, either, never known the feeling of a mortal wound, but he could bear it. Perhaps because he did not despair, not this time. He'd been saved then, by Keller, who had so easily repaired him with his strange Human tools, who had been so eager to help him become a mortal in this world.

But no amount of Human medicine could help him now, and such a hope was not the reason for his complacent acceptance of the pain, of the death that awaited him.

Ayla. He'd wanted to kill her those many years ago, had known his life would be complete when he did. How those feelings had changed, once he'd seen her again. The sight of her, slick with sweat, hair whipping behind her like a thick rope of flame, her every movement calculated and controlled as she slew creatures far larger and more frightening than she, had awakened something in him that had been wholly mortal. The drive to possess her had overcome the need to destroy her, though he did not admit it then.

That moment had changed him, and countless moments after, though he had not recognized it at the time. Perhaps it was only something one could see looking back, not something one experienced as it happened. But now, though he was close to death, he could not despair.

He had loved her, and she him, and he could not despair the end.

He heard a rustling, knew them to be close. He did not wish to go with them, and he would fight, though he did not know how, or if it were even possible. *Go away,* he told them without speaking. *Leave me...I do not want you.*

I am not ready.

He heard his soul cry it—how similar it was to the cries he'd heard from those he'd escorted to Aether, and before that, long, long before that, to the Gates. Ready or not, they would come for him. But they receded now, perhaps out of respect? Did they recognize him? Or did they see his rejection of God on him, as he had seen it on so many souls that did not go to the Gates, but were abandoned for the others to collect?

Let the others come. He would fight them, too.

I am not ready.

He was greedy for more time, more life, but above all, he wanted to see Ayla's face one last time, not in his memory—though she burned through it now, every moment, every glance—but to truly see her.

Let me see her. Then, I will be ready.

They came to the Strip, and no sounds of screaming, no smell of blood, met them. Cerridwen almost sobbed with relief, almost fell to her knees in gratitude that they were delivered from the Darkworld. But Cedric kept going, and so she did not allow herself that moment of relief.

"Keep moving," he said, for the hundredth time.

Keep moving. Keep moving. It had become a chant in her mind, punctuating every step, every motion of her wings. Keep moving away from the darkness that followed, though eventually there would be nowhere to go, and it would catch up to them.

She did not say this to Cedric, because he already knew, and because he did not say it to her, out of fear of frightening her, if she guessed right. If they did not speak of it, the truth could be avoided. They did not escape death now, merely strove to choose the location.

Malachi hung limp over Cedric's shoulders. Once or twice, Cerridwen tried to use the other sight to see if any energy remained in him, but the skill was too new, and not really a skill yet at all. The moment she looked at him, her focus deserted her. Perhaps that was for the best.

She could not make herself acknowledge, not with the word that she knew she must apply eventually, what Malachi was to her. It made her feel ashamed, for the way she'd treated him, and foolish, that she had not figured it out before.

How many hours had she spent staring at the tapestry depicting her mother slaying King Garret, wondering what he was like in life, hating that she had never known? How many nights had she stared into her mirror, trying to find even one feature that resembled the man immortalized in the portraits in the Palace, or some link his sister, the Queene he had murdered?

Too long, it seemed now. No wonder she had not been able to find the King in her plain, mortal features. He was not there, as Mabb's ethereal Fae beauty was not there, for they were not a part of her.

She'd wondered often, as she'd grown, if her father could still watch her, even in death, and if he would be proud of her. Oh, he had been able to watch her, and she was certain he would not have been proud. She'd treated Malachi with nothing but derision, lashed out at him for daring to be mortal. How stupid she must have seemed to him, flaunting her false heritage. Had it hurt him? How had he not hated her?

All of those times she had prided herself on being her father's daughter, as she had spewed bile she had memorized from other Courtiers about the distastefulness of mortals and the superiority of the Fae. Gods, did all of them know her secret?

No, they could not have known. There was nothing in her appearance, apart from her wings, that would have marked her out as his. Was there?

She stole a glance at Malachi's face as he hung, gray and unconscious, over Cedric's shoulders. There was nothing there that resembled her, but he was nearly dead, and surely that was not a recommendation of anyone's features.

Only the wings, which flopped heavily and laden with metal from his back, told her the truth. As they crossed into the tunnels of the Lightworld, she realized why hers had always been hidden. "It was because of me, wasn't it?" she asked Cedric, still keeping her voice low in case the creatures were nearby. "She would not have had you all bind your wings, if it were not for mine."

Cedric took a long time in replying, and what he gave her was not an answer. "Perhaps we did that long before your birth."

"You did not." The pain in her leg was too great, and she rose into the air to give herself some relief. "There are tapestries all over the Palace that depict Faeries with their wings unbound. All except Mabb." A bit of hope sprang into her heart. "Was Mabb...did she have some relation to—"

"She did not know Malachi," Cedric said gruffly. "Mabb was deformed by aberrant Human blood. She hid her wings out of shame. Your mother hid yours, by making all of us hide, in order to protect you."

"Protect me?" She flapped her wings, more conscious of them now that they were speaking of them out loud, to catch up to Cedric's suddenly quickened pace. "From what? Everyone at Court knows what he is."

"But they do not all know what you are." Cedric stopped, obviously exasperated, and faced her. "Your conception was the only thing keeping your mother on the throne. The Court accepted her because they believed that she bore King Garret's child. You are not Garret's child, and that much is obvious, so she did what she had to do."

"That is not protecting me." Cerridwen flew a few feet ahead of him, her mood suddenly irreverent. Perhaps because they were so close to home, and therefore, safety, although they both knew that was not true. "She was looking out for her own interests. I cannot say that I blame her. She has spoken before of her life in the Assassins' Guild, and it is not one I would have wished to return to, either."

"Are you truly that stupid?" Cedric's vitriol took her by surprise. He stalked toward her, grim eyes frightening to behold. "If the Court knew that you were not truly of royal blood, you would have no claim to the throne in the event of her death. And what would have happened to you, then? She did not act out of selfishness or greed. She did what she had to because it was the only way to protect you, to give you a life at all."

Cerridwen could not respond. She had, for just a moment, become her old self again; spoiled, self-centered, dismissive of everyone who did not provide her something she wished for in return. No, she had been dismissive of them, as well.

Cedric stalked past her. "He did what he had to, as well."

It had not occurred to her yet that it might have caused Malachi pain to hide the truth of her birth. Perhaps it hadn't with the way she had treated him. Perhaps he'd been glad to not claim her.

The thought froze her in place, and hot tears sprang to her eyes. Cedric was farther away now; he barked out a command to keep up. She swiped at her eyes with the back of her hand, but she did not want to follow him until her emotions were once again under her control.

He stopped, turned, and angrily called, "I think you wish to be caught by the Waterhorses! I have a mind to let them take you!"

That was the last weight of sadness that could be dropped on her before she crumpled, and a sob tore from her throat despite her best efforts to keep it back. She sank to her knees, tears flowing freely from eyes that burned with soot and fatigue. She expected Cedric to leave her. Or, at least, to angrily haul her to her feet and demand that she pull herself together.

But he did neither of those things. He set Malachi down and limped toward her, though she knew that it pained him to erase the progress of even a few steps.

"Cerridwen," he began, and there was tenderness in his voice, below the terrified urgency. "I did not mean to upset you. I am tired, as you are, and my temper got the best of me. I am not sorry for the things I said, because they are important for you to know. But I am sorry that I told you now, when you have so much else to worry about."

She nodded, wiped her eyes, but the tears would not stop. "I have upset myself," she managed, choking on her sobs. "I have behaved deplorably to everyone who has ever tried to help me, and I have thrown you all to the Waterhorses. I do deserve to stay here and let them find me."

"Self-pity will not help you now," he said, laying a hand on her shoulder, the way she imagined he would comfort a soldier. "Please, get up. We must warn your mother. We must warn everyone we encounter. If you wish to make things right, this would be a good enough place to start."

That, she could not argue with. She climbed to her feet, opened her wings to stabilize herself so that she did not have to step onto her injured leg. She had never used her wings so much, and they ached almost as badly, but she did not wish to ruin what little healing Cedric had accomplished with his energy.

She waited for him as he lifted Malachi onto his back. And though she did not wish to know the answer if it was not the one she hoped for, she asked, "Does he still live?"

Cedric nodded, but did not look at her. "He will not survive much longer."

"So, we must get him to a healer, then?" The hope in her voice sounded very naive.

Cedric shook his head. "Let's just keep moving."

Malachi would die, then. She could no longer fool herself into believing it would not be so. She'd killed him, with her stupidity.

She had killed her father.

"Does he still live?"

What a question to hear about one's self. He waited for the answer, because he truly did not know it, himself.

"He will not survive much longer." So, he was not dead yet. It seemed strange, then, that the pain had left him. Or, at least, that it did not matter to him anymore. He tried to find the pain in the floating pink void his mind presently occupied, and there it was, still far away, throbbing and angry and insistent, but he did not pay attention to it.

"So, we must get him to a healer, then?"

Even he knew that he was too far gone for that. He did not know why he was still alive, wondered if dying took this long for every creature. It was not an unpleasant process, but it was disconcerting.

He knew, for example, that he did not move under his own power. But he did not know how he moved. He did not know why they had brought him along. He knew they were going to the Palace, but did not know why. He did hope that he would hear Ayla's voice, though he hoped it would not pain her too much to see him so injured.

That was foolish. Of course it would pain her. She worried over him more than any immortal creature should worry over a mortal. Should worry over anything. Her life had been difficult, and it should not have been, not when the creatures who'd been created on the Astral had spent their days frolicking and causing mischief and waging pointless wars against each other...

The voices that broke through the void came to him again. A female, and a male. He knew them! Cerridwen, his daughter, and Cedric, his friend. They were still with him, though he was of no help to them in their flight. What did they flee from? He could not recall.

"Why are his wings that way?" It was Cerridwen. She knew now, then, who and what he was to her. That was a tragedy, for she was not supposed to know. And how sad that she found out now.

Cedric answered her question, though Malachi should have been the one to do so. Words. He wished he could rally some strength to open his eyes and see, to make his mouth form words, but all that was left to him was to listen.

"He was a Death Angel. A creature of the Dark-world that was never meant to know mortals. He served the One God of the Humans. Your mother accidentally made him mortal…I am not sure how."

The touch that had made him mortal flashed through his mind. The white-hot of Ayla's skin under his hand, the feeling of, well, not losing immortality, because he could no longer truly remember what it had felt like to be immortal. But the feeling of suddenly…feeling.

"Whatever happened to him, a Human found him, a Bio-mech. There are not so many of those these days as there were then, but you may have seen them on the Strip. They are Humans who fashion new pieces of themselves with metal and gears and other parts. And he did the same to Malachi, to repair whatever injury he had."

Oh, that had been Keller. Malachi wondered why he could remember the dead with such clarity, but could not recall the faces of those at Court. A part of dying, perhaps.

"I never knew." Sadness, an emotion that seemed so bizarre to him now that he inhabited a place where emotions seemed to not touch him, colored Cerridwen's words. "I never knew that he was my father. If I had—"

If she had, she would not have treated him as though he disgusted her. If she had, she would not have avoided him, maligned him. But she had not known, and so he could not blame her for the way she had acted toward him. He wished she would not blame herself.

But that would come in time, he guessed. She would grieve, and she would regret, and then she would move on. It was the way of mortal emotion, and she was more than half-mortal, though cut from strange, immortal cloth.

Far away, in the void, he heard the rustling of their wings, and he chased them away again.

The tunnels near the Palace doors, usually crammed with Faeries selling things, begging for food or goods, an audience with the Queene, an apprenticeship with one of the Guilds, were eerily empty. Cedric could not recall a time, even in the first days that Mabb had worked to establish her Court after the Fae had been banished to the Underground, that this area was not loud and chaotic.

"Where is everyone?" Cerridwen whispered, unsettled by the emptiness, as well.

"Fled." It was his only explanation. "Some had already left by the time we marched on the Darkworld."

"Fled to where?" There was a note of panic in her voice. "To the Trolls? To the Dragons? I heard there are Pixies who live in another part of the Lightworld, but I do not know where that is."

"They have gone to the Upworld, to find Queene Danae's Court." He shook his head. "There is too much to explain, and not enough time, not now. Open the doors, we must get inside."

It was strange to see Cerridwen fly to the doors and try to open them herself. Usually, two guards stood watch there, and would have opened the way for them. Cerridwen pulled on the rusted handles, but the doors did not move.

"Do they lock?" She tugged, stumbled back onto her injured leg and hissed in pain. Rubbing her ankle, she looked up at him. "I think they are locked."

"Halt!" a voice called out, and Cedric turned, saw a spear thrust out in the darkness, brandished by a guard who appeared too frightened to recognize his own kind as they stood before him.

"Lower your weapon," Cedric ordered, and added, when the guard did not obey, "by order of the Queene. I am charged with protecting the Royal Heir, and you are threatening her."

The point of the spear lowered a fraction, but it had never been aimed at Cerridwen. "The Queene is not here," the guard said, and the length of the weapon trembled as he trembled.

Cedric took a step forward. "Where has she gone? We have urgent news that she must hear."

The guard jerked his head in the direction he had come from. "Sanctuary. Everyone in the Quarter is in Sanctuary. There was a runner that came, and he told us—"

In the tunnel behind them, a shriek.

Cerridwen gasped and clutched Cedric's arm, as

though he could bear her weight as well as Malachi's. "They're coming!"

"They are still a ways off," Cedric reassured her. Hopefully, it reassured the guard as well, for he looked just as likely to faint dead away. "But we must hurry. Can you carry the Royal Consort?"

The guard seemed to notice Malachi for the first time, and he blanched further. "Is he dead?"

"Not dead. We need to take him to Sanctuary." In truth, there was no need to take him farther; by the time the Waterhorses reached him, he would be dead already. But they had brought him this far; to abandon him to those fiends while he still lived, only to hasten their flight, seemed wrong.

The guard took Malachi's body from Cedric, draped it over his shoulders in the same way Cedric had carried him. Though relieved of his burden, a new one settled on him, the strange notion that he had done all he could for his friend, and he would not be able to do anymore. This guard would carry him the rest of the journey; for Cedric, Malachi's life was over here.

Behind them, the cries of the Waterhorses grew in number, grew more insistent, and the Fae hurried away, on soft footsteps at first, then, as they put distance between them, pounding harder at the ground for more speed, more haste. Even Cerridwen ran, though she panted and cried out with each step.

"This way!" he called to the guard, as the frightened creature missed a turn altogether. He slid and stumbled, and for a moment it appeared he would drop Malachi. But he regained his footing, and all three of them saw the green of Sanctuary welcoming them.

Though there was room enough in Sanctuary for three times the number of Faeries that assembled there, they all huddled close together on the grass, not daring to go into the trees, content to stay safe in their number.

Ayla could not blame them. For an hour or more she had watched as the guards uncovered their escape route to the Upworld, and now all eyes on the ground eyed the hole warily, waiting, she presumed, for the guards to leave it unattended.

They would not, though, not without her signal. She trusted that, at least. If they had to flee the Underground, they would do so together, so that none was lost in the journey to the boat.

Flidais still glared at her, lying on the ground, her gag bound tighter. But when she'd had the chance, she'd told Ayla all she knew about the Upworld escape that Bauchan had planned. No doubt she believed this assistance would help her, because she believed that Ayla would take her along, and the glory would be all hers when she arrived at Queene Danæ's Court.

There would be no going to the Court of another Queene. Not for Flidais, and not for Ayla.

She looked to the guards at the hole over Sanctuary, saw they had their expectant gazes trained on her, and she looked away.

"Mother!"

The voice cut through the air like an arrow aimed for her heart, and she turned to the entrance to see Cerridwen, wings unbound, hair matted to her face, clothes bathed in blood and grime, flying toward her. She was more beautiful to Ayla now than she had been the moment she'd been born. With a sobbing cry, Ayla ran to meet her.

"I am sorry! I am so sorry!" Cerridwen cried as she came into Ayla's arms, and they embraced as though every harsh word between them had been forgotten, as though no betrayal had ever taken place. Ayla's arms ached with the reminder that they had been empty for too long, now that she finally held her child again.

Cerridwen lifted her head, red eyes rimmed with tears and grime. "They are coming," she whispered, looking fearfully at the Faeries clustered on the grass. Either she did not wish to cause a panic, or she feared for them as genuinely as Ayla did.

"Your Majesty!" Picking their way down the steps were the guard she'd sent back to lock the Palace doors and Cedric. And there was the thing she had not wished to see. Limp over the guard's shoulders, a body with black wings.

* * *

The moment he touched the cool grass, the void lessened. He heard more sounds than just voices. He heard birdsong, the rustle of insects in the soil.

And he felt. The pain was sharp, twisting, bearable only because he knew he would not have to bear it much longer.

"Malachi." Ayla's voice. And her cool hands on his face, her lips on his cheek.

He opened his eyes, saw her face, so close to his, and she looked back at him, all the sorrow of the world reflected painfully in her gaze.

He lifted his hand, the one that still moved. She caught it, brought it to her face.

"It is all right," he said, surprised at his own strength after so long.

And it would be all right. The same, sacred feeling of rightness that had affected him as he lay beside the pool came to him now. The dirt and the grass embraced him, the air covered him like a silken shroud. He looked to the sky, no longer obscured by concrete tunnel, but blue and wide, stretching on forever, and beyond that, black and dotted with all the stars of the firmament. The sun warmed him, the moon smiled down on him. And there were no winged messengers here. Only the feeling that he was ready to leave, that he was meant to.

And so, with a sigh, he left.

Twenty

Ayla heard some distant sound above her.

"They are not far off now, Ayla," Cedric repeated loudly in her ear. Emotionless, almost cruel, Cerridwen thought, that he would break the spell of her mother's grief before she'd barely had time to feel it.

Ayla looked up, nodded, but it seemed she operated with only a part of herself in command. The other part, the wounded part, had retreated, and it made her appear very small and fragile. "I know what to do."

She went to Flidais, hauled her up roughly. "Take this and make it show you the way to the boat. Bauchan plans to leave shortly, he waits only for her return. When you arrive at Queene Danae's Court, you must tell her what has happened here."

"With respect, Your Majesty," Cedric began.

Cerridwen interrupted him. "You are not coming with us?"

Her mother turned to her, looked at her the way she had looked at her when she was a child, woken from a bad dream. She opened her arms and enfolded her, stroked her hair. "Calm yourself. We will see each other again."

It was goodbye. Her mother did not plan to leave this place, not even with the Waterhorses bearing down upon her.

"No!" Cerridwen wrenched away. "We have weapons! We have guards! We can fight them!"

"You do not understand these creatures," Cedric said, sadly resigned to his Queene's words. "Our entire army would not be a match for them."

Desperation clawed in her chest. "No! I will not leave you here!"

Her words were as effective as one of her childhood tantrums, and her mother deftly ignored them. "Faeries," she called out, and the worried gazes of what was left of the Court turned toward their Queene. "The Waterhorses are upon us. You will go to the Upworld, and there be led to the Court of Queene Danae, far across the sea. Serve her well, but do not forget me, and do not forget that you are proud citizens of the Lightworld."

The Faeries mobilized before she finished speaking. They did not need or want a speech; they wanted deliverance. They rose into the sky in a line that stretched like the string of a kite as they streamed out of the hole.

Ayla turned to Cedric, gave him an apologetic smile. "You will have your work cut out for you, I suspect."

"Mother, no!" Cerridwen gripped her mother's arm, tugged at it, but she stayed rooted where she was, and did not look at her.

"Take care of her, Cedric." Ayla embraced him, short, but not unfriendly. "I cannot follow. There will be no hope of asylum from Danae if I do. She will not rest until I am not a threat. It is better to die here, where I can be useful, than fall to an Assassin's blade in a Pretender's Court. The Waterhorses come. I will hold them off for as long as I can."

The guard who had carried Malachi grabbed Flidais, tossed her over his shoulder and rose into the sky. The Faeries rose higher, escaping out of the hole faster and faster.

"Cerridwen, come with me," Cedric said, his expression sympathetic, but resolute as he took her by the arm.

"No!" She pulled away, clung to her mother. This could not happen. Not another death, not her fault. "You cannot stay here! They will kill you!"

How could she stay so calm, with death only a few steps behind her? She smiled, as if a smile would calm her child's fears. "Everyone has a destiny, Cerridwen. And my destiny has to be fulfilled before you can find yours."

"I do not care about your destiny! You are going to *die!*" she screamed, clutching at her mother's robes, but Cedric hooked an arm around her waist, dragged her back, and she could not hold on.

At the top of the steps, the Waterhorses appeared. They looked more horrible in the daylight than they had in the dark, and Cerridwen screamed.

"It was my destiny to protect you," her mother said, drawing two daggers from her hair. "Now, you must protect your race. Do not fail them."

The Waterhorses poured down the steps, and Cerridwen screamed one last protest to her mother as Cedric pulled her into the air. Below them, the creatures swarmed around Queene Ayla. Her daggers flashed, she spun, struck at them. Then Cerridwen could look no more.

An Assassin knows no honor.

I strike out before they can reach me, catch one in the throat. Their hides are tough, and I carve through as best as I can. Another grips me with its claws, and I grab its wrist, pull it toward me to sink a dagger to the hilt in the pit of its arm. The flesh here is thinner, vulnerable. It releases me and staggers back. Another takes its place in the blink of an eye.

If I do not know honor, at least I know humility. I know that my place is to die here. If I survive, my daughter will not fulfill her destiny. If I survive, my race will not.

An Assassin knows no pity.

A lucky strike, and I have felled one of the beasts. I drove the dagger into the curve between his ribs, and caught something vital.

I see Malachi, lying still and destroyed on the grass. I know I am not meant to win this fight, but I must—for him—claim at least one life. A hundred deaths will not replace him, but even one will appease my vengeance right now.

An Assassin is no judge to bestow mercy, but the Executioner of those who have already been sentenced, those Darklings who shun the truth of Light.

There is no reason to save my strength in this fight. I use all of my grief, all of my rage, to fuel me. I grip the scaled head of one creature and turn it sharply, with all the strength I have, to snap its neck. It falls to its knees. Most creatures can be felled this way. I have never given this knowledge to my daughter, and now she may need it.

The fight is over for me. Claws slash my face, and I stumble, my jaw falling open. The pain is more than I expected, and already another set of claws flash at my middle. I feel the spill of my blood and entrails, but see only leaves.

At the end, I am granted a Fae death. I look past the creatures who tear my flesh, up to the trees of Sanctuary and the light of the sky I will never stand on Upworld ground beneath. The light grows, the brilliant-white consumes my vision, and I am free.

For the first time in over a hundred years, Cedric put his feet down on the surface of the Upworld. Chaos surrounded him. The other Faeries, who had perhaps never been aboveground, staggered, blinded by the sunlight. Cerridwen still struggled in his arms, and when he let her go, she fled back toward the hole, but tripped in the forest growth that carpeted the ground and sprawled, cried out in pain.

"Here, let me help you," he soothed, stooping to lift her, but she kicked at him with her injured leg, sank her fingers into the muddy Earth to pull herself back toward Sanctuary. He did not wish to hurt her, but he gripped her legs and pulled her back, climbing over her until he'd pinned her to the ground. Once subdued, she ceased her struggles and sobbed, her eyes squinted tightly closed against the light that assailed them.

It was early morning. Cedric climbed to his feet and lifted Cerridwen into his arms, cradling her like an infant. He called out to the Faeries around them, tried to order them to stop, to regroup, but they fled, all toward the east, as if they knew the way. He cursed himself, and Ayla, for not thinking this through.

The guards, though, responded. They came to his side immediately, as if eager to be ordered about. The one holding Flidais tossed her to the ground and kicked an Earthy clod of loam into her face.

"Stop that," Cedric ordered. "She is not to be harmed until we reach the boat."

Flidais's eyes flickered to his, and he stared her down. Let her feel the weight of his anger. No doubt, she thought she could save herself, and therefore did not take him seriously. But there was no chance for her now. Let her believe there was, let the end come as a surprise. He would dearly love to see her suffer at that moment, when she died at his hand.

"Were any of the Faeries that came up before us healers?" He prayed they were, guessed from the grim expressions of the guards that they did not know, or doubted it. "Then we must move quickly. Can we reach this boat by nightfall?"

Flidais closed her eyes and turned her head. As if that would make him give up questioning her. He kicked her, not hard enough to do any damage, but with enough force to make her fear his anger. "You will answer me or you will march us to the boat on broken legs! Where is it, and can we reach it before nightfall?"

She choked on her gag, and rolled to her side to nod vigorously.

"Get her up. Remove that stupid thing. If she

cannot talk, she cannot tell us where to go." As the guards hauled her to her feet, Cedric turned away from them, bent his head to Cerridwen's ear. "Can you walk now? Or fly, at least?"

She did not face him, but nodded miserably and did not dash back toward Sanctuary when her feet touched the ground. "I cannot see," she sniffed, reaching out for him, and he took her arm, tucked it into the fold of his, and guided her after the guards, who had set off through the trees.

It was slow going, and he whistled to the guards occasionally, signaling to them to wait if Cerridwen needed to rest or had a difficult time navigating an obstacle. They did not complain; if they had, he would not have had the patience not to kill them.

The day wore on, and he could not think of what had happened the night before, or that morning. To do so only increased his weariness, and he knew that the hour of rest was far off. Beside him, Cerridwen said nothing, not even to complain of the pain in her leg. She kept her wings folded against her back and never once attempted to use them to relieve her feet. They were a reminder of her father, no doubt, and her mother, and, were Cedric in her position, he would not wish to be reminded, either.

The sun at their backs cooled and faded, leaving them with only murky twilight to guide them. He called to the guards to stop, and came to face Flidais.

"You said we would reach the boat by nightfall. Where is it?"

"We are not far," Flidais replied, too cooperative. "No more than a mile." She did believe, then, that she would ultimately survive. He nodded to the guards, and they pulled her after them, tripping her so that she had to scramble for balance.

"I do not understand," Cerridwen said quietly beside him. "Why is Flidais treated so?"

"Flidais freed Ambassador Bauchan and led the Faeries of the Court to flee." He hesitated. He did not wish to diminish Cerridwen's guilt at her own part in the Faery Court's destruction, but he did not wish for her to blame herself entirely, not when Flidais had made so noble an effort to betray her race as well. "She did so without your mother's permission, and in doing so depleted our guard. If she had not, then perhaps there would have been enough of a force to destroy the Waterhorses. Perhaps things might have ended differently."

Cerridwen was silent for a long moment. Then, with a bitterness that had not been in her voice that morning, not even after their harrowing flight through the Darkworld, she said, "But it has not ended, yet."

Flidais was true to her word. Just as the total blackness of night fell over the forest, the trees gave way, revealing a Human settlement unlike any that Cedric had ever seen. The dwellings were plain wood, and built so close together as to be nearly on top of each other. Electric lights burned from the windows, the sounds of their strange theater boxes spilled tinny into the night.

"Where there are Humans, there are Enforcers," Cedric warned the guards. "We must move cautiously."

Cerridwen covered her wings, closed her shirt over them, though they were almost more conspicuous poking out below the hem of the garment. If they thought they could fool any mortal with their appearances, they were very foolish, in Cedric's opinion. Flidais was bound, led by Faeries in matching tabards gripping spears. Cedric himself was soaked in blood and caked in grime from battle, and Cerridwen looked much the same, and with an angry wound in her exposed ankle.

Luckily, though, the narrow streets were clear. They passed one or two mortals who gave them strange looks, but said nothing, passed another who gave them a strange look and warned, "Lots of Enforcers around. Not a good night to be playacting."

Flidais led them to where the little houses clustered along one side of the street; a pebbled beach and open water edged the other. Then, she showed them a narrow path, two dirty tracks winding across grass that disappeared into more trees, past a weathered sign with peeling paint that said Salem Ferry in Human letters. A swath of cracking white paint attempted to cover the dark shape of a witch on a broomstick—the Human interpretation of a witch, anyway—and another sign, this one not painted, but printed with large orange letters against black, No Trespassing.

"If this is a trick, I will kill you," Cedric growled. Never mind that he would kill her, anyway.

They followed the trail, found the stand of trees thin and nowhere near as daunting as the forest they had emerged in. A squat, brick building stood out as a black shape against the darker sky, dotted with stars.

Cerridwen clung to his arm and whispered, "What is that sound?"

It struck him as painfully tragic that she had never heard it before, and it hurt doubly to remember that Ayla had not, either. "The waves against the shore. Nothing to fear," he reassured her.

They followed Flidais to the doors of the building, rusted from the salt in the air, and waited as she knocked what appeared to be a code on the hollow metal.

"No trickery," Cedric warned her under his breath. The doors swung open, and a Human woman, short and round, with white hair pulled back from her face with combs, stood before them brandishing a Human weapon that she kept leveled at them. Her expression was friendly, despite the weapon in her hands. "Oh, goodness, I thought you would be Enforcers."

Cedric stood in front of Cerridwen to shield her. "We are not. We seek Ambassador Bauchan and the rest of the Faery Court. We come with Queene Cerridwen, and seek safe shelter and healing for her."

"A Faery Queene?" The woman lowered the weapon and made a clumsy curtsy. "This is truly an honor. I wish my Edward were here to see this, but he's taken the rest of your kind off already."

"We are too late?" Dread tightened Cedric's stomach, and behind him, Cerridwen whimpered.

The old woman nodded, her head tilted slightly to the side, as though it pained her to hold it up straight. She kept on bobbing her head as she spoke. "Off in the ferry with the evening tide, I'm afraid. Meeting up with a boat moored up in Old Maine Country somewhere."

Cedric nodded as though he understood. "And when he returns, will he ferry us there, as well?"

"Oh, I don't see why not. Bauchan told us there would be more of you, he was dead certain of it. Said this one would deliver them." She inclined her ever-nodding head toward Flidais. "Not as many as he expected."

"No, that I am certain of," Cedric agreed. "In the meantime, is there a place where we can stay? We have had a long day of travel, and a trying night before then. And the Queene is wounded, as I say."

"Of course, of course, come in." The old Human stepped back, held the door open wide. "Right in here, and mind your step."

The building had two levels—the one they had entered on and, below the metal grates that made up the floor, another, arranged like a dormitory with beds on one end and a long dining table at the other. The woman led them down a set of rusting stairs, chattering all the way.

"Not much, I'm afraid. Edward and I, we don't sleep here. We have a trailer back the way you came…used to be the office when the ferry still ran to Boston. But people didn't stay there long after you all went underground. The place was deserted by the time I was a little girl. But Edward did love his father's boat, and we've kept it running nice all these years. Now and then we take some people out for a fishing trip, but we do most of our business now with your kind. Oh, not just your kind, specifically, but you understand. The ones who live Underground." She pointed to the beds, indicated one in a corner beside a table stacked with Human medical supplies. "I can tend to her here, if she doesn't mind a mortal's hands on her."

"She will not mind," Cedric assured the woman. "What can I call you?"

"Patricia," the woman answered readily, laughing as she wiped a few strands of her white hair back.

"Sorry, I've got the manners of an old fisherman, myself. And you are?"

"Cedric. I am…" And there he stopped. He did not know what he was, anymore. Advisor to the Queene, but perhaps not, anymore, now that the Queene was no longer Ayla.

"He is the Royal Consort. My betrothed," Cerridwen said, the authority in her voice mimicking her mother exactly.

"Oh," the woman said, her hand fluttering to her chest as she dropped into another curtsey. "Your Majesties."

Cedric left Cerridwen with the old woman, hoping Patricia's hands were more stable than her appearance, and took the guards aside.

"Sleep now, for four hours. Then, fly back to the Lightworld and collect as much as you can, if the Waterhorses have left. We will need food, clothing, goods to trade. Bring these things back before first light." He looked into each of their faces, knew they must think him out of his mind. "Scavenge new clothes for yourself, if there is time. I do not wish to appear before Queene Danae with only guards. I am appointing you all advisors to Queene Cerridwen. Is that understood?"

The absurdity of the announcement was not lost on them, and they laughed softly to themselves, but all agreed, to a man, that they understood.

"What about her?" One of the guards asked, gesturing to Flidais.

Cedric took a deep breath. "Gag her again, and put her in a bed. I do not wish for her to tell lies to the Humans, but I am too tired to deal with her tonight."

It was not a reprieve, he reminded himself as he watched the smirk grow on her traitor's face. It was merely a delay.

By morning's light, the guards had returned, and they'd done more than recover the treasures of the Faery Court. They also brought with them the bodies of the former Queene and Royal Consort.

"It did not seem right, to leave them there," one of the guards, a young one, not just in appearance, but in years, told Cedric. Cerridwen had listened, curled under her blankets, trying to control the wild hitching of her breathing and the sobs that jerked her chest, so that they would not see her crying. She was Queene now, wasn't she? She should not weep in front of her subjects.

When the sun came up, Cedric came to wake her. The guards had brought clothing back from the Palace for her, and Cedric tried to present it in a way that would cheer her, though she could not play her part and accept it happily.

"Your mother and…father—" he stumbled over the word "—have been *brought*. The Humans want to know how you wish to…lay them to rest."

"Lay them to rest?" she repeated slowly. Understanding followed sluggishly. The Humans believed some sort of ceremony was needed. Cerridwen had never known another Faery to die. "What should we do?"

After a long moment, Cedric said, "Faeries do grieve, but our mourning customs are informal. When Mabb died, she lay in state for quite some time, so that Courtiers could pay their respects."

"That will not be necessary, now," Cerridwen said, feeling a bitter smile cross her lips. "I want to see them."

Cedric hesitated. "Your mother died battling the Waterhorses. She is…not whole."

The nightmare thoughts that crossed her mind then made her mind up even further. "I would rather see her than spend the rest of my life tortured by visions that are likely far worse than reality."

Something flickered across Cedric's face, almost like admiration. Her heart twisted inside of her. How much more meaningful that simple look was, considering how much he should hate her.

Cedric helped her up to the beach. The Human had used mortal healing arts on her, but the wound in Cerridwen's leg still ached, and she needed his help to limp through the bed of pebbles that led to the sea.

"No good for the little dear to see her parents this way," Patricia said to one of the guards, as though Cerridwen would not hear her. "When my father passed, the morticians did such a terrible job on him. He didn't look like himself at all. That's not a good memory to have."

The shrouded figures of her parents lay on the stones, and Cedric held her elbow, holding her up, as they approached. He motioned to a guard, who drew back the shroud covering Malachi. He appeared much the same as the last time she had seen him. His features so mortal, but still noble in death. She nodded to the guard, and he covered him again, then moved to uncover Ayla.

In the same horrible moment, Cerridwen wished she had never looked, and wished she never had to look away. Her mother's beautiful hair was gone, transformed to a cascade of fallen autumn leaves. Her face was blue in death, slashed across the mouth by a Waterhorse's claws, and the torn flesh lay blackened and curled. Her eyes were mercifully closed, her limbs the bark-covered branches of a tree.

"What should I do?" she asked, tears creeping into her voice. "Cedric, what do I do with them?"

"I will ask that they are properly disposed of. Discreetly." He looked toward the boatman's wife, then back to the bodies. "I do not believe they would try to profit from the possession of these remains."

The thought had not even occurred to her that they might, and it was that notion that tipped her grief over the edge. She turned her face into Cedric's chest, not caring who it was that held her, only caring for the comfort he offered.

The boat returned with the morning tide, chugging blue smoke into the air and churning water with a sluggish roar.

"We must leave quickly," Cedric told her, helping her toward the wooden pier.

Flidais stood at the edge of the water, unbound for their journey. Perhaps she had been there all the while, and Cerridwen had not seen her. She turned as Cerridwen and Cedric approached, and bowed meaningfully. "Your Majesties."

Though the mocking was not audible in her tone, only a fool would have thought it absent from her mind.

Cerridwen moved, though she could not feel it. She looked to the bodies of her parents, covered once more, waiting to be left behind. She felt her hand going for the knife—she had not remembered taking it with her, yet there it was—before she decided to reach for it. It slashed across Flidais's throat, and Cerridwen knew that blood poured down, turning to garnets that tumbled down the skirt of her gown, though she did not see them. Her eyes stayed on Flidais's face, took in her expression of shock, of disbelief.

Oh, yes, you are so clever. And you did not see this

coming, Cerridwen thought, her rage swelling within her to impossible size, forcing a scream from her throat, one that Flidais could no longer utter. *You did not believe that anyone would catch you out. You thought you could topple a Queene and live to tell of it.*

Flidais's skin crystallized, turned to stone as she fell, her eyes shining as glass as the light in them died. Cerridwen tossed the knife aside, Fenrick's knife, the last bitter reminder of the Underground and her failure, then reached up to smooth her hair. The guards did not move; the Humans stared. She did not look at them, but fixed her gaze on the open sea, watching the waves through eyes misted with tears.

Cedric spoke as though he had not just stood by while she murdered another Fae, as though that corpse did not lay at their feet. "It will be better for them to believe that I am your Consort. That way, when we arrive at Queene Danae's Court, she will not believe you are a friendless, unprotected, exiled Queene."

A single tear escaped now, to roll in solitary mourning down her cheek. "I do not mind." She took a deep breath and hitched her shoulders back. "I am ready now, Cedric."

He nodded. "We must connect with Bauchan's ship before the evening tide."

"No, I do not mean the boat," she said, taking a tentative step onto the dock. Another, and another, until she walked fearlessly toward the open water, toward the sky that she had never seen.

"I am ready now for what comes next."

* * * * *

ACKNOWLEDGMENTS

Without the guiding hand of spellcheck, Mount Gay rum and Adam Wilson, this book would be a mess.

REQUEST YOUR FREE BOOKS!

2 FREE NOVELS
FROM THE ROMANCE/SUSPENSE
COLLECTION PLUS 2 FREE GIFTS!

YES! Please send me 2 FREE novels from the Romance/Suspense Collection and my 2 FREE gifts (gifts are worth about $10). After receiving them, if I don't wish to receive any more books, I can return the shipping statement marked "cancel." If I don't cancel, I will receive 4 brand-new novels every month and be billed just $5.74 per book in the U.S. or $6.24 per book in Canada. That's a savings of at least 28% off the cover price. It's quite a bargain! Shipping and handling is just 50¢ per book.* I understand that accepting the 2 free books and gifts places me under no obligation to buy anything. I can always return a shipment and cancel at any time. Even if I never buy another book from the Reader Service, the two free books and gifts are mine to keep forever.

185 MDN EYNQ 385 MDN EYN2

Name	(PLEASE PRINT)	
Address		Apt. #
City	State/Prov.	Zip/Postal Code

Signature (if under 18, a parent or guardian must sign)

Mail to **The Reader Service:**
IN U.S.A.: P.O. Box 1867, Buffalo, NY 14240-1867
IN CANADA: P.O. Box 609, Fort Erie, Ontario L2A 5X3

Not valid to current subscribers of the Romance Collection,
the Suspense Collection or the Romance/Suspense Collection.

Want to try two free books from another line?
Call 1-800-873-8635 or visit www.morefreebooks.com.

* Terms and prices subject to change without notice. Prices do not include applicable taxes. Sales tax applicable in N.Y. Canadian residents will be charged applicable provincial taxes and GST. Offer not valid in Quebec. This offer is limited to one order per household. All orders subject to approval. Credit or debit balances in a customer's account(s) may be offset by any other outstanding balance owed by or to the customer. Please allow 4 to 6 weeks for delivery. Offer available while quantities last.

Your Privacy: Harlequin is committed to protecting your privacy. Our Privacy Policy is available online at www.eHarlequin.com or upon request from the Reader Service. From time to time we make our lists of customers available to reputable third parties who may have a product or service of interest to you. If you would prefer we not share your name and address, please check here. ☐

New York Times and *USA TODAY* Bestselling Author

HEATHER GRAHAM

When Sarah McKinley is finally able to buy and restore the historic Florida mansion that she has always loved, she dismisses the horror stories of past residents vanishing and a long-dead housekeeper who practiced black magic. Then, in the midst of renovations, she makes a grim discovery. Hidden within the walls of Sarah's dream house are the remains of dozens of bodies—some dating back over a century.

The door to the past is blown wide open when Caleb Anderson, a private investigator, shows up at the mansion. He believes several current missing persons cases are linked to the house and its dark past. Working together to find the connection and stop a contemporary killer, Sarah and Caleb are compelled to research the history of the haunted house, growing closer to each other even as the solution to the murders eludes them.

UNHALLOWED GROUND

MIRA®

*On sale now
wherever books are sold!*

www.MIRABooks.com

MHG2676R

JENNIFER ARMINTROUT

32537	BLOOD TIES BOOK FOUR: ALL SOULS' NIGHT	___ $6.99 U.S.	___ $6.99 CAN.
32494	BLOOD TIES BOOK THREE: ASHES TO ASHES	___ $6.99 U.S.	___ $8.50 CAN.
32418	BLOOD TIES BOOK TWO: POSSESSION	___ $6.99 U.S.	___ $8.50 CAN.
32298	BLOOD TIES BOOK ONE: THE TURNING	___ $6.99 U.S.	___ $8.50 CAN.

(limited quantities available)

TOTAL AMOUNT	$ _____
POSTAGE & HANDLING	$ _____
($1.00 for 1 book, 50¢ for each additional)	
APPLICABLE TAXES*	$ _____
TOTAL PAYABLE	$ _____

(check or money order—please do not send cash)

To order, complete this form and send it, along with a check or money order for the total above, payable to MIRA Books, to: **In the U.S.:** 3010 Walden Avenue, P.O. Box 9077, Buffalo, NY 14269-9077; **In Canada:** P.O. Box 636, Fort Erie, Ontario, L2A 5X3.

Name: _____
Address: _____ City: _____
State/Prov.: _____ Zip/Postal Code: _____
Account Number (if applicable): _____

075 CSAS

*New York residents remit applicable sales taxes.
*Canadian residents remit applicable GST and provincial taxes.

MIRA®

www.MIRABooks.com
MJA1009BL